MURDER ON ICE

Savannah stepped inside the freezer and instantly felt a chill that made her shiver underneath her silk nightclothes. But her shudder had nothing to do with the temperature inside the walk-in.

On the floor to her left lay a body, sprawled on its back, staring with glazed eyes at the ceiling.

"Lance, take a look at this," she called.

A few seconds later, Lance appeared at her side. He gasped when he saw the body. "Oh, my god. What . . . what happened?"

"I don't know," Savannah replied, but the mental computer inside her head was already clicking away, processing the possibilities.

"Should we . . . . ?" Lance said, reaching a hand toward the body, then withdrawing it. "I'll go call 9-1-1, have them send an ambulance."

"No point in that," Savannah said.

"You mean . . . ?"

"Yes." Savannah had seen enough corpses in her life to know this person was no longer among the living. And while the head was covered with blood and the face contorted with whatever pain the victim had felt when exiting the world, the orange hair and tangerine suit were unmistakable.

"Tess is dead," she said. "There's nothing we can do for her now . . . except call the coroner."

Books by G.A. McKevett

JUST DESSERTS

BITTER SWEETS

KILLER CALORIES

COOKED GOOSE

SUGAR AND SPITE

SOUR GRAPES

PEACHES AND SCREAMS

DEATH BY CHOCOLATE

CEREAL KILLER

MURDER À LA MODE

CORPSE SUZETTE

Published by Kensington Publishing Corporation

G.A. McKevett

Murder à la Mode

A SAVANNAH REID MYSTERY

KENSINGTON BOOKS
KENSINGTON PUBLISHING CORP.
http://www.kensingtonbooks.com

KENSINGTON BOOKS are published by

Kensington Publishing Corp.
850 Third Avenue
New York, NY 10022

All Kensington titles, imprints and distributed lines are available at special quantity discounts for bulk purchases for sales promotion, premiums, fund-raising, educational or institutional use.

Special book excerpts or customized printings can also be created to fit specific needs. For details, write or phone the office of the Kensington Special Sales Manager: Kensington Publishing Corp., 850 Third Avenue, New York, NY 10022. Attn. Special Sales Department. Phone: 1-800-221-2647.

Kensington and the K logo Reg. U.S. Pat. & TM Off.

ISBN 0-7582-0461-2

First Hardcover Printing: January 2005
First Mass Market Paperback Printing: April 2006
10 9 8 7 6 5 4 3 2 1

Printed in the United States of America

*This book is dedicated to
Lady Antonette "The First"
who reminds us that life goes on
and is beautiful!*

Chapter

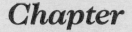

As Raff, the swarthy pirate king, pulled Lady Wimblety against him, she could feel the depth, and more impressively, the length, of his rising need, pressing against her thigh. Or it might have been his sword, she wasn't sure; nor did she care. She was far beyond caring. Trembling—Lady Wimblety that is, not his fingers, because Raff the pirate king's fingers never trembled—his rough, battle-scarred fingers tugged at the lacing on her bodice and—

"I wish you wouldn't read those stupid books when you're on stakeouts with me," Dirk mumbled as he nudged Savannah in the ribs hard enough to make her drop her paperback novel onto the sand beside her.

Swatting his hand away, she reached for the book and brushed away the wet, cold grit, making sure not to smudge the image on the cover. After all, it was the cover art that had enticed her to buy the novel in the first place.

Raff the pirate king in all of his raven-locked, bulging-biceped, sapphire-eyed, burgeoning-manhooded glory had once again seduced her into forking over her hard-earned money. She had run into her local drugstore for a bottle of aspirin and come out with two paperbacks: *Love's Tempestuous Tempest* and *Flickering Tongues of Flaming Passion.*

She simply couldn't help herself; the same male model graced both covers. And whether Lance Roman was dressed—or pretty much undressed, as the case might be—as a ravaging pirate who was ravishing a lust-be-sotted gentlelady with a ripped bodice, or as a New York City fireman rescuing a damsel with scorched hair and ripped T-shirt, he was positively irresistible. If Lance Roman was on the cover, Savannah Reid bought the book. Savannah and a million other faithful, some might say fanatical, admirers.

So, when Detective Dirk Coulter, Savannah's friend and former partner on the police force, called and asked her to accompany him on a beach stakeout, she had welcomed the chance to catch up on her reading.

She brought *Tempestuous Tempest,* knowing that Dirk would never let her live down *Flickering Tongues.* It was the lesser of two evils.

"You're supposed to be keeping a heads-up with me," Dirk said, "watching out for these punks. But you're sitting there, getting off on that junk and ignoring me."

She glanced over at the little pile of goodies he had brought along to while away the boring stakeout hours. On his ragged, Harley-Davidson beach towel lay two empty soda cans, a deflated tortilla chip bag, a CD player and two Grateful Dead CDs.

"You forgot to bring your boxing and wrestling magazines, didn't you?" she observed.

He scowled and nodded, "And I just got the latest edition of *The Ring,* too."

"So, now I'm supposed to sit here and entertain you?"

He reached down and zipped up the front of his leather bomber jacket. The beach weather had been cool all afternoon by Southern California standards, and with the sun setting, the temperature was dropping to downright chilly. "You don't gotta entertain me," he said. "You're just supposed to be helping me keep an eye out for these thugs, not reading about Muscleman Goldilocks there."

Savannah laughed. "He's no Goldilocks. Lance's hair is ebony black, and you're just jealous."

"Jealous? Of what? I got muscles like that."

Savannah could have pointed out that Dirk used to have muscles like that. But in the years she had known him, he had gone from "ripped" to . . . well . . . "not so ripped." But she didn't care. He had never minded her extra poundage. True buddies never noticed such things.

"And the dude's hair looks like a girl's," he continued, poking a finger at the cover, "hangin' down in his eyes like that."

Again, Savannah took the high road and decided not to mention that Dirk's hair didn't exactly hang down anywhere. His remaining precious strands were carefully combed to make the most of an ever-decreasing population.

Lovingly, she placed the novel into her backpack and pulled out a Snickers and a can of Coke. "Looks like this is going to be dinner again, big boy," she told him as she unwrapped the chocolate bar.

"Yeah. I was hoping for better. I thought if I suggested we pose as a couple on the beach, you'd bring along a picnic," he said, "some fried chicken, potato salad, stuff like that."

"Get real," she said, her Georgian drawl thick as she popped open the soda can. "I cooked for you Friday night when you came over to watch the heavyweight bout on my HBO. And I made you biscuits, eggs, and grits on Sunday morning."

"I hate grits."

"You ate them."

"I didn't know what the white goop was, or I wouldn't have."

"Eh, you'll eat anything if it's free." She reached into the pack and brought out another candy bar. It was smashed nearly flat and its wrapper was torn. She held it out to him. "Here, want this?"

He snatched it out of her hand. "Sure."

They both munched for a while, quietly surveying their surroundings. Anchor's Way Beach was one of the favorite playgrounds in the small California seaside town of San Carmelita. And usually it would have been full of sunbathers, even on a day like today, when there were more clouds than sun and a chill wind blowing inland. But the swing sets were empty, the volleyball nets deserted, and the die-hard surfers were hanging ten a few miles south at Pelican Ridge State Park.

A couple of robbers—a pair described by witnesses as "one white male, late teens, wearing a red baseball cap; one black male, late teens, hooded sweatshirt with a Rams insignia"—had been holding up beachgoers, striking randomly, but usually just after sundown. Their favorite victims had been lovers taking a moonlight stroll or snuggling on the beach.

So Dirk, who had been assigned the case, had called Savannah that morning and suggested they do some beach snuggling and see if they could lure the bad guys out of hiding.

Savannah had gladly accepted the invitation to take down the bad guys. As far as the beach-blanket cuddling, she told him she would listen to the weather report and if it was, indeed, a cold day in hell, she was up for that, too.

"How long do you figure we'll have to wait for these guys to show their ugly mugs?" Dirk asked while he licked the remaining chocolate from his thumb and forefinger.

"Five days. A week tops," Savannah replied as she watched a seagull swoop low over their blanket. She covered the top of her Coke can with her hand, just in case. She had gotten over the romance of beach seagulls long ago, after one dropped some "special sauce" on her hamburger. She hadn't eaten a Big Mac or fed a bird a french fry since.

"A whole week? That long?" Dirk said with a whine in his voice that irritated the daylights out of her. To Dirk Coulter, "wait" was a four-letter word.

Actually, she expected they might have a nibble from their teenybopper hoods a lot sooner, but she had learned long ago to prepare Dirk for the worst. That way he would delay his three-year-old, spoiled-baby routine of, "Can we go now? Can we go now? Can we, huh, huh, huh?"

It was a litany that made her crazy and caused her to entertain homicidal thoughts about strangulation and dismemberment. She thought it better to lie to him than murder him.

"Yeah, that long," she said. "Even if they're out here, they'll probably want to check us out a few times before they jump us."

"Assuming they're smart, and they probably aren't, or they'd have real jobs."

Savannah grinned. "Like us?"

"Well, like me."

She slugged his arm. "Hey. Just because I'm self-employed now doesn't mean I don't work. It's not easy being a private detective."

"What's hard about it?"

She sighed. "Not being able to pay the bills when you don't have any clients."

"Yeah, but if you had work, you'd miss out on all this. . . ." He waved his arm wide, indicating the deserted, wind-swept beach. "Not to mention my company."

She looked around at the palm trees, swaying in the evening breeze, black silhouettes against a coral- and turquoise-streaked sky. On the far horizon the Avalon Islands floated on a layer of ocean mist and a lighthouse blinked into the gathering darkness. She smiled at him. "Like I said, it's not an easy life. Sometimes I suffer."

"Yeah, yeah. It sucks to be you. I've heard it all before."

Savannah took a deep breath, drinking in the fresh salt air. For just a moment she could see Lance Roman strolling down the beach wearing nothing but a ragged, bloodstained pair of tights, his hair sweeping back from his rugged face with . . . a red baseball cap turned backward, walking with a guy in a Rams sweatshirt . . . ?

"Don't look now," she said, "but we've got company."

Dirk didn't move, but his eyes brightened, and he smiled a nasty little grin. "Oh yeah? Where?"

"Over your right shoulder about sixty feet back. Salt-and-pepper team walking this way."

"Fit the description?"

"Yep. And they're checking us out." Her mouth had suddenly gone dry. She took a long drink from her cola, then set the can on the sand beside her. "How do you wanna play this one, big boy?" she asked him.

"You mean I get to be in charge this time?"

"It's your gig. You call the shots."

He chuckled. "Since when?"

"Now. And you'd better call it, because they're clos-ing in fast."

"I don't wanna be sittin' when they get here," he said.

"Me either."

"So, let's stroll, act lovey-dovey."

"You got it."

He stood and extended his hand to her. Pulling her to her feet, he said, "You want to walk down to the water or stand here and make-out?"

She moved a step closer to him until they were nose to nose. "I wouldn't want them to think we were trying to get away," she said.

"Me either." He reached out his left arm, wrapped it around her waist and pulled her against him.

He smelled like chocolate, leather jacket, and after-shave, not a bad combination, she had to admit. He was also deliciously warm, she decided as she involuntarily snuggled closer . . . and felt a long, hard object be-tween them.

"Is that a pistol in your pocket, or are you just happy to see me?" she asked in her best Mae West impres-sion, while keeping an eye on the approaching twosome in her peripheral vision.

"Actually, it's my Smith and Wesson," he replied as his hand slipped between them and moved slowly be-neath her breasts.

"Then you'd better be reaching for it, boy, and not coppin' a feel."

"Who? Me? Naw, I wouldn't take advantage of a sit-uation like that."

"Oh yes, you're above all that. You—"

Her words were cut off by his lips covering hers. Before she knew what was happening, Good Ol' Dirk was kissing her. And even though she was trying to concentrate on the pair on the beach and attempting to pull her own 9mm Beretta out of its holster beneath her sweater, she couldn't help noticing that he had a tasty smear of caramel on his lower lip.

Oh yes . . . and that Dirk was an especially and un-expectedly good kisser.

Who woulda thunk it? The words ran through her jangled mind a half-second before she reluctantly ended the kiss, Beretta in hand, but still concealed within her sweater.

"Ready?" she said, a bit breathlessly.

She could have sworn she heard him chuckle. "Sure," he said. "Are you?"

She felt the press of his weapon against her midriff. They were both as ready as one could get to be robbed. "Yessiree."

And the dreadful duo had arrived, stopping about six feet away from them.

The white kid in the baseball cap pulled a knife from beneath his oversized windbreaker and held it out in front of him. "Give it up, bitch," he said. "Your purse and your jewelry. Now!"

The black teen produced a length of chain and began to twirl it in a circle in front of him like a cowboy with a lasso. "Your wallet," he told Dirk, "and your watch." He swung the chain in Savannah's direction. "Do it, bitch, or we'll mess up your face bad."

"Naw," she responded, her drawl even thicker than usual. "I don't think so."

She and Dirk pulled away from each other and turned toward the pair. In one fluid movement they both pointed their weapons in the robbers' faces and enjoyed watching their cocky smirks dissolve into looks of shock and profound dismay.

With his left hand, Dirk produced a badge. "San

Carmelita Police Department, and you girls are under arrest."

The black kid dropped his chain onto the sand. He started to back away, his hands held up in front of his face. "No," he said, "I ain't goin' in. No."

"Freeze!" Dirk shouted. "Right there! Don't you move!"

"You can't shoot us, man," the other boy said, moving away with his friend. "It's against the law for you to shoot us when we're not no threat to nobody and we're not—"

A shot crackled in the air, stunning him into silence. The round sizzled as it hit the surf right next to his foot.

Smoke curled from the barrel of Savannah's Beretta.

"Believe me, darlin'," she said, "I missed you because I intended to. Next shot takes your head clean off."

"But . . . but cops can't—" he argued.

"I'm not a cop. Not anymore." Even in the near-darkness her eyes blazed as she stared the kid down. "I'm just a plain ol' citizen who's sick to death of folks not being able to enjoy their beaches because of the likes of you."

"But you can't just shoot me!"

"Oh, but I will. And I'll say you rushed me with a knife. It was all I could do. And you'll be dead, so who's gonna say otherwise?"

The boy looked to his friend, who simply shrugged. Turning to Dirk, he said, "So, what're you gonna do? I'm a juvenile! Are you gonna just stand there and let her shoot a kid?"

Dirk grinned. "Yep. She's a good shot, too . . . hangs out at the range more than I do. She'll take you down with one, two tops." He moved closer to them, stuck his badge back in his pocket, and produced a pair of handcuffs. "Or you can just turn around, put your hands up and spread your legs."

"Oh, man, this sucks," the black kid complained as Dirk cuffed him.

Savannah did the same to his partner and said, "That oughta teach you guys a lesson: Never bring a knife and a chain to a gun fight. Better yet, get a real job at Burger King and work for a living like everybody else."

Ten minutes later, Dirk was shoving his prisoners into the backseat of a patrol car while Savannah watched, content and cheerful. She was looking forward to the rest of the evening. Dirk had promised to buy her dinner, and after a satisfying meal—okay, it would be a hot dog if Dirk was buying—she would head home where she'd relax in a bubble bath, then cozy up in bed with her Lance Roman paperbacks and her two cats to keep her feet warm.

Could life get any better?

"I can't believe it!" she heard one of the robbers say just before Dirk slammed the door in his face. "The cops are having their girlfriends shoot people now! Man, that's not even fair!"

She laughed and laced her arm through Dirk's. Yes, life was good. Very good, indeed.

By the next afternoon, Savannah's pleasant "catch-the-bad-guys buzz" had worn off and things were back to their mundane humdrum. She sat in her overstuffed, rose chintz easy chair, her feet on an equally overstuffed ottoman, with an enormous black cat in her lap.

The feline was as cushy as the chair and footstool, but not nearly as comfortable.

"Ow!" Savannah yelped as needle-sharp teeth sank into her thumb. "Dang it, Cleopatra! You've got to take this medicine! Now open up those jaws before I skin you alive!"

Another black cat, as well-fed as the one being dosed on her lap, sat on a sunlit window perch nearby, grooming itself and oblivious to the drama in the chair. Savannah gave it a nasty look. "Yeah, Diamante, just wash your face like nothing's happening. But you're next."

Across the living room, a slender young woman sat at a rolltop desk, a computer screen in front of her. With her long blond hair pulled back in a ponytail, she looked like a teenager, but the expression on her face as she studied the screen was all business. Tammy Hart took her job as Savannah's assistant in the Moonlight Magnolia Detective Agency far too seriously, much to Savannah's amusement. Savannah was convinced that the kid had read too many Nancy Drew books in her lackluster childhood. Tammy was the only person Savannah had ever known in law enforcement or private detection who actually referred to themselves as a "sleuth."

As Tammy pecked at the keyboard, she said, "Too bad you don't want to expand the agency's horizons a little, try something new. We could make a bundle."

"I've told you before," Savannah said, grimacing at the drop of blood appearing on her thumb, "the day I have to resort to taking dirty pictures of wayward wives, I'll go get a job cleaning hotel toilets." To the cat, she said, "Look at that! You hurt Mommy. And if it gets infected, Mommy's gonna take you to the pound and tell them she doesn't know you, that you're a good-for-nothing varmint that she found rummaging in her garbage can."

The cat growled and laid back her ears.

"Don't you sass me, young lady!" Savannah told her. "There are plenty of good cats in the world who don't bite their owners. You'll find yourself walking that long green mile yet."

"Yeah, yeah," Tammy muttered. "Like you don't threaten those panthers of yours every day. Yesterday, if they didn't stop scratching the sofa, you were going to stretch their hides out to dry on the barn wall. And you don't even have a barn."

"Well, they don't know that, and the garage would do in a pinch." Having successfully shoved the pill down the cat's throat, she gave it a kiss on its glossy black head. "There you go, sweet pea. That wasn't so bad, huh?"

"Really, Savannah," Tammy said, "you should try to think outside the box with this business if you're ever really going to succeed. I've been researching all morning, and I've found something that would be a lot of fun."

Savannah placed the cat on the rug beside her chair, rose and walked over to the window perch. "I'm afraid to ask," she said, "but what is it?"

"Well, like I said, it would be fun. We'd get to role-play, dress up, and go to fancy bars and clubs and——"

"I'm getting too old to play hooker. Those four-inch heels kill me, and I swore that once my leather miniskirt didn't fit anymore I'd find a new undercover persona."

"No, we wouldn't be posing as hookers, just really hot chicks. And we'd be doing the community a great service."

Savannah raised one eyebrow. "The community? A service? What are you talking about, girl? Spit it out."

Taking a deep breath, Tammy launched into her spiel. "Some detective agencies are making handfuls of money by sending out females to . . . well . . . sorta 'test' certain men . . . to see if they're faithful husbands and boyfriends. They come on to the guys in bars and see if they'll go for the bait. And, of course, the whole thing is being taped so that the wife can hear what her man says when he's presented with a temptation that—"

"No!" Savannah reached out and snatched the preening cat off the perch, grabbing her in mid-lick. "I'd rather hose out the dog cages at the pound. I'd rather test urine and stool samples at a local lab. I'd rather—"

"Okay, okay. You don't have to be gross. I get the point. Sheez, try to suggest something novel around here and you get shot down every time."

"We catch bad guys," Savannah told her. "We don't use our God-given feminine wiles to turn good guys— or even morally mediocre guys—into bad guys."

"It wouldn't bother me," Tammy said. "If they weren't already bad, they wouldn't go for it."

Savannah grinned. "Hey, with legs like yours, and boobs like mine, no man could resist, good or bad. With the way you and I look, darlin', it would be pure entrapment."

Laughing, Tammy said, "So true, so true."

Savannah had just settled down in her chair, Diamante tucked tightly in the crook of her left arm, a pill in her right hand, when the doorbell rang.

"Tarnation!" she said. "Would you get that, Tammy?"

"Sure!" With a high degree of energy and enthusiasm that frequently irritated Savannah, Tammy bounded from the desk, across the living room, and into the foyer, leading to the front door.

Savannah's grumpiness evaporated instantly at the sound of a couple of familiar, deep voices.

"Hi, Tammy," said the first, decidedly male, visitor. "How's it going?"

"Good afternoon, my dear," added the second man, his voice dripping with a deliciously classy British accent. "We were in your neighborhood and thought we'd call on Savannah. Is the lady at home?"

"Ryan! John!" Savannah heard Tammy say, followed by an embarrassing amount of adolescent giggling.

Tammy was a sucker for handsome hunks. Unlike Savannah, who was cool, calm, and collected no matter the circumstance.

Savannah jumped out of her chair, spilling Diamante onto the floor, and shoved the pill into her jeans pocket. Running her fingers through her hair and tucking in her T-shirt, she hurried to the door, nearly stumbling over the indignant cat.

"Hey, fellas! What a great surprise!" she said as she rounded the corner and soaked in the sight that always made her a bit weak in the knees. To say that Ryan Stone and his life partner, John Gibson, were easy on the eyes, was a monumental understatement.

Long ago, she had decided that one look at Ryan, the quintessential "tall, dark, and handsome" romantic leading man type, could set her world right. And John, though older than Ryan, was no less debonair with his mane of thick silver hair, lush mustache, and aristocratic, English manners.

The gorgeous twosome was always dressed impeccably. Today they apparently intended to play tennis and were smartly attired in white shorts and polo shirts that set off their tans to perfection.

"Come in," Savannah cried, throwing the door open and ushering them inside. "When did you get back from New York?"

"This morning," Ryan said, his shoulder brushing

Savannah and giving her a thrill that—she hated to admit—was so intense as to be pathetic. "We caught a red-eye and got into LAX about three."

"You must be exhausted! We're just so honored that you'd rush over here right away like this. Let me make you a pot of coffee . . . a cup of Earl Grey for you, John . . . and I've got some chocolate pecan pie that I baked last night. I could—"

"No, no, love," John said, taking her hand and ushering her like a princess to the sofa. "We didn't drop by to have you entertain us."

"Or feed us either," Ryan added, "although I can't believe I'm turning down anything you baked!"

"We have a birthday gift for you." John pulled a small box from behind his back. It was white and tied with a lavender ribbon.

Savannah sat on the sofa, and they settled on either side of her. Tammy perched herself on the edge of the ottoman, an excited grin on her face.

"But it isn't my birthday," Savannah said, grabbing the box with an eagerness that could hardly be considered ladylike. "Not for another eight months."

"We know," Ryan said, "but some presents can't wait, so consider it a harbinger of gifts to come."

She studied the label affixed to the box. The silver lettering read: *Li-Lac's Chocolate, Greenwich Village, NY.*

"I think I'm going to like this. A lot!" she said as she untied the ribbon and opened the lid.

"They're truffles," Ryan said. "The French creams and amarettos are our favorites."

"Yes, we've long been admirers of Li-Lac's," John told her. "When we lived in New York, years ago, I must admit we became shamefully addicted to them."

"And now you're sharing your vices. How generous

of you!" Savannah took a long, deep smell and felt herself ascending to chocolate heaven.

"But are you intending to share?" Tammy asked her. "That's what I want to know."

Ryan laughed. "We bought twice as many, figuring she would."

Holding the box close to her chest, Savannah said, "Since when do you eat junk food, Miss Celery Sticks for Breakfast and Carrot Sticks for Lunch?"

"I make an exception for gourmet candies . . . or any other kind of food that these two recommend."

"It's my birthday present," Savannah said, "but maybe I'll share. We'll see how good they are first."

"Actually, the candy is for both of you." John grinned mischievously. "And your real gift, Savannah, is tucked there, under the candies."

"There's more?" Savannah peered inside and shuffled the chocolates around until she saw a small white envelope underneath.

"Much more," Ryan told her. "And when you open it, you'll see why we had to rush over here this morning."

"Oh, this is fun." Savannah recognized the fine white linen stationery as one of Ryan's standard notecards. And her name was written across the front in his stylish handwriting.

She opened the wax seal on the back, reached inside, and pulled out what looked like a formal invitation, also penned in Ryan's calligraphy.

Her eyes quickly scanned it, and she frowned as she tried to make sense of what she was reading.

"Well, what is it?" Tammy asked breathlessly. "What does it say?"

"It's an invitation to . . . some sort of audition," Savannah said, still reading. "Tomorrow . . . here in town . . . for a . . . Is it a television show?"

John smiled, terribly pleased with himself. "It is, indeed. I'm afraid it's nothing so highbrow as an educational program, but it promises to be fun, if you're game."

Savannah squinted at the paper. "The name of it is *Man of My Dreams,* and I can audition to be some sort of contestant?"

"It's one of those reality shows," Ryan told her, "like *The Bachelorette* or *Joe Millionaire.* You can be one of the ladies who's competing to win a hunk's heart."

Savannah's expression went from confused to shrewd in a half second. "What's the prize?"

"A diamond tiara and a two-week spa vacation with the guy," Ryan said, "to see if, well, you know . . . true love can really blossom."

"To heck with romance blooming and all that rigmarole. I could use a diamond tiara."

"What for?" Tammy giggled. "Are you going to wear it on a stakeout with old Dirko?"

"No, I'll sell the sucker and use the money to patch the holes in my roof before rainy season starts."

"Rainy season?" Tammy looked confused. "This is Southern California."

"Yeah, where it rains like cats and dogs for a couple of weeks every March. And I'm getting tired of climbing around in my dusty old attic on my hands and knees, setting out pans and bowls to catch the drips. I'm telling you, I need that diamond tiara. I'm going to go to this audition, and I'm going to win the contest, too. You wait and see."

"And maybe you'll fall in love, find your true soul mate," Tammy said, a sappy grin on her face.

"Yeah, yeah, whatever."

Ryan chuckled and nudged Savannah's arm. "You haven't asked who he is."

"Who who is?"

"The star of the show, the man of your dreams, the guy whose heart you have to win."

She shrugged. "Eh, who cares. If I set my cap for him, I'll get him. I just turn on the old Southern charm spigot and he's a dead duck. He'll—"

"Lance Roman."

Savannah sat, stunned, not believing her ears. "No," she whispered.

Ryan nodded. "Yep. Lance Roman, the model, the guy on the covers of those books you like to—"

That was when Savannah started screaming, shrieking incoherently—emitting cries that sounded like exclamations of ecstasy one moment and wails of agony the next.

It would only be much later, when she was reliving the moment in her memory, that she would recall somebody saying, "Uh, oh! Is she all right?" and someone replying, "I don't think so. I'm afraid she's gone. What should we do? Somebody throw water on her! Or maybe slap her!"

Chapter

2

As Savannah left her house the next day, suitcases in hand and a joy born of greed and lust in her heart, she paused beside Tammy's classic Volkswagen bug. Looking back at the modest Spanish-style house with its white stucco walls draped in flowering bougainvillea and its crumbling red tile roof, she said, "I'm doing this for you, you know. I've got every piece of sexy lingerie I own in those suitcases. I'm going to prostitute myself by going on a television show and pretending to fall madly in love, just so that you can have a new roof. I hope you appreciate it."

Tammy popped the trunk on the front of the bug and motioned for her to hurry. "You and I and your house know exactly why you're doing this," she told Savannah as she helped her place the suitcases inside. "And it's got a lot more to do with lechery than a diamond tiara."

Savannah grinned. "Whatever are you implying, young lady? You know full well that my intentions are completely mercenary in nature."

"Baloney. You're hoping to lock lips with Lance

Roman, and *you* know it, so don't try to pretend you're
doing it for a roof. I've seen how you look at those
book covers with his picture on them."

"How?"

Instantly, Tammy arranged her face into a dreamy,
sappy, brainless grin that made Savannah slightly nau-
seous.

"I do not!"

"Do, too!"

"Huh-uh. Liar, liar, pants on fire."

"Oh, well, since you argue your point so intelli-
gently. . . ." Tammy opened the driver's door and said,
"Get in. You're going to be late for your audition."

A few minutes later, they were following a winding
road along the foothills that bordered San Carmelita on
the east. Below them and to the west, they could see
the little town spread along the coastline, five times as
long as it was wide. The ocean was mostly obscured by
a haze of winter fog, created by the warm, inland air
meeting the cooler sea breezes. As usual, the overcast
would burn off by the afternoon, giving way to the famous Southern California golden sunshine.

"Are you nervous?" Tammy asked as they left the
city limits and headed east into a long, deep valley that
ran perpendicular to the coast.

"A little, but not much," Savannah replied. She
reached into her purse and pulled out a compact.
Applying a third layer of powder to her nose, she said,
"John and Ryan said this audition is more of a formal-
ity than anything. Apparently one of the five contestants dropped out at the last minute, and they're
supposed to start filming tonight. John recommended
me so highly that they said they'd take me sight un-
seen."

"He and Ryan are friends of the producers, right?"

"Yes. It's a husband-and-wife team, Alexander and Tess Jarvis."

"I've heard of them," Tammy said. "Aren't they the head honchos of the Romance Network, that cable channel?"

"They're the ones. This show is going to play on their network, which isn't like being on HBO or Showtime, but still. . . ."

"It'll be fun."

"It will. Especially with John and Ryan part of the party. John is going to play the butler—or manservant, as they called them back in the olden days. The show has some sort of medieval theme. And Ryan will be the head coachman."

Tammy's lower lip protruded slightly. "I wish I could play some part and hang out with you guys. All I get to do is stay at your house and feed the cats."

"Ah, don't pout. You'll have fun. Don't forget; you have to give them their medicine, too."

"Gee, I can't wait. Better check to make sure my tetanus shot is current."

Savannah reached over and gave her a sisterly pat on the shoulder. "Don't worry. As soon as my foot's firmly in the door, I'll see if we can get you in, too."

"Really?"

"Sure. Maybe you can be my scullery maid. You can play Cinderella, and I'll be one of the ill-tempered stepsisters who's got all the cool clothes."

"Gee, thanks," Tammy said as she turned off the main highway and drove into a small canyon. The road ran beside a meandering, rock-strewn creek that was lined with ancient, gnarled oaks. Several miles from the ocean, there was no sign of morning haze, only brilliant sunlight that streamed through the oak leaves, dappling the ground beneath the trees in a thousand shades of brown and green. The breeze flowing through the car's open windows smelled of dust, wild sage, and eucalyptus.

"We should be just about there," Savannah said, studying a piece of paper with the map that Tammy had downloaded for her on the Internet. "Right after the curve up there, we should see a road on our right. Ryan says the entrance gates are distinctive."

"A distinctive entrance? What's that supposed to mean?"

Savannah shrugged. "He wouldn't elaborate, said we'll know it when we see it. The place has a name: Blackmoor Castle. Sort of romantic, don't you think?"

"Castle?" Tammy thought for a moment. "Wait a second. I think I've seen pictures of this place. A few months ago, the Sunday paper had an article about it, and. . . ."

"And?"

Shooting Savannah a quick, evasive look, she said, "Uh . . . it wasn't a very long article. I don't remember much about it."

"You're such a lousy liar. Spill it."

Tammy cleared her throat. "I think they said something about some eccentric guy from Texas building a mansion that looked like an old castle. He was . . . you know . . . into that sort of thing."

"Medieval history?"

Tammy grimaced. "Well, maybe more like . . . Dracula."

"Dracu—?" The word caught in Savannah's throat because they had rounded the curve and to the right was, indeed, the distinctive entry to Blackmoor Castle. Two enormous marble columns stood on either side of the gravel road, and the pillars were topped with a pair of hideous, snarling gargoyle-like statues. The monster on the left held a dove in its talons and the bird looked as dead as the proverbial duck. His equally evil twin held what appeared to be a squirming cherub in his jagged teeth.

"Yikes," Tammy said.

"Yeah, just charming." Savannah glanced around . . . hoping. "Maybe this isn't it. Maybe . . ."

But then she saw the words carved into the marble of the pillar on the left: "Blackmoor Castle."

"Wishful thinking," Tammy muttered.

"Yeah, well, one could hope. Especially since *one* is going to have to hang out here for a couple of weeks. Eat, sleep . . . or try to."

"Gargoyles are supposed to scare away evil spirits."

Savannah shuddered as they drove past the columns, and she got a close-up look at the beast who was chowing down on the little fat angel. "Yeah, right. These things are so scary-tacky they'd frighten away anything—bad or good. Maybe the rest of the place isn't so hideous. I mean, we're supposed to be filming something romantic here, not *Frankenstein Meets the Werewolf.*"

As they drove down the gravel road, the Volkswagen stirred up a cloud of dust in its wake, obscuring the grim greeters at the entrance. But new horrors quickly appeared in the form of seven statues that lined the right side of the road.

At first, the sculptures simply looked like an assortment of oversized human figures wearing hooded robes. But on closer examination, the expressions on the faces of what turned out to be monks were hideously contorted.

"Boy, that guy looks madder than a wet hen," Savannah said of the first one.

"And that one seems to be soused," Tammy commented.

The third one had his tongue lolling out and a dirty-old-man leer on his face.

"Oh, I get it," Savannah said. "They represent the seven deadly sins. So far we have Rage, Envy, and Lust."

"And that one's got to be Gluttony." Tammy pointed to the fourth figure, which had a plump face and a rotund tummy.

His glazed, sated expression reminded Savannah of the look on Dirk's face after she fed him a rack and a half of her famous barbecued ribs.

"I don't think I'll be taking any moonlight strolls down this road," Savannah said as they passed Jealousy, Greed, and Sloth. "Not even with Lance on my arm."

"Lance Roman on your arm . . . has a certain ring to it, huh?" Tammy giggled. "Do you think you'll get a chance to, like, make out with him?"

"I don't want to even think about it. I don't dare." Savannah sighed. "If I get my hopes up and then I get voted off the first night, I'll have to kill myself."

They passed through a thickly wooded area and when they emerged they got their first glimpse of the castle. From the actual moat with a drawbridge to the battlements and corner round towers with fluttering pennant flags, Blackmoor was the quintessential medieval fortress—at least, at first glance.

"Is that a real moat and drawbridge?" Tammy said as they drove onto the narrow bridge that crossed the ribbon of water circling the structure.

"Looks pretty wet to me," Savannah said peering out the window at the sparkling water below. "But I think I see some goldfish swimming around in there. Are moats supposed to be stocked with goldfish?"

"A crocodile or two would be more effective, protection-wise."

"Maybe they're gold piranhas."

Tammy leaned forward, squinting through the dusty windshield and studying the massive iron gate that hung high above them. Its lower edge sprouted a row of sharp spikes. "That reminds me of the reverse spikes in a parking lot entrance, only more lethal."

"Yeah, if that sucker dropped on you a time or two it'd sure cure you of illegal parking."

Once through the arched entrance, they found themselves in a cobblestone courtyard. Several buildings filled the enclosure created by the protective stone walls that encircled the complex. Most of the structures had steep, granite-tiled roofs and plastered walls with Tudor beam crosshatching. But in the center of the courtyard, the largest of the buildings was shaped more like a traditional castle, with stone walls and arched windows. The top of the edifice was flat and rimmed with a row of giant gargoyles perched on the edge, glaring down on those in the courtyard below.

In front of the structure stood an elegant black carriage. Two huge, white draft horses were hitched to the front in harnesses of crimson leather with shiny silver buckles.

A tall and gorgeous male, wearing a royal blue tunic, black leggings, and knee-high boots stood at the head of one of the horses, stroking its ears and speaking to it soothingly.

Savannah rolled down her window as Tammy pulled the VW alongside the carriage. "Hey, Sir Ryan . . . lookin' good in those leggings."

Leaning across her, Tammy said, "Hi, Ryan. Where should I park?"

He pointed to a barnlike structure behind the main building. "Over there, in yon garage . . . I mean . . . stable."

"Thanks." Tammy gave him a thorough once over. "Savannah's right; you look awesome in tights. You should wear them more often."

"Like to Home Depot?" he asked. "Hooters, maybe?"

Savannah laughed. "Yeah, you spend a lot of time there."

"Hey, I'm on a first-name basis with the paint department and the plumbing section at my Home Depot." He waved them on. "Go park. They don't want automobiles in front of the keep."

"The keep?" Savannah asked.

"That's the main building of a castle," Tammy announced proudly. "The heart of the compound, the most secure area where precious things were kept. Hence the term 'keep.' I've read up on all that stuff."

"I knew that." Savannah turned back to Ryan. "But we can't park here, huh?"

Ryan shook his head. "Nope. Ruins the ambiance, if you know what I mean."

"I guess there's nothing like a hot pink VW bug to jerk you right out of the seventeenth century," Savannah said as they pulled away and headed toward the "stable."

"Seventeenth? If it's the Middle Ages, I think we're talking a lot earlier than that."

"Seventeenth, tenth, eleventh . . . whatever." She shrugged. "I never was any good with dates."

Tammy found one of the garage's six parking spots empty, and she quickly pulled into it. When they got out and looked around, she said, "I don't think the architect who designed this place was too good with his dates either. You've got fifteenth-century Tudor over there, along with the more Norman lines of those battlements, which are from . . . say . . . the turn of the millennium. And those steep, granite roofs with the round turrets and decorative ironwork are reminiscent of a French chateau."

Savannah stuck out her tongue. "Show-off."

Tammy laughed. "You want your suitcases now?"

"We'd better leave them in the car for the moment, just in case I flunk the audition. It cramps your style if you have to lug luggage when you're stomping away in a huff."

"Good thinking."

As they approached the keep, Tammy pointed to a door toward the rear of the building. "Do you suppose we should use one of the back doors . . . you know . . . a servant's entrance?"

"Shoot, no. I'm going straight to the front door. No time like the present to start acting like the lady of the manor."

Tammy shook her head. "You know, Savannah, if you could just come out of your shell. . . ."

"Hey, people only treat you as good as you treat yourself, Tammy darlin'. And you and I just aren't service-door kind of girls."

The front door was an impressive, eight-foot-tall, arched affair with hammered iron hinges and a pewter door knocker shaped like a snarling lion's head. Savannah grabbed the ring that dangled from his bared teeth and gave it a hard rap. The sound echoed across the cobblestones, and from the far end of the courtyard Ryan waved to them from his seat on the carriage and gave them a thumbs-up.

They waited for what seemed like a long time before the door swung open with a deliciously creepy creak. But the woman greeting them was anything but spooky. A young thing, probably less than thirty, wearing a baggy blue dress that reminded Savannah of one of Granny Reid's old flour sacks, she peered at Savannah and Tammy through thick-lensed glasses. She blinked her nearly lashless eyes as though trying to focus. "Yes?" she said, a suspicious tone in her voice.

"This is my friend, Tammy Hart, and my name is Savannah Reid." Savannah extended her hand. "I'm here for an audition."

"Audition?" The woman's pale face was a blank.

"Yes, for the television show."

Recognition dawned in her eyes, and she blinked twice. "Oh, right. You're the replacement for the one who dropped out."

"Ah, yes, I think so."

Suddenly more interested, the woman gave Savannah a thorough once-over from head to toe, taking in her navy blue suit and simple white blouse. The suit wasn't expensive, but the cut was smart, emphasizing her hourglass figure. Her shoes and purse weren't designer either, but they were high-grade leather and stylish. And Savannah had actually taken half an hour to apply her make-up, rather than her usual slap-dash of lipstick.

Apparently, the woman liked what she saw, because she smiled, accepted Savannah's outstretched hand, and gave it a hearty shake. "I'm Mary Branigan," she said, "personal assistant to Mrs. Jarvis. Come inside."

Savannah and Tammy passed through the arched doorway and into a dark, cavernous foyer. It took several seconds for Savannah's eyes to adjust to the low light, and when they finally did, she had to restrain herself to keep from running back outside into the sunshine and fresh air.

The stone walls seemed to close around them, in spite of the immense size of the room and the torch sconces that flickered at ten-foot intervals along each side. The vaulted ceiling was so high and dark that it appeared to disappear into the shadows. Savannah half-expected to be attacked by a swarm of vampire bats at any moment.

To her right, at the bottom of a curved staircase stood a suit of armor. Its body plates were silver-colored metal, but the helmet was black and had things that looked like horns sticking out the top of it. On its chest was a blood-red crusader's cross.

Not nearly as friendly-looking as the greeter at Wal-Mart, Savannah thought as they walked by him, instinctively not getting too close.

She gave Tammy a quick, sidewise look and saw from the expression of dismay on her face that she shared the same opinion of the new accommodations.

"Grim," Savannah whispered to her.

"I beg your pardon?" Mary asked.

"Ah . . . dim," Savannah said, plastering a semipleasant smile on her face. "It's a bit dim in here, but I suppose it's for atmosphere."

"Ambiance," Mary said. "It's the perfect location for the show, don't you think? So romantic."

"Um-m . . . sure." *If you're filming* The Bloody Bride of Dracula, Savannah added mentally.

"Mrs. Jarvis is in the dining hall with the camera crew," Mary said. "It's this way. Follow me."

"The dining hall . . . that sounds sorta neat," Tammy said with that overly optimistic tone that made Savannah want to shoot her at sunrise, when Miss Pollyanna Hart was at her most irritating perkiness.

"Yeah, well, we shall see," Savannah muttered under her breath as they followed Mary Branigan down a long, dark corridor lit by torches.

Savannah noted as they passed one sconce after another that they were lit with electricity, their "flames" produced by small, flickering lightbulbs. She supposed the artificial fire was much more practical and far safer than the real thing, but she couldn't help thinking it looked a bit cheesy.

"It probably looks really good on camera," Tammy whispered, as though reading her thoughts.

Ahead of them, Mary paused and said over her shoulder, "Don't you just *love* Blackmoor? Don't you just feel as if you've stepped back in time inside these walls?"

Savannah looked at a tapestry hanging on the wall to her left, a forest scene where hunters on horseback were plunging spears into a bloody, writhing unicorn. *Yeah, really cozy,* she thought. *I'll never see a unicorn the same way again; thank you very much for ruining a childhood fantasy.*

On the wall to her right hung a collection of swords, axes, knives, crossbows, and other nasty-looking weapons with assorted blades and spikes that she couldn't name. Over the armory was a carved wooden sign that read: "Death or Glory."

"Aye, positively jolly," she replied in her best old English. Then she whispered to Tammy, "In a Madame Tussaud's 'Chamber of Horrors' sort of way."

The corridor was so long that Savannah was convinced they had walked all the way back to the Middle Ages when they finally reached the dining hall. And their guide didn't have to announce the location for them to realize they had arrived.

This wasn't your average breakfast nook, Savannah decided the moment they stepped inside. "Wow," she said. "You could hold a jousting tournament in here and still have room for a three-ring circus."

"No kidding," Tammy said, her eyes wide. "I always wanted a dining hall of my own. I think I'll have one built in my apartment. This is neat!"

"Nothing like a fireplace you can walk around in," Savannah said, "and chandeliers that trapeze artists could swing from."

Jewel-toned pageantry banners hung from the coffered ceiling, illuminated by half-a-dozen wrought-iron, spoked-wheel chandeliers. Tapestries softened and warmed the stone walls, hanging alongside groupings of shields bearing heraldic crests.

The wall to their left was lined with a row of elaborately carved mahogany chairs and several austere monk's benches. A pair of matching marble-topped buffets were decorated with gleaming brass candlesticks and sculptures of everything from angels to dragons.

The immense stone fireplace dominated the wall to their right and was flanked by two suits of armor. Savannah allowed her mind to wander as she imagined Lance Roman in one of those suits, riding toward her on a white stallion, sweeping her into his. . . .

"Come along," Mary said, breaking the spell and jerking her back to the present. "Mrs. Jarvis wanted to see you as soon as you got here."

She was pointing to the far end of the room where a woman stood talking to two men and gesturing wildly. As they approached the threesome, Savannah could hear the woman say, "That's it! That's all! If I could afford a bigger crew, I'd have one. But, like it or not, you're it. Do you want the gig or not?"

Both men grumbled but nodded, shifting from one foot to the other, staring at the floor.

Mary, Savannah, and Tammy paused ten feet from the group and waited for Tess Jarvis to acknowledge them. But she continued her rant, informing the unhappy men that she didn't have Martin Scorsese's budget, and if she did, she would hire *his* camera and sound crew, not the two of them.

Savannah took the opportunity to study the woman, and she had to classify her initial impression as "a giant pumpkin." From the unnatural marmalade tint of her short, unevenly cropped hair, to the tangerine shade of lipstick that Savannah hadn't seen in stores for twenty years, to the orange pantsuit that was much too tight for her plump figure, Tess Jarvis looked like a spokesperson for a citrus juice commercial. A very hyper spokesperson.

From her hands, that were fluttering in the air around her like skittish parakeets, to her feet, that were tapping, shuffling, jigging around as though she were standing barefoot on an old-fashioned furnace grid . . . Tess Jarvis was a bundle of nerves.

Savannah decided she could get thoroughly sick of her in two minutes. Possibly ten seconds.

Tess turned her attention from the unhappy men to Savannah, as Mary introduced them. She looked Savannah up and down, conducting her own quick evaluation, and from the slight nod of her head, Savannah surmised she might have passed Jarvis muster.

Then Tess frowned as though reconsidering. "How old are you?" she asked brusquely.

Savannah lifted one eyebrow and chuckled. "My Granny Reid taught me that a lady never answers a question with a number—you know . . . age, weight, income. . . ."

She bit back the rest of Gran's quote: "Or *asks* a question requiring a number."

"You're over forty, though, I'll bet," Tess persisted.

"A bit."

"I guess that's okay, but I wish John Gibson had told me that. He was right, though, when he said you're fat."

Savannah bristled. Yes, she was thoroughly sick of Tess Jarvis. Sick enough to smack her silly.

She lifted her chin a couple of notches and fixed Tess with an icy blue stare. In a low but chilly voice she said, "I've known John Gibson for years now, and he is the quintessential gentleman. I'm absolutely certain he would never refer to me or any other woman as 'fat.' "

Tess looked a bit taken aback by Savannah's tone. Apparently, she wasn't accustomed to being contradicted. After a long and awkward pause, she shrugged and waved a dismissive hand. "Well, maybe he didn't use that exact word. He might have described you as something like·... deliciously voluptuous or delectably bodacious."

Savannah grinned. "Now *that* sounds like John."

"Of course, we all know what *that* means. It's like 'plump' and 'chubby.' It's just a nice way of saying 'fat.' And I should know; I'm not exactly a toothpick myself."

Savannah placed her hands on her waist and struck a Mae West pose. "Who wants to be a toothpick?" she said. "I'd rather think of myself as overly blessed with an abundance of feminine fascinations."

Tess thought for a moment, then smiled and nodded. "Not bad. I can see why John recommended you. And Lance will like you, too. He likes feisty women with a little extra meat on their bones."

Lance will like you. The words shot through Savannah's brain, making her knees wobbly and causing other, more intimate, parts of her anatomy to feel warm and tingly. A dozen pirate/ knight/ fireman fantasies flashed across the screen of her imagination.

"Take Lady Savannah upstairs to her ... ah ... bedchamber, Mary," Tess said. "Get her settled in." She turned to Savannah. "You'd better rest while you can. We're going to start taping about six this evening, and for the next couple of weeks, you won't have time to breathe."

Breathe? Breathe? Savannah thought as she and

Tammy followed Mary Branigan out of the dining hall, past the banners and tapestries, past the family crests, stained glass windows and suits of armor. *Who can breathe and think about Lance Roman at the same time?* she thought. *Hell, I'm not even sure I've got a measurable pulse.*

Chapter

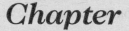

3

After spending only three hours in the "Middle Ages," Savannah had already reached a conclusion: The good old days weren't all they were cracked up to be. In fact, the romantic era of knights and ladies pretty much stunk.

Standing in her costume, an ensemble that she wouldn't wear to a dog fight—or, as the case might be, a *cat* fight—she cursed the man who invented laced bodices. No woman would have dreamed up such a torture device; she was certain of that.

When the make-up/wardrobe woman, a cute young thing named Kit Eckert, had laced her into it, Savannah had complained bitterly, only to be told that she'd better get used to it. She'd be wearing a medieval costume for the next two weeks. Then Kit had put a silly-looking hair net thing that she'd called a snood on the back of Savannah's head and slapped an obscene amount of make-up on her face before sending her on her merry way.

Many times, Savannah had fantasized about meeting Lance Roman. But in none of those erotic scenarios had she been looking like a gothic hooker with a fish-net on her head.

The only upside to the outfit was the cleavage. Looking down at her uplifted and overflowing bosom, she had to admit that the costume made the most of her womanly charms. And Tess's words, "Lance will like you," kept running through her mind, making the need to breathe seem a little less important. *What sacrifice for love?* she kept telling herself. Not to mention a diamond tiara.

But that was before she had been told to go stand in the courtyard and wait. That was before she had seen the horse that Ryan had led out of the stable—a horse as tall as a building with a stupid contraption called a sidesaddle on its broad back. And Ryan was holding its bridle and telling Savannah she was supposed to climb aboard.

"Yeah, right," she whispered, trying to avoid having her words picked up by the tiny microphone they had clipped to the inside of her blouse. "Like there's a chance I'm going to get on that beast. No way."

She fought the urge to glance right, toward the big, shaggy guy who had a camera trained on her. Tess had warned her a dozen times that she wasn't to look at the camera. She had to pretend that woolly Leonard with the mop of long, curly hair and the scraggly beard wasn't even there, pointing a lens at her.

Also, she had been told to ignore Pete the soundman, who could appear at any minute carrying a long boom with a fuzzy "sock" on the end of it. Even if the wind sock was practically hitting her on the head or if Pete was shoving it up her nose, she was supposed to pretend it didn't exist.

Pasting a phony smile on her face, she leaned closer to Ryan and whispered, "I can't do it. I'm afraid . . . I mean . . . I'm not big on horses. One bit a plug out of me when I was a kid."

Ryan smiled down at her, reached over and placed a hand on her shoulder. His expression was that of a supportive, caring, older brother. But it wasn't nearly enough to convince her to start playing Annie Oakley at her age.

"John told Tess you could ride," he said. "You can't?"

"Sh-h-h-h," she said, nodding toward the microphone clipped to his tunic front.

"They aren't recording us," he told her. "This scene is just visual. They'll play some schmaltzy music in the background when and if they show it."

"How's it going over there?" Tess shouted across the courtyard. She was standing near the front door of the keep, waiting for Savannah to ride over to her.

"Fine," Ryan called back. "I just have to adjust the saddle." He pretended to busy himself with a strap beneath the horse's belly.

"No, I can't ride," she said, nearly choking on the admission.

"Have you ever been on a horse?"

Ever been on a horse? Her mind flashed back to a summer day back in Georgia when she was thirteen. Trying to impress a boy she liked, she had attempted to ride his father's farm horse. After two unsuccessful attempts to launch herself onto the enormous animal's back, she had given it a mighty third effort. She had sailed over the horse and promptly fallen off the other side. And then the horse had reached around and bitten her on the rear end.

But . . . for half a second, she had technically been *on* the horse.

"Of course I've been on a horse," she replied with what she hoped was just the right touch of righteous indignation. "I just don't particularly like riding them. They smell and attract flies."

"You'll be fine," Ryan said, again flashing her a sweet, big-brother smile. "I'll give you a boost up onto the saddle, and you'll be on your way over there to meet Lance."

Savannah looked across the courtyard at the keep where Tess, Mary, and John waited. The directions had been simple enough. "Get on the horse, ride straight toward us and wait on your horse. Lance will ride through the gate and across the courtyard to greet you."

Only one ride on a flea-bitten mule stands between you and your prince, she told herself. Then she took another look at the exquisite black horse in front of her, odor free, fly-less, and dignified. She chided herself for her cowardice. *Since when did you sprout wings and start clucking, Savannah girl?* asked a voice in her head that sounded a lot like her Granny Reid's. *Get up on that horse before you're a minute older!*

"Let's do it," she told Ryan. "Daylight's a'burnin'."

Ryan placed his hands on her waist, and much more smoothly than she had expected, lifted her onto the horse. From her seat, which felt at least ten stories aboveground, she said, "I can't tell you how stupid it feels to be sitting sideways on a horse."

"But that's the way fair ladies sat in days of yore," Ryan told her.

"Yeah, well, if straddle was good enough for Dale Evans, it should be okay for me. I'm afraid I'm going to slide off."

"I'll walk beside you, and if you do, I'll catch you."

At any other time, Savannah might have been tempted to fall off intentionally, just for the chance to land in Ryan's arms. But the prospect of meeting Lance Roman was even more enticing. Realizing that those were her two worst possible scenarios, she decided she might just be the luckiest woman on earth, sidesaddle or not.

Her only scare was when the horse first began to move, but before she knew it, she was across the courtyard and standing near Tess, who was hidden from the camera's view behind a hedge.

"That's it," Tess was saying. "Just wait right there. Leonard—the gate! Lance should be coming through it right about . . . now!"

The cameraman and everyone else turned toward the castle wall's arched gateway. Anticipation built by the second, until Savannah felt as though she would pass out cold, then and there. Then she realized she wasn't breathing, and she knew it wasn't because of the bodice.

She was about to see *him*. Lance Roman himself. And if she didn't stop shaking she was going to fall off the horse and onto her face. And having that happen twice in a lifetime—in front of a male she was in lust with—would simply be more than a body could bear. She'd wind up shopping on eBay for a hara-kiri knife.

Fortunately, the suspense was quickly broken by the sound of a galloping horse, coming toward the castle entrance. She heard the thundering of its hooves on the wooden drawbridge, then suddenly, a white horse and its rider burst through the gate and into the courtyard.

It was Lance all right, dressed in blue and black medieval garb, racing toward her, his dark hair streaming out behind him, wearing thigh-high leather boots, leggings that hugged his famous muscular thighs, a blue suede doublet that accented his broad shoulders and narrow waist, a white cavalier's shirt that was open just enough to reveal a sprinkling of hair on a deeply tanned chest. He was the living embodiment of Savannah's favorite highwayman fantasy. And he was riding straight to her.

The next few minutes were a hazy pink blur for Savannah as he pulled his horse to a halt beside hers and jumped down from his mount. In a couple of strides, he was standing beneath her, looking up at her with the bluest eyes she had ever seen.

"Lady Savannah," he said, extending his hands to her, "what a pleasure to meet you. May I help you down from your horse?"

"Ye-es, please," she managed to croak.

She was going to place her hands in his, but he reached for her waist instead, and a moment later she was on the ground in front of him, her hands on his broad shoulders, gazing up into those amazing eyes.

He smiled at her, and she felt herself melting into a puddle at his feet. "You're just as lovely as they said," he told her. "I'm looking forward to getting to know you."

Know me? she thought. *Know me intimately? Know me in the biblical sense of the word?* Her eyes traveled over his face, taking in the high cheekbones, the patrician nose, the strong jaw and chin line that would have been perfect for a shaving commercial. *Oh, yes . . . know me, darlin'! Know me good!*

But Granny Reid had raised her to be a lady . . . or at least to act like one when being filmed for a television show, so she batted her eyelashes, smiled demurely and said, "Why, kind sir, it will be *my* pleasure, I'm sure."

He offered her his arm. "Would you join me this evening at my banqueting table?"

"I would be delighted." She laced her arm through his, and together they strolled through the front door of the keep.

As they walked together she momentarily forgot everyone and everything around her: grungy Leonard with his camera in her face, Pete the soundman with his fuzzy microphone over her shoulder, even Tess and Mary . . . they all faded into oblivion as she savored the touch of her hand on his arm, the warmth that radiated through his shirt, the hard, rounded muscles just below the cloth.

And the way he looked down at her, his sapphire eyes aglow, locked with hers as though they were the only two people in the wor—

"Cut!" Tess yelled. "That should do it."

Do it? Do what? What do you mean, "Cut"? Savannah thought.

"Let's go get the other girls. We've got a lot to do this afternoon before we lose the light," Tess said, motioning to Lance.

Other girls? What other girls? He was looking at me like I was the only woman on earth.

Instantly, Lance dropped her arm and walked away from her without a backward glance, let alone a lovelorn gaze.

The spell had been so abruptly broken that Savannah felt a bit like a princess who had been changed into a frog. And Tess was the wicked fairy godmother who had given her warts.

"Well, if that ain't a fine how-do-you-do," she muttered.

She sensed someone standing behind her and turned to see Mary Branigan watching her, a sympathetic look on her face. "You did that well," she said, "for someone without acting experience."

"Who was acting?" Savannah said. "I mean, he's so gorgeous."

Mary looked over Savannah's shoulder at the retreating figure and sighed. "How true! Every woman between the ages of eight and eighty must fall in love with Lance at first glance," she said dreamily. Then she shook her head as though coming out of a trance.

"You'd better go upstairs and get some rest while you can. It's going to be a long, long night for all of us."

"No more horseback riding, I hope."

Mary shook her head. "No. Tonight's the royal banquet."

Savannah brightened at the thought of food. "A medieval feast? Warm, honeyed mead, roasted venison, and all that?"

"Well . . ." Mary gave her a quick, sideways glance that didn't inspire confidence. "I don't know how much eating and drinking anybody will actually do, but that's the impression we're supposed to give . . . for the camera, that is. And you'll get to meet the other girls."

"Ah, yes, my competition." Savannah looked around and leaned closer to her. "What do you think of them?"

For just a second, Savannah was certain she saw a flicker of disgust cross Mary's face, but it disappeared just as quickly. The young woman shrugged her thin shoulders. "They're okay, I guess. A diverse group. A little bit of this, a little bit of that."

"What do you mean?"

"You'll see tonight. Like I said, you'd better get some rest. Knowing Tess and Alex, they'll work our butts off this evening."

Work? Savannah thought as she climbed the stairs to the third story, where her assigned bedroom was located. *Feasting, drinking, making merry, and looking at Lance Roman's face. How much work can that be?*

"I've gotta tell you," Savannah whispered to her nearest competitor, a petite redhead named Brandy, "I don't recall when I've been so aggravated, tired and hungry."

Brandy sat to Savannah's right, and a pretty Asian woman named Leila sat to her left at the banqueting table—a table where not a lot of banqueting had been going on. At least, not nearly enough to suit Savannah, who hadn't had a decent meal since breakfast, and that seemed like years ago.

Platters of bread, cheese, and all sorts of fruit had been placed before her, the other four ladies who were vying for Lance Roman's attention, and the lord of the manor himself. Ryan, John, and Mary, dressed in medieval garb, had also poured great mugs of golden and dark red liquids that looked like rich ale and wine and placed a suckling pig with an apple in its mouth in the middle of the table.

While Savannah was a bit turned off to the head—never having been fond of letting her food watch her while she ate it—she was ready to devour the wee-wee piggy, even if he was still oinking.

But then she had realized that all the "food" was fake, plastic stuff, like one might see displayed in the window of a really bad deli, which explained why the sumptuous fare had no aroma, sumptuous or otherwise.

Even the beverages were nothing more than kiddy fruit punches of the powdered variety.

"I know what you mean," Leila said, tugging at the bottom edge of her laced bodice. "I'm tired of doing this same old scene over and over again, and I'm sick to death of this stupid corset thing!"

From the other side of the room, Pete Woznick, the soundman, motioned to them, then laid his finger across his lips. Apparently, the sensitive microphones clipped to the necklines of their blouses were picking up their whispers. He looked as irritated as Savannah felt.

So much for a romantic dinner with Lance Roman. He sat at the opposite end of the table, flanked by a blond sexpot called Roxy Strauss to his right and a lean black beauty named Carisa Middleton to his left. Both women had dominated his attention and the conversation since the taping began. Savannah had heard far more about Roxy's lingerie modeling career and Carisa's television commercial auditions than she would ever want to know.

Tess Jarvis had been standing on the sidelines for a change, allowing her husband to run the show. A stout, bald fellow in a gaudy tropical shirt and baggy Bermuda shorts, Alexander Jarvis looked at least ten years older than his wife. But he was as energetic and nervous as she. His voice was high and nasal with a whining quality that gave Savannah the jitters.

"Cut, cut, cut!" he shouted, waving his arms wildly. "This isn't anything we can use—a total waste of tape. Start over. And this time could we have some scintillating conversation, please? I'm not seeing any chemistry here, Lance. Wake up, man. You look like you're about to fall asleep on us."

Tess stepped forward and added her bit. "Roxy, enough about the underwear modeling already. Carisa, deodorant commercials are not the stuff great TV is made of, okay?"

Roxy's lower lip stuck out in a pout, and she turned to Alex with a plaintive expression that clearly asked him to intervene. He pretended not to see, but Tess shot her a hateful look so intense that Savannah was startled. Apparently, there was bad blood between the two women.

Carisa bristled, too, and said, "Yeah, well, you try to think of something cutesy to say when you've been at this for five hours and haven't had anything to eat all day. And these stupid costumes suck! Nobody told us we'd have to wear these tight girdles that—"

"Corsets," Roxy interjected. "They're corsets. Don't you actresses know anything?"

"Actually, they're bodices," Kit, the make-up and wardrobe woman, said from her position behind the cameraman. "And—"

"I don't care what they're called!" Carisa shouted. "I'm not going to wear this thing for two weeks. It's so damned tight it's choking me."

"Too bad it's not around your neck," Roxy muttered, loud enough for everyone to hear.

Savannah gouged Brandy and Leila in the ribs. "Okay, girls, that's our cue. Enough of this crap already. Come on."

She stood, pulling Brandy out of her chair, then hurried around the table to the other side where Lance sat. With not-so-gentle pressure, she placed one hand around Roxy's upper arm and pulled her to her feet. "You're outta here," she told her. "Our turn. Same with you, Carina or Catrisa or whatever your name is. You've been hogging the spotlight long enough. Brandy, sit down there in her place. Leila, scootch closer over here, and let's get this show on the road."

Other than a couple of soft gasps, nobody objected. Even Carisa and Roxy cooperated, surrendering their chairs and retreating to the other end of the table.

Savannah patted her hair, adjusted her bodice and its contents for the maximum effect, licked her lips and turned to the cameraman. "Let her roll, Leonard."

Leonard looked at Tess and Alex; they nodded. The camera started to purr.

Savannah scooted her chair next to Lance's and leaned against him, making sure he had an unobstructed view of her décolletage. Placing one hand on his sleeve, she ran her fingertips over his world-famous biceps and said in a hushed, breathy voice, "So, Lance . . . I have a lot of fantasies about you, but my favorite is from *Pirate of Wolf Cove* . . . that steamy scene in the lighthouse where you . . . ah . . . pillage the heroine's treasure chest."

Lance's blue eyes widened, then he gave her a suggestive smile.

Our cover boy's wide awake now, she thought a moment later when she glanced down at his lap.

From the corner of her eye, she could see Alex and Tess Jarvis cheer up instantly. Even Kit and Pete the soundman looked acutely interested.

So far, so good. She trailed her hand up to Lance's throat, where the deep vee of his shirt revealed a sprinkling of dark chest hair. "Tell me, darlin'," she breathed, "what's *your* favorite fantasy?"

When Savannah woke at one-thirty in the morning, she wasn't sure where she was. The canopy hanging over the bed confused her, as did the unfamiliar shadows cast by the moonlight shining through a stained glass window to her left. The mattress beneath her felt like wooden planking compared to her cushy feather bed at home—courtesy of Granny Reid. And the pillow under her head was twice the size of her usual one, causing a major knot in her neck muscles.

But those were only small discomforts compared to the major rumblings and grumblings of her near-empty stomach. Although she was known for her larger-than-life appetite, she couldn't recall when she had been so ravenously hungry.

I wonder if there's the makings of a bologna sandwich in that kitchen downstairs, she thought. *Or maybe a fried peanut butter and banana sandwich, some macaroni and cheese, and a big bowl of ice cream and some chocolate chip cookies.*

Just a little something to take the edge off her hunger—that was all she asked.

The two measly pizzas that Tess's assistant had ordered earlier in the evening hadn't gone far with the famished girls and crew. One and a half slices of a thin-crust pepperoni pie wasn't Savannah's idea of a meal . . . not unless it was chased by a pint of Ben and Jerry's Chunky Monkey.

She threw back the lace-trimmed sheet and the pink satin duvet and got out of bed. After fishing around in the dark for her slippers, she stubbed her toe on an accent table and decided to turn on a light. It took her a while to remember that she hadn't yet unpacked her robe. Pulling it out of her suitcase, she again congratulated herself for having at least a few nice pieces of sleepwear.

Although she operated on a cotton and rayon budget, she had treated herself to a few silk gowns and matching robes. This set was a particularly becoming shade of sapphire, a rich brocade that set off her dark hair and accented her blue eyes.

She didn't really think she would happen to see Lance Roman during this next two weeks when she was dressed in her nightclothes, but it never hurt to be prepared.

Slipping the robe on over her gown, she tied the sash with its satin fringed end and glanced at her reflection in the dresser mirror.

"You look fine, darlin', " she told the woman looking back at her with soft eyes and hair that was just bed-tousled enough to be moderately sexy. "Yep, just fine and dandy. That's you!"

Her morale bolstered, but her stomach still empty, she left the bedroom.

Although she generally had a keen sense of direction, Savannah wandered around the dark halls of the keep's third floor quite a while before she finally located the staircase that led to the lower levels. And, although she didn't usually spook easily, she had to keep a tight rein on her imagination as she passed the castle's creepy props. A suit of armor made her jump as she hurried by it on the stair landing, and a panther's skin stretched on the wall of the second set of stairs gave her the shivers.

"I wouldn't want to try to shove a pill between your teeth," she told the trophy as she stared at the bared yellow fangs and golden taxidermy eyes.

As well as its eccentric décor, the keep had a thick, heavy silence about it that was broken only by the occasional creak of Savannah's footsteps on the wooden stairs and the far-off yelping of some coyotes in the distant hills.

But that was fine with Savannah, who wanted complete solitude on this little excursion. If she could just find her way to the kitchen, score a triple-decker sandwich and a dessert of some sort, and return to her room undetected, she would be a happy wench, indeed. The last thing she needed right now was to run into one of those other—

"Roxy!" she said as she reached the bottom of the staircase and nearly ran headlong into the blonde, who was headed up, an apple in one hand and a bottle of water in the other.

Like Savannah, Roxy was in her nightclothes, but as Savannah might have expected of a professional lingerie model, her gown and robe were a cut above anything in Savannah's wardrobe. Upon closer inspection of Roxy's plunging neckline, Savannah decided that the black silk gown with its strategically placed lace inserts was definitely a few cuts *below* anything she would wear . . . even on a hooker stakeout.

For a moment Roxy looked flustered to be running into anyone, even a bit guilty as she stammered out an explanation. "I, um, was still a little hungry, and I'm on this ten-day, apple-and-water-only diet and didn't eat any of the pizza tonight and . . . ."

Savannah shook her head in disgust. "Shoot, girl, you don't have to apologize to me for what you eat. If you want an apple, have one. But you need a big hunk of cheese and a glass of wine to go with it, and maybe a handful of cashews, too."

Roxy's eyes widened and her jaw dropped, as though she had just heard a string of blasphemy. "Why . . . why . . . no! I couldn't. I . . . oh. . . ." Then Roxy took a long look up and down Savannah's figure and a nasty smirk appeared on her face. "But, I guess you could," she said, "and do . . . quite often."

Savannah gave her a too-sweet smile in return. "I do," she said, "and I highly recommend it. How do you think I got this divine cleavage? It sure wasn't from eating apples and drinking water. I have better things to do than spend my life in a bathroom."

Leaving Roxy to ponder the possible disadvantages of her apple diet, Savannah made her way through the dark maze of the downstairs hallways to the back of the building, where she had caught a glimpse of a kitchen during their brief tour.

As she approached the kitchen's open door, she heard the murmur of lowered voices coming from inside. And her heart skipped a beat as she got closer because, even though she couldn't hear their distinct words, she recognized the male voice as *his*.

Apparently Lance himself couldn't sleep tonight either.

When she entered the room, she saw Lance and Mary Branigan sitting on high stools at the center island. A large stained glass lamp shade, suspended over the marble-topped counter, lit Lance's dark hair and bronzed skin, giving him an aura that was almost other-worldly. Savannah had to fight the urge to just stop dead in her tracks and stare at him for an hour or two.

The fact that he was wearing a simple gray UCLA sweatshirt and a pair of well-worn jeans did nothing to detract from his appeal. In fact, Savannah considered it all the more amazing that this Grecian god of gorgeousness would deign to walk among them, dressed like a mere mortal.

He and Mary didn't seem to notice her at first, so intent were they on their conversation. When, finally, Mary looked her way, she jumped and said, "Oh, hi." She nudged Lance's forearm. "Look, Lance; it's Savannah."

He turned his head and locked eyes with Savannah. Again, her knees weakened, and the thought passed through her head that if she were to just fall down on the floor for no apparent reason, it would be most embarrassing, indeed. How could you gracefully explain how you tripped over your own feet when you weren't even walking? It was about as difficult as trying to look cool while choking on your own spit during an important and tense conversation—something she had done more often than she cared to admit.

Legs, don't fail me now, she thought as she walked across the flagstone floor to the island where they sat. She noticed that Mary was also in her nightclothes, a simple white gown with a cheap purple velour robe. Her hair was mussed, as though she, too, had just rolled out of bed.

A heavy silence hung in the air, along with a whiff of tension. "Hope I didn't interrupt anything," she said, looking from one to the other.

Mary and Lance glanced at each other, then Mary giggled and covered her mouth with her hand. "Just some gossip," she said.

"Something juicy?" Savannah asked.

Lance shrugged. "Just your standard, on-set rumor mongering."

More interested in food than gossip, Savannah looked around the kitchen with single-minded purpose. Ordinarily she might have taken time to admire the rustic ambiance: the giant, stone fireplace with its iron spit, the stained glass-fronted cabinets, the marble counters and copper sinks. But not with her stomach growling and her blood sugar level dropping by the moment.

It was only when she had stuck her head into the double-wide refrigerator that she realized—this was the perfect moment to score some contest points.

She looked over her shoulder and gave Lance one of her most beguiling, deep-dimpled smiles. "So, tell me, big boy," she said, "are you as hungry as I am? If you are, I'd be happy to dish you up something tasty."

He grinned, and his blue eyes twinkled. "I'll just bet you could. What did you have in mind?"

"Oh, I have an extensive repertoire." She waggled one eyebrow. "But judging from the contents of this ice box, I'd say you're lookin' at steak and eggs. Maybe some home fries. . . ."

"You can do that?" He looked highly impressed . . . just the way she wanted him to be.

"Darlin', you'd be surprised what I can do." She turned to Mary. "And how about you, Miss Mary? I'd be glad to scare up some for you, too, while I'm at it."

Mary shook her head. "Not for me, thanks. I think I'll head back to bed . . . if I can get some sleep, that is," she added, giving Lance a sideways look.

"Am I missing something here?" Savannah asked as she assembled the ingredients for thcir late night breakfast on the counter. "If I'm willing to slave over a hot stove, the least you two could do is share your gossip with me."

Mary cleared her throat and glanced toward the kitchen's front and rear doors. Seeing no one else about, she said, "Lance and I both heard Alex and Tess arguing earlier. Woke us up from a sound sleep, in fact."

Savannah grabbed a copper skillet from an overhead rack and plopped it onto the eight-burner gas stove. "Oh? What were they fighting about?"

Lance looked uncomfortable with the topic as he shifted on his stool. "Who knows?" he said. "Something about the way the taping's going so far. I think Alex is happier with the results than Tess. But that's nothing new."

"Tess is a bit harder to please?" Savannah asked.

Mary gave a sniff. "Tess is impossible to please. And I should know. I've been her personal assistant for five years. I have the battle scars to prove it."

"I hope you're speaking figuratively, not literally," Savannah said as she hauled some potatoes and onions out of the pantry.

"Sure," Mary replied dryly. "Not all scars are on the outside."

Lance nodded. "Tess knows how to hit you so that the cuts and bruises don't show."

"Sounds like you have a history with the Jarvises, too," Savannah observed.

"Even longer than Mary's," he said. "Tess got me my first book cover ten years ago. You might say she 'discovered' me."

"Working a soda fountain in Hollywood?"

"No, nothing so glamorous." A shadow crossed Lance's face. Savannah noted the brief sadness in his eyes, but she wasn't sure how to interpret it. He didn't elaborate.

"Well, like I said, I'm going back to bed." Mary slid off her stool and patted Lance's shoulder as she walked away. "You two have a nice breakfast and get some sleep. Tomorrow's going to be worse than today."

"Ah, something to look forward to," Savannah said as she began to scrub the potatoes in the sink.

"By the way," Mary said, pausing in the doorway. "I don't suppose you'll have room for dessert after all that, but if you do . . ."

"Yes?" Savannah perked up. "There's always room for dessert."

"Then you might want to raid the big walk-in freezer downstairs, next to the wine cellar. Tess always has a big bowl of gourmet ice cream after dinner. She's bound to have some stashed down there. Just don't let her know I told you about it."

"Mary, you're a gem of a woman!" Savannah said. "I owe you one."

"You'll owe me more than that before this is all over." With that, Mary disappeared, leaving Savannah deliciously alone with Lance.

"Sounds ominous," Savannah told him.

"She's just been on locations before with Tess and Alex. She knows the score."

"Sounds like you do, too."

"Let's just say it's been a long ten years." He watched her quietly for a few moments as she popped the potatoes into the skillet and the steaks under the broiler. "What do *you* do, Savannah? Are you a chef?"

She laughed. "Not even close. Although sometimes I feel like a greasy spoon short-order cook when I'm feeding a batch of my friends. Actually, I'm a private investigator."

"A private detective? Really? Wow!"

She was accustomed to a bit of surprise when she told people her occupation, but not shock. Lance looked like she had just told him she was an international spy and then socked him in the solar plexus.

"Yep," she said. "That's how I earn the cat food and

potatoes around my house. It's a living . . . most of the time."

"How did you get into that line of work?"

"Well, a million years ago I was a cop, and then—"

"A cop? You? Really?"

She gave him a sly grin. "Handcuffs and everything."

Before he could respond, someone walked into the kitchen, and Savannah silently cursed them before even turning to see who it was.

"What's going on down here?" asked an abrasive voice that Savannah instantly recognized. Carisa swept across the room, wearing a marabou-trimmed, hot pink negligee with matching high-heeled slides.

"Savannah's making us some breakfast," Lance told her. "Would you like to join us?"

Savannah didn't particularly like the gleam of interest in Lance's eyes as he watched Carisa sashay over to the stool where he sat. And she certainly didn't appreciate him offering her services to someone she didn't even like. Cooking for Mary was one thing, but Miss Priss Carisa could rustle up her own grub.

"Breakfast?" Carisa said, instantly interested. "What are we having?"

"*We* are having steak and eggs," Savannah replied coolly.

"Oh, good." Carisa sat on the stool next to Lance and began to play with a strand of her long, black hair. "I'm on a high-protein diet. I can have steak and eggs, but no toast."

"Then you're in luck," Savannah told her, "because there are at least three more steaks and a dozen eggs there in the refrigerator. Help yourself."

Carisa flipped her hair to the right, then the left, while batting her eyelashes at Lance. "But I don't cook," she said in a breathy tone that Savannah had only heard in cheap porn films.

"Then you'll be eating your steak raw," Savannah said, "because I'm starving, and these suckers are about ready to eat."

Lance appeared to take pity on the starving actress. "Mary said that there's some ice cream in the freezer downstairs," he told her. "It's Tess's, but I won't tell."

"That's so-o-o not on my diet," Carisa said. Then she reconsidered. "But I'm really hungry, so. . . ."

She glided across the kitchen, a pink cloud of feathers and billowing chiffon. After searching several cabinets and drawers, she found a bowl and spoon and disappeared through the rear door.

Savannah grabbed a couple of plates and began to dish up their meal, while Lance looked on with acute interest. As she slid it under his nose with the panache of a diner waitress, she said, "There ya go. Sink your choppers into that, Sir Lance, and tell me if it hits the spot."

He cut off a large chunk of steak, and when he bit into it, his eyes rolled back in ecstasy. "Ah . . . oh . . . Savannah this is absolutely—"

A terrible shriek split the air, cutting off his words, followed by another and another, coming from the direction of the rear door.

"What the hell?" Savannah said.

Lance jumped off his stool. "Carisa?"

Another scream seemed to answer his question.

Savannah dropped her plate onto the counter and raced to the door with Lance right behind her.

They opened the door and saw a long flight of stairs that led down to the cellar. Another scream echoed upward from the darkness below.

Instinctively, Savannah reached to her side for her Beretta and realized she was unarmed.

Don't enter a dark room and face a threat unarmed, she told herself.

But the cries below were too horrible to hesitate. Someone was in trouble. Savannah took only a few seconds to make her decision . . . and run down the stairs into the castle's dank, gloomy cellar.

Chapter

4

One small, bare lightbulb suspended from the ceiling halfway down the staircase did little to illuminate their path as Savannah and Lance hurried down the steps into the cellar. Savannah reached the bottom first where she stopped and raised her hand, signaling Lance to wait. She leaned forward and ducked her head quickly around the edge of the wall to get a fast look and to evaluate the situation.

She got only the briefest glance and only a limited impression of a large, dark room with strange equipment hanging from the walls.

"Carisa?" Lance called out. "Are you okay?" When there was no response, he said, "I've got to go help her. She could be—"

"I know. I know. Hold on just a second." Savannah stuck her head around again, this time taking a slightly longer look.

About thirty feet to her left she could see an open door and a dim light shining from it. Beside the door stood Carisa, her pink peignoir glowing even in the semi-darkness. Carisa had her hands clamped over her mouth, but she was whimpering and shaking.

Seeing no one and nothing else, Savannah hurried toward her. But Lance rushed ahead and reached her first. Carisa threw herself into his arms, crying hysterically.

"Were you the one screaming?" Savannah asked her.

Carisa nodded, still sobbing against Lance's chest.

"What's wrong?" he asked, gently shaking her by the shoulders. "Carisa, what's the matter with you?"

"In . . . in there," Carisa stammered, pointing to the door of what they could now clearly see was a walk-in freezer. "I was going to get some ice cream, but I opened the door and saw . . . that!"

Savannah left Lance to comfort the weeping Carisa and walked over to the freezer door.

At first, all she saw were shelves stacked over more shelves holding boxes and plastic bags full of all types of meats, vegetables, fruits, pastries, and miscellaneous snacks. For half a second she wondered if the tycoon who owned Blackmoor was a Southerner. Surely no Yankee would stock this much food.

Then she remembered he was a Texan. Mystery solved. If anybody could put away more food than a Georgia girl, it was a Texas cowboy.

She stepped inside the freezer and instantly felt a chill that made her shiver inside her silk nightclothes. But her shudder had nothing to do with the temperature inside the walk-in.

On the floor to her left lay a body, sprawled on its back, staring with glazed eyes at the ceiling.

"Lance, take a look at this," she called.

"But," he replied, "but Carisa. . . ."

"She'll be all right. Come here."

A few seconds later, Lance appeared at her side. He

gasped when he saw the body. "Oh, my god. What . . . what happened?"

"I don't know," Savannah replied, but the mental computer inside her head was already clicking away, processing the possibilities.

"Should we . . . ?" Lance said, reaching a hand toward the body, then withdrawing it. "I'll go call 9-1-1, have them send an ambulance."

"No point in that," Savannah said.

"You mean . . . ?"

"Yes." Savannah had seen enough corpses in her life to know this person was no longer among the living. And while the head was covered with blood and the face contorted with whatever pain the victim had felt when exiting the world, the orange hair and tangerine suit were unmistakable.

"Tess is dead," she said. "There's nothing we can do for her now . . . except call the coroner."

Savannah had always thought of medical examiner Jennifer Liu as a cheerful person, especially considering her occupation, but Dr. Liu wasn't her customary sunny self after being called to a scene at two-thirty in the morning. Usually pristinc in a crisp lab coat and a dress short enough to show off an impressive expanse of legs, her long black hair pulled back and tied with a colorful scarf, this pre-dawn M.E. wasn't someone Savannah would have immediately recognized.

Wearing a rumpled pair of jeans and a T-shirt that bore the words "Born to Rock," her hair hanging limp around her face, this grumpy version of the professional doctor was kneeling beside the body, gently examining the head. With gloved hands she was carefully parting the bloody hair, trying to locate the wound that had caused the bleeding.

Savannah stood patiently behind her, wearing a pair of slacks, an Aran sweater, and loafers, having changed before the coroner arrived.

Next to her was an even less cordial Dirk. Savannah had phoned him before her call to Jennifer Liu, and he was no happier about having been hauled from a warm bed than anyone else.

But once he had arrived and looked at the body in the walk-in, he had stopped complaining and was now as engrossed in the scene as Savannah. Human drama was a more powerful stimulant than the most potent cup of espresso.

"This isn't right," he said, keeping his voice low so that the others standing behind them just outside the freezer couldn't hear.

"I know," Savannah whispered. "That's why I wanted you to get here as soon as you could."

In her peripheral vision she watched the threesome behind them as Ryan Stone and John Gibson attempted to comfort the distraught husband. Savannah had gone upstairs to give Alexander Jarvis the bad news about his wife just before the M.E. had arrived, and from the moment he'd heard, he had been crying and asking questions.

"But what happened to her?" he said for what seemed like the hundredth time. "Why is her face all bloody? Did she fall? Did she hit her head on something? She was just coming downstairs for some ice cream before she went to bed like she always does! Damn it, what happened to my wife?"

"We don't know yet, Alex," Ryan replied, as he had again and again. "That's why we called the coroner. She's checking right now, and she'll be able to tell you something soon, I'm sure."

"Won't you please come upstairs with us?" John

asked, his hand at the man's elbow. "I'll pour you a spot of brandy to calm your nerves."

"No! I don't want anything to drink." He shook John's hand away. "I want to know what happened to my wife!"

"Yeah," Dirk grumbled under his breath. "That's what we all want to know."

He pulled a pair of surgical gloves from a packet in his coat pocket and handed them to Savannah. Then he put on a second pair himself.

While Dr. Liu continued to examine the corpse, he knelt on the floor nearby and reached out to touch a large, round, cardboard container that lay on its side about a yard from the body. Beside the container lay a silver spoon and some broken pieces of white china that looked like a shattered bowl.

But Savannah was more interested in the cardboard carton. She had seen that sort of container before, but it took her a moment to recall where . . . at her local mall ice cream shop. "Is that one of those giant tubs of ice cream?" Savannah asked.

Dirk studied the writing on the opposite side of the carton. "Seems so. It says, 'Gourmet Ice Cream.' "

With one finger he carefully rolled the container over. "Looks like one side here is bashed in."

Savannah knelt beside him and took a look herself. "Not only that," she said, "but this has to be blood." She pointed to a thick smear of a dark red substance on the lower metal rim of the tub. A couple of orange hairs and what appeared to be a small patch of skin were congealed in the gore.

"I think we've found what hit her," Dirk told Dr. Liu. "We've got blood and tissue on this ice cream carton."

Dr. Liu simply nodded in reply without looking up from her own work.

Savannah read the writing on the crushed side of the tub and nearly laughed. Though she felt a bit ghoulish, she couldn't resist chuckling at the irony. "Check out the flavor," she whispered to Dirk. "Can you believe it?"

Dirk read aloud, " 'Killer Fudge.' Yikes, that's creepy."

Savannah stood and studied the interior of the freezer. "But how could something like that hit her on the head . . . un-less. . . ."

"Somebody whacked her with it," Dirk whispered.

"Or . . ." Savannah studied an empty spot among the frozen goods on a high shelf directly above them. "Or maybe she was reaching up to get it off this top shelf and it fell on her."

Dirk stood and glanced up at the shelf, then down at the body and the tub. "Maybe."

They turned and looked at each other for a long, long moment. Then, Savannah said, "Not likely, though."

"Nope."

"I'm thinking that's what somebody intended for us to think."

Dirk glanced out at the others in the cellar. "Yeah. I suspect that's exactly right."

Savannah took a step closer to the body. "What do you think, Doc? Did she die from getting smacked on the head by a big carton of ice cream?"

"I don't know. I'm still looking for the wound." She glanced up at Dirk. "Did you take your pictures yet?"

"Yeah, already took them before you got here," he said, patting the small camera in his jacket pocket.

"Then help me roll her onto her side."

As Dirk leaned over and assisted the doctor in repositioning the body, Alexander called out, "What's going on in there? I have a right to know what's happened to my wife."

Savannah stuck her head out of the freezer and said,

"Yes, you certainly do, Mr. Jarvis. I know this is a terrible time for you, and I'm so sorry you have to go through it, but we'll tell you something just as soon as the doctor has completed her examination. Really, we will."

Ryan slipped his arm around the man's shoulders. "Please, Alex, come upstairs with us. There's nothing we can do down here, and we're interfering with their work."

This time Alex acquiesced and allowed Ryan to lead him away.

John stayed behind just long enough to tell Savannah, "If we can assist you in any way, my dear, you need only ask."

"Of course, John. I'll bring you two up to speed when we're done."

Turning back to the body, Savannah asked Dr. Liu, "See anything yet?"

"Yes, cause of death," the M.E. replied. "The back of her skull is crushed. And there's a gaping wound over the fractures."

"Crescent-shaped?" Dirk asked, looking at the curved bottom edge of the round ice cream container.

"No," Dr. Liu replied. "Straight, wide open, and bloody. That tub of ice cream didn't cause this wound. The weapon had to be a lot more substantial—heavier and straight."

"Weapon," Savannah repeated under her breath. By speaking the word, Dr. Liu had changed the investigation. Now they all knew for certain what they had suspected all along. This was no accident; although someone had tried to make it appear so.

Tess Jarvis had been murdered.

Dirk straightened a kink out of his back. Sighing, he said, "Well, good doctor, you'd better call in your C.S.U."

Dr. Liu stripped off her gloves, reached into her pocket and retrieved her cell phone. As she was calling the crime scene unit, Dirk and Savannah walked out of the freezer and into the dark, musty cellar.

For the first time she had a chance to look at the weird contraptions hanging from the walls. It was a strange and ominous assortment with a distinctive medieval flavor: manacles and bondage mechanisms, rusty metal objects with spikes and chains—all sorts of devilish devices that appeared to be designed for warfare and torture.

In spite of her thick Aran sweater, Savannah shivered.

"Cold?" Dirk asked.

She nodded. "And creeped out by this room, not to mention exhausted." She glanced at her watch. "It's nearly four, and I'm feeling my lack of sleep."

"You hungry?"

"Nope. Funny how the sight of that much blood and a crushed skull can take the edge off your appetite."

"Let's go talk to Jarvis," Dirk said. "Get it over with."

Savannah felt for Dirk. It was never easy delivering terrible news to a family member. And if there was anything worse than telling someone that their loved one had died, it was having to inform them that the deceased had been murdered. In fact, it was the one part of being a cop that she had always hated the most.

Nevertheless, she said, "I can do it if you want. He sort of knows me. It might be easier coming from me."

Dirk shook his head. "No. It's miserable no matter who informs you. And I'm the one getting paid to do the dirty work." He slipped his arm around Savannah's waist as they headed for the stairs. "Thanks though. You're a good gal, Van . . . no matter what anybody says."

"Thanks," she replied. "I guess."

* * *

When they reached the top of the stairs and entered the kitchen, Savannah and Dirk found the entire cast and crew of *Man of My Dreams* standing around, looking at each other with an awkward, heavy silence. They jerked to attention as Dirk took out his badge and showed it to them.

"I'm Detective Sergeant Dirk Coulter, San Carmelita Police Department, and I'm investigating a . . . situation . . . that's happened here tonight. I'd appreciate your cooperation, and—"

"Is Tess dead?" Roxy Strauss demanded as she elbowed her way through the group to stand in front of Dirk. "Carisa says she saw her down there in the cellar, and she's dead."

The blonde was still wearing her black nightgown with its deeply cut front, and with her hands on her hips, the edges were spread wide, revealing even more. Savannah noted with a bit of humor how deftly Dirk averted his eyes. She knew he was as warm-blooded and as boob-obsessed as any other adolescent/middle-aged American male, but he was, above all, a professional. Dirk knew when to look away.

"Well," he told Roxy, while staring at the top of her head, "I would have put it a bit more delicately than that, but yes, Mrs. Jarvis has . . . passed away."

Gasps and exclamations of astonishment and dismay rippled through the group. Some clamped their hands over their mouths; others turned to their neighbors, their eyes wide with shock.

Pete, the soundman, stepped forward and pushed Roxy aside. "What do you mean, passed away? Did she have a heart attack?"

"Yeah, what happened?" his partner, Leonard, demanded. "Did the ol' gal fall down a flight of stairs?"

Savannah couldn't help noticing the lack of respect

and the almost gleeful light in the cameraman's eyes. He didn't exactly look broken up over the news . . . unlike Carisa, whose wails could still be heard in the distance, coming from somewhere in an adjoining room.

Dirk ignored the pointed questions as he looked around the kitchen. "Where's Mr. Jarvis?" he asked.

"I think he's upstairs," Brandy said, her voice soft and tremulous. "I saw the butler and the carriage driver—I mean, the guys who are playing those parts, you know—take him upstairs. He was really upset, and. . . ."

Tears were brimming in her eyes as her voice trailed away. Savannah reached over and placed her hand on her shoulder. She could feel the woman shaking beneath her terry bathrobe.

"Thanks, Brandy," she told her. "You can go back to your room if you want to. There's nothing to see down here." Savannah thought of the fact that the coroner's team would eventually be bringing Tess's body up from the cellar, and she silently added, *Nothing that you'd want to see, anyway.*

"Yeah, you can all go back to your rooms," Dirk told them gruffly. "But nobody goes down into the cellar and nobody leaves the property, at least until I get a chance to talk to you."

Ignoring the indignant mutterings around them, Dirk and Savannah left the kitchen and proceeded through the hallways on their way upstairs. In the foyer they passed Carisa, who was standing at the base of the main staircase, still shrieking and clinging to Lance.

Savannah resisted the urge to tell her, "Aw-w, hush your bawling," because she realized her own annoyance wasn't wholly because the woman seemed to be milking the drama from the situation. It had a lot to do with the fact that Carisa was having her prolonged hysterics against Lance Roman's burly chest.

When Savannah and Dirk reached the second floor,

she said, "I think the Jarvises' rooms are here. I over-heard somebody say that they have a whole suite to themselves."

"How did you read Jarvis downstairs?" Dirk asked as they walked down a hallway past one closed door after another.

Savannah shrugged. "Couldn't really tell. But you know what they say. . . ."

"It's always the husband or the boyfriend or the ex."

"Well, at least we know this time the butler didn't do it. Or manservant, as John prefers to be called."

Dirk paused beside one of the doors and cocked an ear that way. "Speaking of John, I think I hear him and Ryan in there."

He rapped sharply on the door, using his best "Open up, police!" knock.

It was promptly answered by Ryan Stone, who ushered them inside.

"We were just talking to Alex," he whispered.

"Anything?" Savannah asked.

"Nothing remarkable," he replied.

Once inside the suite, Savannah looked around and couldn't help noticing that Tess and Alex had definitely chosen the best accommodations for themselves—or at least the most ostentatious.

The canopy bed in the middle of the far wall looked as big as a football field—a field spread with blue and gold damask. Bed curtains of the same flashy fabric enclosed the antique bed and still more of the heavy material hung at the windows. In the center of the floor an enormous medallion rug displayed the same colors and a similar design. Much of the other furniture and accessories were covered in gold leaf, giving the room a certain Las Vegas panache.

Savannah quickly decided she liked her own smaller

room that was more tastefully decorated with its un-
gilded antiques.

To their right, John and Alex Jarvis sat on a dia-
mond-tucked sofa that looked more Victorian than medieval to Savannah. Alex held a snifter with a large
amount of brandy in it. As soon as Alex saw them, he
jumped to his feet and hurried across the room to inter-
cept them.

"Well?" he wanted to know. "Have you found out
what happened to my wife yet?"

"Not yet," Dirk replied.

Savannah could hear the forced patience in his
voice. A few years back, he might have snapped at
Jarvis, something about needing more than half an
hour to solve a homicide case. But the years had mellowed him, and Savannah liked to think her constant
harping on his shortcomings had, too. She didn't mind
at all taking credit for his personal growth.

"But you're sure she's dead? She couldn't just be. . . ."

His words trailed away, and Savannah searched for a
delicate way to speak the ugly truth. But there was no
way. Dead was dead. "She's gone, Alex. The doctor
pronounced her at the scene."

"So, they won't be taking her to the hospital, just to
see if they could maybe—"

"No, I'm afraid not." Savannah reached out to him
and put a hand on his shoulder. "I'm so sorry for your
loss. If there's anything we can do, just ask."

Alex shook his head as though still unable to grasp
the thought, and said, "You can tell me what happened
to her. How does somebody die just getting a bowl of
ice cream? Did she have a heart attack and fall down
or . . . Where did all that blood come from?"

"A wound on the back of her head," Dirk told him,
his investigator's eyes narrowing as he studied the hus-

band for any reaction that might be considered out of the ordinary. "She suffered a devastating, fatal blow."

"Blow? Are you saying that somebody hit her? Somebody *murdered* her?"

"We don't know anything for sure yet," Savannah said. "The M.E. will have to conduct an autopsy to determine the exact cause and manner of death."

Alex gripped his brandy glass with both hands and stumbled back to the sofa, where he collapsed, spilling part of it onto the floor. John quietly rose and went into an adjoining bathroom. He returned with a towel and wiped the floor clean.

"This is all so . . . unreal," Alex said. "She and I were here in this room talking not that long ago, and everything was fine. And now she's dead. I can't believe it."

Savannah sat down on the sofa beside him and donned her most innocent, benign mask, the one she used to interrogate suspects who weren't yet on her bad side. "Forgive me for having to ask this, Alex," she said, "but were you and Tess on good terms just before her death?"

"What?" he said, bristling. "Why would you even ask me something like that?"

In her peripheral vision Savannah could see Dirk, John, and Ryan all perk up at the question, obviously curious as well.

"Because," she said, choosing her words carefully, "several people said they heard you and your wife arguing earlier this evening. So loudly, in fact, that you woke them from a sound sleep."

She glanced over at Dirk and saw he was all ears as he took a couple of steps closer to them.

"We didn't argue about anything tonight," Alex said, swiping his hand over his perspiration-damp, bald head. "We were getting along just fine. Tess and I had a good marriage. The best. Who said we were fighting?"

Savannah hesitated, having no intention of revealing confidences, and Dirk quickly filled in the blank. "I notice you're dressed, Mr. Jarvis," he said as he pointed to the husband's tropical print shirt and shorts. "Had you gone to bed yet?"

"No. Tess and I are both night owls. We would have worked well into the night except for, well . . . you know . . . what happened to her."

"You said she was going downstairs to have some ice cream just before she went to bed," Dirk told him. "Like she usually did. That was what you said earlier."

"I didn't say that!" Alex's eyes darted from Dirk to Savannah, then to John and Ryan. "I didn't say anything like that."

"Well, actually, Alex," Ryan interjected. "That's exactly what you said down in the cellar tonight."

"So, what is this? You're all questioning me now? You think I did something to my wife? You know us, Ryan. So do you, John. You know I'd never do anything to hurt Tess." The sweat on his head began to roll in rivulets down his forehead and into his eyes. His already ruddy complexion turned a couple of shades redder.

"We don't know who did what to who," Dirk said evenly. "We're just trying to find out what happened here tonight. *Everything* that happened. I'll be questioning everybody."

"Well, I want to know, too!" Alex assured him. "I want you to stay on this until you find out what happened to Tess." Tears flooded his eyes again as he choked over his words. "Tess wasn't everybody's cup of tea, because she always said what she thought. But she was a good person, and she sure didn't deserve to have anybody hurt her . . . if somebody did, that is."

"I absolutely agree," Dirk replied. "And we'll get to the bottom of things. I suppose you'll want to cancel this show you're doing, what with—"

"Hell no!" Alex jumped up from the couch so suddenly that they were all surprised. "Tess would have wanted the show to go on. And it will."

"But . . ." Savannah stammered. "But under the circumstances—"

"If my wife was murdered, I want the killer caught. And since that person is probably someone on the show, the best way to catch them is to keep everybody right here under our noses, right?"

They couldn't argue with him. That would be ideal, if everyone were willing to cooperate. Savannah's mind began to whir, thinking of strategies to accomplish that. Having one's main suspects under one roof was a luxury she was unaccustomed to. And besides, that meant she still had a chance at a diamond tiara.

Of course, she told herself, it didn't matter that she would also still have access to Lance Roman. *Naw,* she thought. *Continued contact with the man of my dreams, an easygoing, rather pleasant and conversational hunk of burning love like that . . . nope . . . never crossed my mind.*

"Savannah, I know that you're a private investigator," she could hear Alex saying as though from afar as her mind spun its webs. "You and Ryan and John here, you're all members of a detective agency, right?"

"Yes, that's right." Savannah had a feeling something was coming. Something to add a star to the top of her Christmas tree of delights.

"I'd like to hire you, all of you," he continued, "to help Detective Coulter here. I'll pay you to help him find out who killed Tess. You do your detective routine and report everything you find out back to me. Okay?"

Okay? Okay? Savannah thought. *Okay to do what I*

love to do and would do for free ... for pay? Whoa, howdy!

But she fixed him with blue eyes as calm as the Pacific and said in her peach-sweet Georgian drawl, "Well, I reckon we could work out something, Mr. Jarvis. We don't work cheap, the Moonlight Magnolia Detective Agency, but for you . . ."

Chapter
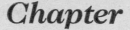
5

Ten minutes later, Dirk and Savannah had a quick huddle with Ryan and John in the hallway outside Alex's suite.

"This could work out very nicely," Savannah said. "I get a paying gig, which I could really use right now, and you"—she turned to Dirk—"could profit from our collective expertise." She waved a hand, indicating herself, Ryan, and John.

"Eh, get over yourself," Dirk grumbled.

Savannah lifted one eyebrow. "Oh? You don't need our help? The department has finally assigned you a partner that you can actually work with without coming to blows?"

"Well, no. With the budget cuts and all that . . ."

"Ah, then you're a one-man wonder who wants to go downstairs and canvass . . . let's see . . . no less than nine potential suspects in what's bound to be a high-profile case, what with Lance Roman involved and all."

"Yeah, yeah. All right. I guess you can help. But don't screw nothin' up."

She batted her eyelashes at him. "Why, kind sir.

Your generosity is surpassed only by your boundless optimism."

"Watch it."

Ryan held up his hand like a cop directing a traffic jam. "Uh . . . if you two are finished, I'd like to add my two cents' worth."

Savannah nodded. "The voice of reason speaks. Spit it out."

"You're probably going to have to 'out' yourself right away, Savannah, as an active investigator to the rest of the cast and crew. And once it's common knowledge here that you're a P.I., they'll be expecting you to be snooping around, in some sort of official or unofficial capacity."

Dirk gave a little sniff and said to Ryan, "Well, you're the expert on the finer points of 'outing' oneself."

Savannah gouged him in the ribs with her elbow.

Ignoring Dirk, Ryan continued, "But as for John and myself, we've been represented to the ladies and crew as nothing more than elite bodyguards. They don't know about our FBI backgrounds, and they don't need to. We'll probably learn more if we ask our questions in an unofficial capacity."

John smiled, his silver mustache tipping upward at the ends. "Gossips and snoops, as it were, plain and simple."

Dirk gave a derisive little chuckle. "So, you two will remain 'in the closet' for now? Is that what you're saying?"

Savannah reached for Ryan's arm with one hand and John's with the other. "Come on, guys. Let's go downstairs and get to work. As soon as we get this case solved, we can put a certain somebody back in the attic where he won't embarrass the family."

*   *   *

"Hey, what's all this?" Savannah asked when they found a mob in the foyer at the bottom of the main staircase. From the mountain of luggage piled in front of the door, it appeared that everyone was leaving en masse.

"We're getting out of here," Roxy said, tossing a garment bag onto the heap. "Tess is dead, the contest is over, and there's no point in the rest of us hanging around until something happens to us, too."

"The show isn't over," Ryan told her and the others who were standing around, some with suitcases in hand. "We just talked to Alex, and he says the taping will continue."

Mary gasped and shook her head. "No! It can't. It would be disrespectful to Tess!" Tears flooded her eyes. "Someone has died. We can't just continue as if nothing's happened."

"Oh, I don't know. . . ." Leila stepped forward. "It's a shame about Tess and all, but we're here, we've started taping, and if Alex wants to go on, why shouldn't we?"

"But what if it turns out that Tess didn't have an accident?" Leila said. "What if she was . . . you know. . . ."

"Murdered?" Pete said.

Savannah couldn't help noticing the lack of revulsion in his expression as he spoke the word. In fact, he looked ghoulishly delighted at the idea. And, for that matter, so did his partner, Leonard.

"It's possible," Leila said. "Carisa told me she looked pretty murdered to her, lying there on the floor with blood around her head."

"I thought you said there was a big thing of ice cream right beside her," Brandy said. "Maybe it just dropped on her head accidentally when she was pulling it off the shelf."

"Or somebody smacked her on the head with it,"

Pete said, again beaming with macabre delight. "Maybe Tess died . . . murder à la mode."

Several unpleasant snickers circulated in the group. Savannah held up her hand. "We don't know what happened yet," she told them, "but I can tell you right now that Detective Coulter will be down in a few minutes, once he's finished with Alex. He'll want to interview Carisa, and then he'll want to talk to every one of you before you traipse off to parts unknown. So, we might as well go on as usual, the best we can. For the time being, we're all stuck with each other . . . as unpleasant a prospect as that might be."

Savannah looked around the room. "Where is Carisa? Anybody seen her?"

"Last time I saw her," Brandy said, "she was with Lance, still crying. He said he was taking her upstairs to her room so that she could lie down."

"Hey, the show's going to go on!" Leila shouted, practically jumping up and down. Turning to Roxy, she lowered her voice and added, "Meanwhile, let's find a crowbar and go upstairs and pry that crybaby Carisa off Lance's chest."

"Yes, for sure," Roxy whispered. "Enough with the drama queen routine. Sheez! Like . . . how long does it take to get over finding a dead body?"

Sighing, Savannah turned to Ryan and John. "I think I'll go down to the cellar," she said discreetly, "and see how the crime scene techs are doing. If you see Dirk, tell him Carisa's in her room. I'm afraid it's up to you two to deal with the grieving masses here."

"I think they're beyond consolation," Ryan replied dryly, "but we'll do all we can."

Leila followed Savannah as she made her way down the hall to the kitchen and on to the door leading to the cellar. "What do you think happened to Tess?" she asked, prodding her in the back with her forefinger as they walked. "I hear you're some sort of private detective or whatever. Do you think it was an accident, or did one of us kill her?"

Savannah stopped at the cellar door, where Dirk had strung yellow police barricade tape across the entrance and turned to the woman, a scowl on her face. She didn't like being poked, and she didn't like pushy contestants who were competing against her for the hunk of her dreams and the possibility of a new roof.

"I am a private investigator . . . or whatever . . ." she replied evenly. "At the moment, I have no idea what happened to Tess. But I aim to find out."

Savannah ducked under the tape and started down the stairs.

"Hey!" Leila called to her. "You're not supposed to cross the line. It says so right on that ribbon-thing there."

"That's absolutely right," Savannah called back. "So, make sure you don't! You could wind up in a whole mess o' trouble."

"Hi, Savannah! You're looking better every time I see you!" Sam Ruston looked up from his work long enough to give her a once-over, then returned to dusting for latent fingerprints on the freezer door handle.

"You're only saying that 'cause it's true," she replied.

"How's it going upstairs?" he asked as he expertly twirled the brush with its black dust across the stainless steel handle.

"Don't ask," she said, bending over to watch. "They're a bunch of cold-hearted hyenas. I've seen deeper grief over a road-killed skunk."

Sam chuckled. "I've heard the deceased was a bit of a stinker. Maybe there's a reason why they aren't exactly mourning her passing."

"Tess was okay," Savannah replied. "She was a tough gal, but that didn't make her an altogether bad person. There's plenty of room in the world for another lady with some grit in her craw."

"Grit in her craw?"

Savannah shrugged. "A Southern poultry reference. Don't trouble your mind about it." She pointed to the handle. "Anything?"

"Yeah. Looks like we've got something." He reached into his kit and pulled out a square of clear plastic sheeting. After peeling off the backing, he pressed the adhesive side onto the dusted handle. Carefully, he pulled it off and replaced it on the white backing. He held it close to his face and peered at his results. "Yep. It's just a partial, but it's clear. Looks like a thumb."

"Good." Then she added, "Although I don't know how much help it'll be. A gal named Carisa, the one who found the body, she was the last person to open the door before we came down here. Chances are, it's hers."

Savannah knelt beside a broken crystal bowl and spoon that lay on the floor just outside the freezer door. She recognized it as the kind of bowl that Carisa had taken from the kitchen cupboard before coming downstairs earlier. "That's probably hers, too," she said, pointing to the broken glass. "Must have dropped it after she opened the door and saw the body."

Photo flashes inside the freezer told Savannah that one of her favorite crime scene investigators was at work. Eileen wasn't all that good at her job, but she was friendlier than most.

Savannah poked her head inside the freezer. "Hey, Eileen, how's it shakin', sugar?"

"Shaking, rocking, and rolling," came the reply. Eileen stood on tiptoe and focused her camera on a place on the freezer wall, high and near the door.

"What 'cha got? Anything juicy?" Savannah asked.

"Blood splatter. Juicy enough for you?"

Savannah couldn't resist the temptation to step inside. *What the heck?* she told herself. She'd already contaminated the scene to some degree by going in earlier. Her hair and fibers were probably all over the place. Some transfer was inevitable.

"I've got to see," she said as she studied the spots on the wall near the ceiling.

Eileen handed her a flashlight, and Savannah pointed the intense beam onto the tiny red dots. "We've got a couple of dozen spots here that are a millimeter or larger," she said. "Medium-velocity blood splatter with tails. Looks like castoff to me. There and on the ceiling, too."

"Where?" Eileen asked.

"Up there." Savannah trained the light on several more spots almost directly over their heads.

"Oh, yes. I saw those," Eileen said, clearing her throat. "I was going to shoot those next."

Sure you were, Savannah thought. She had learned long ago to double-check a scene when Eileen was on duty. The woman was good with a camera and pretty thorough when it came to swabbing blood evidence. But unfortunately, she had an active social life and had been known to rush a job in order to return to the arms of her dearly beloved soul mate . . . whom she might have met that night at a local club.

As Eileen took more photographs of the wall and then proceeded to the ceiling, affixing reference numbers and rulers next to the drops, Savannah watched and thought. And she didn't like the images that were flashing in her mind. Violent, cruel pictures of a woman being murdered . . . the old-fashioned way . . . bludgeoned to death.

"More than one blow was struck," she said, thinking aloud.

"What?" Eileen asked.

"The victim had a wound on the back of her head, a nasty, bloody one. That could have gotten the blood on the weapon. But the killer had to strike again or there wouldn't have been castoff." She demonstrated, lifting her arm up and coming down with an imaginary weapon, then coming up again, as though splattering the ceiling with the action.

"Unless they missed the second time," Eileen suggested.

"Not likely. She would have been a stationary target after that first crushing blow to the head. Dr. Liu will probably find another wound under the clothing that wasn't obvious before."

"So, why does that matter?" Eileen asked as she climbed onto her portable stool to take a ceiling shot.

"The first blow, the one to the head, would have been plenty to kill her. Hitting her again shows anger. It was personal. Especially since they intended to try to make it look like an accident with the ice cream container. The second blow was out of control. Not smart."

Eileen nodded. "I see what you mean."

"Yep. You can't blame it on the ice cream. Tubs of ice cream—even those named Killer Fudge—don't hit twice."

By the time Savannah was finished in the cellar and had come upstairs, it was five-thirty, and the adrenaline rush that had fueled her nightly activities was long gone. But Dirk was still at it, interviewing those members of the cast and crew who were still awake and milling about the castle. And, weary as they had to be, Ryan and John were doing their part—mingling and gleaning bits of gossip.

So, in spite of her burning eyes, aching body and woozy head, she decided to resist the urge to sneak upstairs and crawl back into bed. It certainly wouldn't be the first night's sleep she had lost on a job. But when she had been twentysomething, she had found it much easier to make up for lost pillow time. Now, solidly into her forties, she had to admit: The old bod just didn't spring back with as much vim and vigor as before.

Oh well, she thought as she went to the kitchen and made a strong pot of coffee, *I wouldn't go back. Not if it means trading some hard-earned life lessons for a bit more vim. Vigor is overrated when it includes "stupid."*

A few minutes later, mug of coffee in hand, she decided to step outside for some fresh air to clear her head.

Exiting the keep through a back door leading off the dining hall, she found herself in a charming, informal garden. Lit with the pale golden-pink light of the rising sun, the setting was so romantic that for a moment, she could lose herself in the fantasy of Blackmoor Castle.

A cobblestone path wound among beds of lavender, wild poppies, nasturtium, star jasmine, geraniums, and hollyhock. Passing beneath wisteria-draped arbors and several arched trellises covered with climbing roses, she breathed in the early dawn scents of dew-damp earth and growing things, and she felt her spirit renewed.

Even in the midst of death and cruelty, there were always new beginnings and examples of nature's beauty. And speaking of nature's beautiful creations. . . .

Lance Roman himself.

He was standing next to a pond in the center of the garden, staring into the water with a look of sadness so profound that Savannah said nothing, but just watched him for several moments.

She wasn't surprised. The sight of a corpse had a sobering effect on almost everyone, reminding them of their own mortality. And if the dead person was murdered, it stirred even deeper feelings of sorrow, fear, and anger.

At first, she considered turning away and quietly leaving him to his solitude. It would be the most respectful thing to do.

But as an investigator she wasn't being paid to be respectful. And, she had to admit, it wasn't really her nature either. She had been a cop and an investigator too long.

Besides, this was the "Man of Her Dreams" and she was still in a contest for his affections . . . not to mention a diamond tiara. Chances to be alone with him might prove few and far between.

"Lance," she said softly. "Mind some company?"

He turned and gave her a blank look, as though his thoughts were still elsewhere. Then he forced a smile and nodded. "Sure. I'd like that."

She walked over to a wrought-iron park bench and sat down. Patting the seat beside her, she said, "Rest your bones a spell. It was a rough night for us all."

When he sat next to her, she tried not to notice what a large man he was, at least six-three and extraordinarily broad through the shoulders. Even through the thick material of the sweatshirt she could see the results of what had to be a strenuous workout routine. She had assumed that the artists who painted him for the book covers exaggerated his physique. But they hadn't at all. Lance Roman was just as big a hunk in person as he was on the front of romance novels.

And it was difficult for her not to think about that with him so near on the cozy bench, his hard, warm arm pressing against hers. It wasn't easy to slip into investigator mode. Her mindset was more inclined toward "Captured Victorian Virgin Heiress" or "Savannah, Virgin Piratess of the Seven Seas."

She was trying to push those tantalizing little fantasies aside and think of a graceful way to begin her interrogation, when he opened the conversational door himself. "I guess you're used to it," he said, "seeing dead people and all that."

"Not really," she said. "It's always a bit of a shock."

"The difference . . . in dead and alive?"

"Yes." She sighed. "How dead 'dead' is."

He ran his fingers through his thick dark hair, pushing it back from his forehead. "I was raised on a farm," he said. "I saw a lot of animals die."

"Me, too." Savannah smiled, recalling the bittersweet memories. "My Granny Reid used to kill a hen about once a month on a Saturday night so that we could have fried chicken for Sunday dinner."

"Your grandmother raised you?"

"She raised all nine of us kids. We've nominated her for sainthood."

"I'll bet you have! Where were you in the lineup?"

"Oldest."

He turned and gave her a long, searching look. "Granny killed one chicken for Sunday dinner? One bird for nine kids?"

Savannah shrugged. "You can cut a chicken into eleven pieces, if you count the back and the neck. And with a batch of mashed potatoes, a mess of gravy, and some greens that you picked along the railroad track . . . you've got dinner."

"Hm-m-m. . . ."

Savannah saw the pity in his eyes and rushed to set

the record straight. "We weren't starved at all for love or attention. That matters a lot more than getting a drumstick *and* a wing."

"And where were Mom and Dad Reid?"

"Mom held down the bar stool under the signed picture of Elvis at the local tavern. Dad was a truck driver who forgot to come home except maybe once a year, long enough to get Mom pregnant . . . again. But enough about all that." She nudged his arm with hers. "Tell me about your family."

"I had a good childhood," he said. "Dad was a dairy farmer in Ohio, retired now. Mom died when I was eighteen. Dad raised my kid brother and me the best he could, considering how hard he worked. He did a good job."

"Is he proud of your success?"

He chuckled dryly. "Not that you'd notice. He tells people I'm an actor—can't bring himself to say 'model.' Not macho enough, I guess. He's pretty happy with the checks I send him."

"I'm sure he is. He's probably proud, too. Some parents are just a bit sparing with their praise. They're afraid their kid will get too big for their britches."

She didn't mention the fact that he was, frequently, a bit too big for his pants on the book covers. It was a large part of his appeal.

But as appealing as the fit of his trousers might be, she had to get back to business. "Lance," she said, "would you mind if I ask you a couple of questions about what happened tonight?"

He gave her a sideways grin that nearly took her breath away. "I wondered when you'd get around to that—you being a private investigator, a former cop and all."

Damn, he's better-looking than a man ought to be

allowed to be, she thought as he flashed his perfect teeth, his blue eyes warm and friendly.

"Sure," he said. "I don't know what I can tell you that you don't already know, but ask away."

"When we were talking there in the kitchen, you and Mary said that you overheard Tess and Alex arguing earlier. Can you tell me any more about that?"

He shook his head and looked away. "No," he responded quickly. "I think I heard them, but I'm not sure."

"Mm-m-m. I thought you were pretty sure earlier."

"Not really. I think it was Alex and Tess, but I couldn't swear to it."

"Was it a man and a woman you heard?"

"I think so."

"What were they saying?"

"I didn't hear actual words. I couldn't tell you anything for sure that was said."

"Nothing?"

"Nope."

"Okay."

Over the years, Savannah had questioned hundreds of people who genuinely didn't know anything and hundreds of others who knew something but weren't willing to talk about it. Sitting there next to her dream hunk, she was pretty certain that he fell into the second category.

Not a pleasant thought.

"About what time was it that you overheard this argument?" she asked.

"I don't know."

"No idea at all?"

"No. I was asleep. They woke me up, but when they stopped, I went back to sleep. I didn't look at the clock. Later, I woke up again and was thirsty, so I went down to the kitchen to get something to drink."

"When you went downstairs, did you see anyone other than Mary?"

"Yeah, Roxy. She was in the kitchen already when we got there."

"What was she doing?"

"Washing an apple at the sink."

"Did she hang out very long?"

"Yeah, with that low-cut gown, I'd say she was practically hanging out the whole time."

Savannah laughed. "And about how long was she downstairs—after you showed up, that is?"

"Five minutes maybe. Just long enough to make a nuisance of herself."

One contestant down, Savannah thought, reminding herself that she could investigate and play the game, too.

"Roxy not your type?" she asked.

"Naw. Girls like Roxy are a dime a dozen in my business. Pose with one of them bent backwards in your arms for ten hours and they tend to lose their appeal."

She gave him her best, deep-dimpled grin. "Yeah, some of those positions look pretty uncomfortable."

"You have no idea."

"I hear you do a lot of guest appearances at book fairs and signings, and the ladies line up to have their pictures taken with you."

He sighed. "Yes. And they all want the traditional pose."

Savannah could mentally picture the row, stretching around the bookstore, of women—all ages, all sizes— waiting for their chance to be bent backward by this mountain of sex appeal. A glorious chunk of manhood whom Savannah was quickly realizing was just a guy . . . a person like anyone else, playing a part.

"Is that difficult?" she asked softly. "Treating the

older ones or the less attractive ones like princesses no matter how they look?"

Instantly, his eyes softened and he shook his head. "No, not at all. I love that part. Holding that stupid pose two hundred times a day is exhausting. But the ladies . . . I love them all. They aren't airhead models like that Roxy gal. They're real women who, for whatever reason, like me so much that they'd stand in a line for hours just to talk to me, to have their pictures taken with me. If I can make them feel special, give them a nice memory, that's a gift—a gift to me, that is."

"Oh, I think it's a gift all the way around."

He glanced her way and their eyes met for a long moment . . . long enough for her to sense a real connection and to know that he felt it, too.

She liked Lance Roman. Not just his biceps. Him.

And she had a feeling he liked her, too.

"Did I mention that I'm really glad you came out to the garden this morning?" he said, his face only inches from hers.

She looked down at his lips, so full and so near, then back up at his eyes. Her heart gave an extra beat when she saw that he was looking at her mouth, too.

"Ah . . . no, you didn't mention that," she whispered. "Did I mention that I'm particularly glad we had this conversation?"

"And is this *Detective* Savannah Reid I'm talking to right now, or Savannah the contestant?"

She grinned. "I'm a complex woman, Mr. Roman. I'm a whole bundle of women rolled into one, and let's just say they're all pretty darned happy to be sitting on this bench right now."

He returned her smile, reached up and traced her jaw line slowly with his fingertip from just below her earlobe to her chin.

The simple gesture went through her like a warm

liquid that washed her from head to toe, but settled in the more intimate parts of her body. She could feel herself melting into a big puddle there on the bench.

Then he cupped her chin in his palm and brushed his thumb over her lower lip.

She tried to remember to keep breathing.

"And do you suppose," he asked, "that any of the women in this intriguing bundle would object if I stole just one kiss here in the early morning light?"

That was it. She was over the edge, sure that she had no measurable pulse, respiration, or brainwave activity.

But Granny Reid's teachings were deeply ingrained. "Don't give it away too quick, Savannah girl," she had told her a thousand times as young Savannah had headed out the door to a date. "Keep your treasures close to your heart like the precious jewels they are. Dole 'em out slowly and wisely. The boys who're worth a hoot will keep comin' back for more. And the ones who don't . . . they can go sit on a fence post and spin."

He ran his thumb along her upper lip and Gran's warnings seemed to fade to whispers.

But not completely.

"That depends on who I'm talking to," she said, giving him a teasing grin.

He looked confused. "What do you mean?"

"Is this the guy who's an expert at making every woman feel special, or is it the teenage boy who got up at dawn and helped his dad milk a zillion cows?"

He thought for a moment, then said, "Depends."

"On?"

"On who's the most likely to get a kiss."

She laughed at his honesty, then raised one eyebrow. "Well, I've always had a liking for those farmer boys. You know, salt of the earth, strong and steady . . . hay lofts. . . ."

Chuckling, he turned toward her on the bench and said, "That works out great, because I've always had a thing for dairymaids."

He reached up and touched her hair, then gently brushed it back from her face. "You're a very pretty woman, Savannah," he said. "And you're . . . different. I like you a lot."

She glanced over his picture-perfect features, taking in the deep blue eyes with their dark lashes, the rugged cut of his chin, the breathtaking smile that had charmed so many. She reached up and ran her fingers through those famous raven locks and wondered how it must feel to be so incredibly beautiful. So beautiful that your appearance was all anyone could see.

"Well," she said with her slow drawl, "you're a bit on the homely side for me, but you're kinda sexy . . . in a rough and tumble sort of way."

He gave a low growl deep in his throat, then took her face in both of his hands. "I'll show you homely. I'll show you rough."

But he didn't kiss her roughly. He gave her the longest, sweetest kiss she could remember, nicer than Dirk's on the beach, better than those teenage make-out sessions in the Georgia peach orchards, and certainly better than any she'd had in the years between.

Then, when she thought she might absolutely die from the sheer delight of "sweet," the kiss turned deep and passionate and lasted—she was sure—for a year and a half.

When they finally pulled away, both were breathless, and Savannah was sure she was experiencing her first bona fide hot flash. What a time for menopause to arrive!

"Mmmm, that was great," he said, more to himself than to her. He even sounded a bit surprised.

Savannah wasn't sure if she was surprised or not.

She was too stunned for any meaningful self-examination.

Gran's advice about dispensing the goodies in a judicious manner went out the window. At that moment she could have gladly thrown the treasures right at him. The whole chestful.

Apparently he was thinking along the same lines, because he looked around at the dew-damp cobblestone path, the crowded, wet flower beds, and the tiny bench where they were sitting and said, "Damn. Speaking of rough . . . speaking of tumbles . . . where's a good hay loft when you need one?"

Several ridiculous thoughts flew through Savannah's mind that included: *Would it really be all* that *uncomfortable to do it on cold, wet cobblestones?* But the sound of someone clearing his throat behind them jerked her back to reality.

She turned around and saw Dirk standing there, a strange look on his face, as though he had just been forced to drink a glass of pure lemon juice.

"Oh, uh . . . hi," she stammered as she jumped to her feet and smoothed her hair with both hands. "What's up?"

"I've finished talking to that Carisa gal," Dirk said, his voice low and strained. "Didn't get much out of her. Was wondering if you'd have a go at her." He gave Lance a quick look that Savannah could only classify as dark and threatening. "If you're finished here, that is," he added.

Savannah hated the fact that her face was getting hotter and no doubt redder by the moment. Why should she care that Dirk was standing there with the most pained and angry look she'd ever seen on his face?

And why should she feel like she'd just been caught

in the act? For heaven's sake, it wasn't as if she and Dirk were married or even a couple.

It wasn't as if Dirk had ever expressed any desire for a romantic relationship. And if he had, she wasn't at all sure she would have returned his interest.

Standing there, looking at the pain and anger on his face, she wanted to just walk over and slap him upside the head and tell him to grow up.

She also wanted to go hug him and tell him not to worry; she was just enjoying a hot kiss with a handsome hunk because . . . because . . . well . . . hell, why shouldn't she?

Instead, she lifted her chin, turned to Lance and said, "That was lovely, Lance. Enjoy the rest of the sunrise. I have to get back to work." Then, to Dirk she said, "I'd be happy to talk to Carisa. She was next on my list anyway."

With that, she left them both and made her way carefully over the cobblestone path back toward the keep. Her legs were still wobbly and her head spinning from the unexpected romantic encounter. She really preferred not to fall on her face.

She didn't want to spoil her dignified exit. And nothing could ruin a graceful departure like doing a dive, face-first, into a bed of English lavender or wrestling with a rosebush and losing.

It wasn't until she was well out of their sight that she paused in the middle of the garden walkway and closed her eyes. She could still taste him on her lips, smell the faint scent of him on her clothes, and feel his touch as he had pulled her close against him. Warm. Hard. And deliciously close.

"Nice," she whispered. "Very, very nice."

But no sooner had she summoned the memory and felt the joy of it wash over her than she recalled a second mental picture: Dirk, her dearest friend in the world, standing there looking jealous and wounded.

Jealous. That didn't bother her. He'd get over *jealous.*

Wounded. That was another story.

Promising herself a phone call to her Granny Reid to get her head straight later in the day, she shook off both memories.

Dad-burn men anyway, she thought. *They're always messing things up. Who needs 'em?*

Me, she added as she continued to walk the rest of the way on lust-weakened legs. *Oh, mercy! Me-e-e!*

Chapter

6

When Savannah entered the keep, she tried to leave the garden behind, along with her jumbled emotions. A murder investigation conjured plenty of unpleasant feelings on its own; she didn't need to add a false sense of betrayal or a dash of adolescent infatuation to its already potent cocktail.

And as she passed through the gloomy hallways of Blackmoor Castle, she reminded herself that—in spite of the show's hype—she didn't need a romantic entanglement to complicate her life right now.

No matter how good a kisser Lance Roman might be.

The situation was depressing enough already without adding an irked, hurt Dirk to the mix. And in the garden he had looked about as irked as she'd ever seen him.

He'll get over it, she told herself. *Like he wouldn't lock lips with one of those contestant beauties if he had a chance.*

Although she had to admit that the very thought of him smooching someone like, say, Roxy, caused her hackles to rise just a tad.

Okay, a little more than a tad, she had to admit. And why that might be, she didn't even want to hazard a guess. Some places the mind shouldn't even go.

As she negotiated the maze of hallways, trying to find the main staircase that led to the upper floors, she rounded a corner and heard a female voice speaking in a tone that caused her to stop and listen. The woman, whoever she was, was trying to whisper, but she was loud enough for Savannah to hear her clearly. Her pauses between sentences told Savannah that she was probably speaking on a phone.

"Yeah, she's dead. This morning. Your freezer. The coroner took her body out. Yes, the medical examiner. No, I didn't hear anything yet. Sure, I'll let you know when I do. Love you. Miss you. This is a lot harder to do than I thought it would be. No, I'm not complaining. Just saying."

Savannah sneaked a quick look around the corner and saw Brandy Thomas sitting on a monk's bench in a dark alcove beneath the staircase. She was wearing a dainty, floral sundress and was talking into a hot-pink cell phone. Her thick auburn hair was pulled back into a ponytail, and she looked as sweet and innocent as a society debutante. But there was something in her voice, an underlying harshness that belied her soft exterior.

And her words, while not exactly incriminating, didn't exactly have the ring of mundane gossip either.

"Okay, baby. I have to go upstairs now and put on my face. Oh, come on. I'm not interested in him. I'm not. You wanted me here. So, I'm here. Yeah, I will. Bye."

Savannah listened to Brandy's retreating footsteps until they died away completely before following her up the stairs. She heard a door open and close at the end of the hallway as the redhead went into her room.

Hm-m, interesting, Savannah thought as she filed the telephone conversation away for future consideration. Something told her that Brandy hadn't been talking to her sister or mother about the morning's events. And more than anything else that had been said, the phrase *"your* freezer" had caught Savannah's attention.

Was she speaking to the owner of the castle, the crazy Texan who had built this monstrosity? And if so, why did he put his own girlfriend into the contest?

When Savannah reached the top of the stairs she turned left and proceeded down the hall to the third door on the right. Yesterday, she had seen Carisa entering that door, and she was fairly certain it was her room.

She knocked gently on the door, then harder when no one answered. After her third knock, it opened an inch, and Carisa stuck her nose out through the crack.

"What do *you* want?" she asked Savannah. "I'm busy, and I want to be left alone."

Savannah was a bit surprised at the woman's appearance. Amazing what a few hours of crying, mussed hair, and copious lines of mascara streaking one's face could do toward turning a pretty person into a plain, ugly one. The massive Rudolph nose didn't help either.

"I'm sorry to bother you," Savannah said. "I know you had an awful night. But I really need to talk to you for a few minutes, if you don't mind."

"I mind," she replied. "I mind a lot. I've been talking to that police detective friend of yours for the past hour. I don't know what he thinks I can tell him. I went downstairs for ice cream, I opened the freezer door, and there she was. I screamed my head off, and Lance came down to rescue me. That's it, that's all."

"When you went downstairs, was the freezer door open or closed?"

"I don't know! Why are you asking me this stuff? Why are you bothering me? You and that detective have no—"

"Because a woman died last night," Savannah said. "And she was murdered. If you were the one who'd been killed, I'd be asking Tess about you. As unhappy as you are right now, aren't you glad it's the other way around?"

Carisa blinked her swollen eyes and swallowed hard. "Yeah . . . okay. Let me think." She bit her lower lip, concentrating. "I think it was closed. Yes, closed. I remember opening it."

"Did you step into the freezer?"

"I think so. Maybe a step or two until I saw her. Then I ran out."

"Did you touch the body?"

She shuddered. "Heavens, no!"

"I didn't think so, but we needed to know for sure."

"Is that all? I want to get back to my packing."

"Packing? You're leaving?"

Carisa's face twisted into a grimace, then she started to cry again. "Of course I'm leaving. I mean, isn't everybody? It's over."

"Actually, it isn't. Mr. Jarvis says we're going to continue."

Carisa brightened instantly, her face a wreath of smiles. She threw the door open wide. "Really? You mean the contest is still on?"

"That's right. He said it's what Tess would have wanted. We're going to do the show in her honor."

"Cool! That's great! That's fantastic!"

Savannah had never seen such a transformation, from grief-stricken and traumatized to positively giddy in an instant.

Carisa left the doorway and practically danced over

to the bed where her suitcases were open and half-filled. She started pulling the clothes out and shaking them to get rid of the wrinkles. "It's back on again!" she said as she hung them in a giant armoire. "And here I thought it was all over because of that"—she glanced over at Savannah and with an effort, dampened her enthusiasm just a little. "You know. Because of that awful thing that happened downstairs."

"Yes, it was pretty awful, someone we know getting murdered like that. And then you being the one to find the body. But we'll all just have to bear up as best we can," she added dryly.

"Yes, as best we can."

"And you can be thankful that Lance came downstairs to rescue you like that. And that he was there to comfort you . . . for so-o-o long."

"Um, yes, that was nice. Nice of him."

"Yeah, right."

Savannah left Carisa to handle her own sorrow in her own way—gleefully unpacking.

Hey, everybody expresses their heartfelt grief differently, she thought as she walked away. And something told her that, devastated though she was, Miss Carisa was going to be fine. In fact . . . just peachy.

If the *Man of My Dreams* production team had an office at all, Savannah figured it must be in the dining hall. The day before, she noticed that Tess and Alex had set up a table at one end that appeared to function as a desk, with a telephone, some stacks of papers, and a couple of notebook computers. When she didn't find Alex in his suite, she decided to look for him there.

Instead, she found a tearful Mary Branigan sitting at

the desk, talking on the phone and typing on one of the computers.

Savannah sat on a nearby bench and waited while she spoke to someone, saying things about "the bird" and "making sure our girls don't get hurt" and "make sure it's safe."

Savannah couldn't resist speculating as to what the conversation might be about. Another artificial dinner like last night's perhaps? A plastic turkey that they might break their teeth on if they weren't careful?

When Mary finally ended the call, she turned to Savannah and said, "Hi. Sorry about that. I'm having a little problem with . . . well . . . never mind. I'm not supposed to tell you ladies yet."

Mary sighed and rubbed her hand across her face as though she were simply too weary to function any further.

"Have you had any sleep?" Savannah asked, using her kindest, big-sister voice.

"I got about an hour last night, before . . ."

Savannah nodded. "Yes, if anybody got any rest, it was *before*. Certainly not afterward." She glanced around to make certain they were alone, then stood and walked over to the desk. "If you don't mind me asking, Mary, how did you find out about Tess?"

"Roxy told me. I was sound asleep and woke up to her pounding on my door. When I opened it, she told me."

"What did she say, exactly?"

"The truth, ugly as it was." Mary closed her eyes for a moment, then shook her head as though trying to escape the grim reality. "She said, 'Tess is dead. Somebody killed her.' "

"Those were her exact words? 'Somebody killed her'?"

"Yes. I'll never forget it. You know how you remember every little thing at a time like that, when you're hearing terrible news? You'll *always* remember *everything,* like even hearing the clock ticking in the background. The exact look on the person's face who told you."

"Yes, I know what you mean. What *was* the look on Roxy's face?"

Mary hesitated, giving her answer some thought. "I'd say excited. She seemed more excited than scared or upset. But then"—her words were cut short by a sob. She grabbed a piece of tissue from a box on the table and blew her nose. "But then Roxy wasn't a big fan of Tess's. She didn't really see her as a person with feelings and. . . ."

"And?" Savannah prompted, trying to hide her own excitement.

But Mary seemed to sense she was saying too much. She wadded up the tissue and tossed it into a wastebasket under the table. "And, nothing. Roxy just didn't know her as well as I did. Tess was a tough gal when she needed to be. Maybe even sometimes when she didn't need to be. But she had a good heart."

After taking a few moments to compose herself, Mary said, "I'm sorry. You must have come down here to see me. What can I do for you?"

"Actually, I was hoping to find Alex. He wasn't in his suite, and I wanted to check on him, see if he's okay." *And squeeze him for a little more info while I'm at it,* she added silently.

"I think he went for a walk," Mary said. "I saw him heading out toward the garage . . . I mean, the stables. He may be around there somewhere."

"Thanks, Mary."

"No problem. Oh, by the way," she called after

Savannah, "breakfast will be served at a table in the garden. If you see any of the other girls, let them know, would you?"

"Sure. Is it real food this time?"

"Bread, cheese, and wine."

"For breakfast?"

"Yes. We have to stay in character. Everyone has to come in costume, too. We'll be shooting it."

"Oh, goody," she mumbled as she walked away. "If I'm going to squeeze into a corset, I want something better than cheese and bread—like a slab of Virginia bacon and a tall stack of flapjacks."

As Savannah made her way across the courtyard toward the stables, she ran into Ryan and John, who were headed toward the keep. They were each carrying a box full of strange things that looked like giant gardening gloves.

"What have you got there?" she asked. "Rose-pruning gloves?"

"Nope. It's a surprise," Ryan said, turning his back so that she couldn't see into the box.

John did the same, so she stood on tiptoe, trying to see over their shoulders. "Come on. What is it? I just lo-o-ove surprises."

"Then you're going to continue to love this one," John said, "because we've been sworn to secrecy. And, honorable knights that we are, we will guard this secret with our very lives."

"Aw, don't get up in arms. I'm not curious enough for bloodshed."

She nodded toward the white van with the crime scene investigation team's logo on the side. "So, they're still here?"

"Oh, I think they're going to be here until the cows

come home—as you would say," Ryan told her. "They're still dusting and taking blood splatter pictures, not to mention checking the floor for footprints."

"So, what brings you out here, love?" John asked. "Other than spying on us, that is."

"Ah, I've got more important people to spy on than you two."

"Like Alex Jarvis maybe?" Ryan said.

"How did you know?"

"Just a guess," Ryan replied, "since Dirk came by thirty seconds ago asking for him. You two seem to travel in pairs."

"Mm-m, maybe not anymore," Savannah mumbled.

"What's that?" John said.

"Nothing. Never mind. How did Dirk look?"

"Look?" Ryan shrugged. "I don't know, sort of grumpy, I'd say. What would you say, John?"

"Without a doubt. Quite out of sorts, indeed. In other words, he looked quite like himself."

"Oh, goody. That bad, huh?" she said. "And which way was he headed—Dirk, that is?"

Ryan shifted his box to the other arm and pointed toward the stable area. "We sent him that way to find Alex. But after we'd sent him on his way, we saw Alex heading toward that other building; I think it's the hawk house."

"A hawk house. Like with real hawks? Birds with sharp teeth and talons and—"

"Beaks, dear," John said. "Beaks, not teeth. And I don't know if there are any actual birds in there. I'm afraid on this estate it's a bit much to expect the authenticity of a real hawk in the hawk house."

Savannah remembered the plastic pig served at the banquet the night before, and she agreed wholeheartedly. "Thanks a lot, guys. Although you really could have shared your secret with me."

"But that would have spoiled the surprise," Ryan said.

"It better be a good one," Savannah called over her shoulder as she walked away.

"Oh, it is," John replied. "I'm sure it will be a once-in-a-lifetime experience for you."

"Unless she's had an encounter with a chicken hawk in Georgia," she heard Ryan say as they entered the keep.

"True, how true," John replied.

At first, Savannah was reluctant to open the door of the small building, for fear of releasing a flock of rabid raptors. But after pressing her ear to the door for awhile and hearing nothing, she decided to take a risk and open it an inch or so.

Once the door was open, she stuck her head in and breathed a smell that took her back to her childhood, the warm, cozy, dusty scent of birds. For a few seconds she was back in Georgia, a ten-year old child, collecting eggs in her grandmother's henhouse.

Certainly, birds had been kept in this building, and judging from the freshness of the droppings that littered the floor, they had been here recently. But other than some black, white, and gray feathers here and there, she saw none of the hawk house's former inhabitants.

And she saw even less of Alex Jarvis.

It was when she was re-closing the door and fastening the latch that she heard the voices, a man's and a woman's, coming from behind the building.

Recognizing Alex's distinctive nasal twang, she decided to investigate.

But halfway around the building she heard Alex say, ". . . can't be seen together. It wouldn't look right. Not now. Not this soon." And she decided not to investigate after all. She would snoop.

She tiptoed a few more feet to the corner of the building. Plastering her back against the wall, she listened, hardly daring to breathe, because she could tell by the sound of their voices that they were only a few feet away.

"Okay," a woman replied. "If not this soon, when? After all, you're free now, aren't you? We shouldn't have to sneak anymore."

"Free? I guess I am. But if they find out about you around here, that'll raise suspicion, and we don't need that right now on top of everything else," Alex said.

"You told me that if Tess wasn't in the picture anymore we'd be free to do whatever we want. You said we'd get married. You promised me when we were in Key West last summer."

"I know what I said. I also know that the husband is always the one they suspect first when a woman is murdered, and if anybody finds out I've been having an affair with you, I'll wind up with my butt in jail for the rest of my life. And then neither one of us will be free to do what we want."

"So what are you saying? Are you telling me that we have to keep going on the way we've been for the last two years, pretending we don't even know each other?"

"That's exactly what I'm saying. And if you're as smart as I think you are, you'll listen to me, too."

Savannah could hear some sniffling. It sounded like the woman was crying; it also sounded a bit phony, not unlike Carisa's caterwauling the night before.

"Sh-h-h, stop that," she heard him say. "We'll be together soon. Just not now. We lay low for a few months—"

"A few months!"

"Okay, okay, at least a few weeks. Until the coroner's report is done, and I'm in the clear."

Savannah was absolutely dying to stick her head around the corner and see who he was talking to. She had heard the voice recently, but she couldn't place it.

"And then we can get married?" the woman asked between sniffs.

"And then I'll buy you a ring."

"A big one! I want a really, really big one! At least two carats, a princess cut."

"Whatever. Just don't ask me to meet you like this again. I mean it."

The sniffling stopped. "Okay. As long as you promise about the ring. Two carats. No less. And as long as you say you love me."

"I love you. Okay?"

Savannah had to stifle a snicker. She had heard more enthusiastic expressions of affection from ten-year-old boys greeting their maiden aunties.

"Okay."

The woman actually sounded convinced.

Moron, Savannah thought as the sounds of lovemaking replaced the conversation. *You'll never get a ring out of that guy, unless it's blackmail jewelry, given to keep you quiet.*

But in spite of her disgust at yet another example of female naïveté, Savannah couldn't help feeling a rush of adrenaline. What she had just overheard would have been nearly enough to convict Alex Jarvis of murder, had it been on tape.

Not enough for a conviction, but certainly enough to steer their investigation in his direction.

Still, she had to know the woman behind the voice. She had to take a look and hope to God she didn't get caught doing it. There was nothing worse than having your number-one suspect know that he was your number one suspect.

She waited as the panting and groaning on the other side of the building escalated. It didn't sound like old Alex was exactly going to score a home run, but from the level of female noises she would bet that he had made it at least to second base. If she was going to sneak a peek, this was the perfect time.

She squatted, and with her head low, took a quick half-look around the corner.

Alex had his lady friend pinned to the wall and was devouring her face while his hands mauled her chest area.

Safely back behind her corner, Savannah paused a second to marvel at some women's taste—or lack thereof—in men. Who would have thought anybody would get the hots for Alex Jarvis? It would take far more than a tropical shirt to turn this guy into Tom Selleck. And that nasal, whiney voice—who could stand it?

And the answer—Savannah decided as she hurried away—was a woman who was pretty darn sure of getting a two-carat, princess-cut engagement ring.

A woman who was actually glad another woman had been murdered that day.

A brazen, blond hussy named Roxy Strauss.

As Savannah headed back to the keep, she passed the stables and glanced inside. Dirk was sitting in his old Buick, as she had thought he might be. Frequently, when working a case, he would retreat to his battered jalopy to think and make notes in the crime scene log. Something about the interior of the car—she suspected it was the assortment of fast-food wrappers that littered the floor—helped him to think.

As usual, he had the radio on and was listening to classic rock . . . the only form of classical music he enjoyed, other than some occasional classic Johnny Cash.

She dreaded an encounter with him, but the longer she put it off, the worse it would be. And she wasn't prepared to get ulcers over some innocent, or even not-so-innocent, kisses.

As she approached the passenger door, she noted that he had the radio turned up to deafening decibels. Dirk only blasted his music when he was extremely jovial—an event that occurred less frequently than the planets aligned—or when he was in a bad mood. And judging from how loudly Elvis was belting out "Hound Dog," she decided that old Dirk obviously had his tail in a serious twist.

He was concentrating on scribbling on a pad, which he was holding in his lap, and didn't notice her until she opened the passenger door and slid inside. After giving her only the briefest nod, a scowl, and a muttered, "Hmphf," he went back to writing.

"How's it shakin', sugar?" she said.

He mumbled something that she couldn't distinguish above Elvis's loud complaints about never catching rabbits.

"I can't hear you," she yelled. She reached for the volume knob on the radio. "Do you mind if I—"

"Yes, I mind!" he shouted. "I'm listening to that!"

"Well, excu-u-use me!"

She sat, staring straight ahead while he scribbled furiously on the log and Elvis finished his lament.

As soon as the last note had faded, she reached over and flipped the radio off.

"What have you got there?" she asked, nodding toward the pad on his lap. "Anybody look good for it yet?"

He kept writing, as waves of heavy silence rolled from one side of the car to the other. Savannah decided she could have surfed those waves.

"You're not going to believe what I just overheard," she said.

"I'm still having a problem believing what *I* overheard this morning," he said, "or what I saw."

Savannah could feel the muscles in her shoulders tying themselves into two half-hitch knots. The whining tone in his voice made her want to bludgeon him to death with his writing pad. The hurt in his eyes made her want to hug him and call him a big, sweet fool.

In the end, she decided to do neither, but to use her tried-and-true method of handling Dirk's moods: Ignore them. Ignore him.

"Roxy and Alex, behind the birdhouse over there," she said, pointing to the hawk house, "playing suck face and—"

"Gee, there's a lot of that going around today."

Savannah took a deep breath and tried not to wonder just how far she could cram that pen up his. . . . "And saying that they've got to lie low and not be seen together until the M.E.'s done with the autopsy and he's in the clear."

His eyes widened and his jaw dropped. All traces of Mr. Surly gone. "Really? Really? Wow!"

"Yep. It's been going on for a couple of years. He promised to marry her once Tess was out of the picture."

"Out of the picture, like *dead*?"

"He didn't say 'dead.' So he could have meant divorce, but the conversation was very interesting, nonetheless."

"It sure is." His eyes glimmered with the delight of a bloodhound who—unlike Elvis's—had caught a fresh scent. "Anything else?"

"He's promised to buy her a two-carat ring. Princess cut."

"What's that?"

"Something every girl wants and most never get."

"To keep her quiet?"

Savannah shrugged. "Don't know, but I'd keep my mouth shut for one carat."

"You'd keep mum for a box of Godiva."

"We all have our price."

Savannah sat quietly for a moment, enjoying the companionable vibes that had replaced the tension. Ah, this was her friend, her buddy, her. . . .

"And apparently, *your* price is a friggin' diamond tiara," he said, totally ruining the moment.

"Damn it, Dirk!" she shouted, turning in her seat to face him. "Just stop! Don't even go there! You have no right to say squat about nothin'! So, just shut your yap before I—"

"Double negative," he said softly, staring at the steering wheel in front of him.

"What?"

"You said, 'no right to say nothing.' That's a double negative. You're always yelling at *me* for that."

She shook her head, incredulous. "Are you kidding me? You're going to fight with me about grammar at a time like this?"

He looked up at her, his eyes full of something that looked a lot like love mixed with pain. "If we're going to fight about anything right now," he said, keeping his voice low, his tone gentle, "it probably oughta be about grammar."

Something caught in her throat . . . something that felt like a big, suffocating rock. "That's true," she whispered. Then, after a long moment, she added, "I hate to see you upset . . . about double negatives . . . or whatever. You mean a lot to me."

To her surprise, he reached for her hand and squeezed it. "You mean a lot to me, too, Van. Just . . . you know . . . be careful."

She returned the squeeze and smiled at him. "I will, buddy. Don't you fret. This ol' girl ain't never not careful."

Chapter

7

Back in her room, Savannah stood beside the unmade bed and thought how lovely it would be to just slip back into it, pull the covers up over her head and sleep for a day or two. It seemed like some former life when she had rolled out of bed in search of something to satisfy her hunger pangs. Pangs that were now returning with a vengeance, since her adrenaline high had subsided.

Thank goodness it'll be breakfast time soon, she thought as she reached into an antique armoire and pulled out the day's costume—yet another medieval ensemble with the inevitable corset. She figured it was too much to hope for biscuits and gravy at Chez Blackmoor, but surely something like bacon and eggs would be on the menu.

She glanced at her watch. Eight-thirty. *Tammy should be up by now,* she thought, reaching for her cell phone. And, as she had expected, the voice that answered on the other end was bright and perky.

"Hey, sugar," Savannah said. "Been up long?"

"Of course! I've already done my three-mile run. I'm in the middle of a protein smoothie."

Savannah could picture the thick, goopy drink that Tammy called breakfast—some sort of concoction that she whipped up in a blender that was the lovely, appetizing hue of gray-green and smelled like seaweed. Even as hungry as she was, that didn't sound appealing.

"Yum," she said without enthusiasm.

"How's it going? Are you having fun? How's Lance? Is he as gorgeous in real life as he is on the book covers?"

"We had a murder last night."

There was a long silence on the other end. Then, "Murder? You mean like a murder mystery game or—"

"Nope. The real thing. Tess Jarvis was killed last night. Found her in the cellar's walk-in freezer this morning, colder than a frog on a mountain and about as responsive."

"Get out! That's awful! Have the cops come yet? Dr. Liu?"

"Yeah, come and gone. Dr. Liu, that is. Dirk and the techs are still here. Alex Jarvis hired me to investigate. He wants to continue the shoot in spite of his wife dying. Do you want to come out here and help me?"

"Do I?! Of course I do!"

"Then pack a bag and hightail it over here."

"What about the kitties?"

"Ask Mrs. Fischer next door to look in on them a couple of times a day. She's got a spare key to the place."

"Wow! Cool! I can't believe I get to hang out there, see the filming and—"

"And investigate. As in, work."

"Sleuthing! I love it! I mean, I'm sorry Tess Jarvis

got killed, but I'm so glad I get to join you there and help out!"

Savannah smiled and mentally hugged and kissed her friend long distance. The kid was sweet. "There's just one more thing I want you to do before you come out here."

"Sure! Anything! What is it?"

"Drop by the morgue and talk to Dr. Liu. See if she's started the autopsy and if she knows anything yet."

The long pause on the other end indicated a drop in the level of enthusiasm. "But, but . . . Dirk's always bugging her, calling her before she's done. She gets really mad."

"So?"

"So, I'm sorta afraid of Dr. Liu."

"Not to worry. She just gets mad at Dirk because . . . well, because he's Dirk. If you tell her I sent you and bring her a box of Godiva chocolate, she'll welcome you with open arms."

"I don't want her to welcome me with open arms if she's in the middle of an autopsy. You know I can't stand that sort of thing. I don't have the stomach for it like you do."

"Oh, don't be such a tender buttercup. What's a little blood and guts? The body's fresh. None of that awful decomposition smell."

"Ugh."

Savannah laughed. "See you later. Okay, Honey Bunny?"

"Yeah, okay."

"And while you're at it . . . could you stop by the Patty Cake Bakery and get me half a dozen maple bars?"

* * *

"Bread and water? Bread and water? Are you kidding me?" Savannah stood beside the long dining hall table, her hands on her hips, a scowl on her face, as she stared down at the large, round loaves of bread and the pewter pitchers full of water.

To her right and left, the other contestants voiced their own indignation with cries of "No way!" and "Enough with this crap. Where's the *real* food?"

Mutiny was thick in the air, and even Alex Jarvis seemed to sense his precarious situation. He stepped from behind the cameraman and approached the table. "We're trying to tape here!" he shouted. "Do you mind?"

"We're starving plumb to death here," Savannah replied. "Do *you* mind?"

"For your information," he said, "this is what people in medieval times had for breakfast. We're trying for authenticity here!"

Savannah took a few steps closer to him, her eyes blazing. "And . . . in medieval times every now and then the starving masses would rise up against their callous lord and perforate his hide with a pitchfork!"

"At least put a platter of fruit out," Roxy suggested. "Some apples and oranges, maybe or—"

"Screw the fruit," Savannah said. "Either put something on this table that we can seriously sink our teeth into, or set up another table over there out of camera range and get a caterer to put on a decent showing. I've heard all about how it's done in Hollywood. Real productions have craft tables that are virtual feasts."

"But we're on a limited budget here," Alex whined. "And we need to stick to the schedule. I don't have time to arrange for anything else right now."

"I'll take care of it," Mary said. From her position behind Pete the soundman, she gave Alex a gentle but authoritative nod. "I'll call a caterer and set up a nice lunch."

He opened his mouth to protest, but she ignored him and continued. "Let's get this scene under way, ladies, and I promise you'll have something substantial to eat later, off camera."

The women looked at each other and mumbled their acquiescence.

Mary smiled. "That's it. Now, why don't you all take your seats and let's get started. While you're eating, I'm going to explain the morning's activities, and I think you're going to just love it!"

Savannah didn't love it. She loathed it.

"I hate pigeons," she whispered to Ryan as they and the entire cast stood in the middle of the courtyard, awaiting the promised arrival.

"This isn't a pigeon," he replied. "It's a falcon."

"A pigeon with talons. Goody."

"What have you got against pigeons?"

Savannah shuddered. "My Grandpa Reid used to have some of them living in his barn. One of them would fly down out of the rafters every time you went in there, and try to land on your head."

"Doesn't sound too threatening . . . just landing on your head."

"Yeah, well, you had to be there. It wasn't fun."

Ryan gave her that kindly, big-brother smile. "Poor little Savannah, terrorized by a mean old pigeon. How old were you when this happened?"

"Nineteen . . . twenty."

"Oh."

"I still have nightmares about it."

"Okay."

She looked up and saw the twinkle in his eyes. She

knew he was stifling a giggle. "Laugh it up, Chuckles," she said. "You have a monstrosity like that flapping on your head, slapping you silly with its wings, and then you tell me it's no big deal."

"I'm sure it was perfectly dreadful. I don't know how you ever survived!"

"Oh, shut up."

"But this bird won't be landing on your head. He's a beautiful, well-trained raptor. That's why we gave you ladies the gauntlets, to protect you from his talons."

Savannah looked down at the heavy leather gloves on her hands. They were extra thick and went all the way up to her elbows. The other contestants were wearing them as well and looked only slightly happier than she about the coming attraction.

"You know," he said thoughtfully, "I figured that a farm girl like yourself would be more comfortable with animals than you are. I mean, the horse yesterday, and now—"

"It doesn't always work that way," she said. "Sometimes having contact with certain critters can make you leery of them. It's easy for citified people to be all sentimental about preserving a wild bobcat . . . until they've tangled with one."

Ryan looked at her with surprise and renewed respect. "You've tangled with a wild bobcat?"

She grinned and shrugged. "Well, two-footed ones. And I've *seen* wild bobcats. Granny Reid's bloodhound, Colonel Beauregard, tangled with one and lost, big time."

Her narrative was cut short by the sound of horse hooves, clip-clopping over the wooden drawbridge. A rider on a black horse burst through the gate. His long purple robe billowed behind him as he rode toward them. On his head sat a pointed hat that sparkled with silver moons and stars.

"Oh, Lord help us," Savannah muttered. "Don't tell me that's supposed to be Merlin."

"I'm afraid it is," Ryan said. "I tried to get Alex to at least ditch the hat, but . . ."

As the rider drew closer, Savannah saw that his arm was raised to shoulder level in front of him, and he, too, wore a leather gauntlet. On his forearm sat an exquisite bird with feathers of silver, black, and white. The animal had a leather hood over its head and was tethered to the man's gauntlet by a long strip of leather.

The "wizard" pulled up short in front of them, raising a small cloud of dust that added a bit of dramatic flair to his entrance. Savannah had to admit that, in spite of the dorky hat, the character had a certain panache.

And the falcon was so regal in its bearing, sitting there on the man's arm, looking both elegant and dangerous, that Savannah instantly regretted her comparisons to pigeons.

"Hear ye, hear ye!" shouted Wannabe Merlin. "All maidens who would contest for the affections of his lordship, draw hither."

"That's your cue," Ryan said, nudging her. "Good luck."

"Thanks," Savannah replied as she left his side and walked over with the other women to stand in a semi-circle in front of the horse. The closer she got to the rider and his falcon, the more nervous she felt. The bird looked as big as an eagle, although a calmer voice of reason inside her head whispered that it wasn't much larger than the pigeon that had tormented her. And standing nearer to the bird, she could see the sharp beak and deadly talons, the tools of a raptor that would seize, shred, and devour its prey alive.

Savannah glanced right and left at the other contestants, and she could see her own apprehension mirrored on their faces.

All except for Carisa, who was wearing a cocky little grin that Savannah recognized. It was the smirk of somebody who was up to no good. As the oldest of nine siblings, Savannah knew the look well and decided to keep an eye on Miss Carisa.

"The contest will be thus . . ." Merlin was proclaiming in a loud voice. "Each lady will stand in her appointed position and extend her arm, like so. I shall release his lordship's royal falcon, and the bird will choose which lady shall win the prize."

"What's the prize?" Leila asked. "Jewelry? A car?"

"Yeah, what are we playing for?" Roxy wanted to know.

Savannah saw Alex wince as he watched off to their left, out of camera shot. He had told them to use as much old English as possible when speaking, and she was pretty sure that "Yeah" and references to automobiles weren't what he wanted from his contestant-actresses. She was equally sure that if he resisted providing them with anything beyond bread and water for breakfast, he wasn't going to be handing out a new Lexus.

"The prize," Merlin said, his theatrical voice booming across the courtyard, "is a romantic afternoon, an enchanting, fantasy date with his lordship, in a boat on yon lagoon."

"Lagoon?" Brandy said, looking around, confused. "What lagoon?"

"I think he means the goldfish pond out front," Savannah told her. "The moat thing."

"I don't care where it is," Carisa said. "It's a date with Lance."

"True, true," the rest agreed, nodding, recalling their mission.

"So," Merlin continued, raising his arm a notch, "take your positions, and may the best lady be chosen."

From her appointed spot, a balcony overlooking the courtyard, Savannah watched the other contestants take their places. Brandy was perched on an outer-wall turret; Leila on the roof of the stable; Carisa on a balcony similar to Savannah's, directly behind her; and Roxy was stationed near the hawk house, which Savannah feared might give her an unfair advantage.

Now that she knew about Roxy's little liaison with Alex, Savannah was suspicious of her on a number of levels.

If they had murdered Tess, Savannah might forgive them eventually . . . after they had served a couple of life terms in prison. But if they fixed the contest, she would hang, draw, and quarter them. Plain and simple.

Not that she wanted the bird to come to her. If there was a way to win other than having that creature land on her arm she would have felt more competitive. But the thought of those talons, that beak, the flapping wings—the pigeon in Grandpa Reid's barn—all served to take the edge off her appetite to win.

But then, there was the thought of spending the afternoon with Lance on a boat in a moat. The memory of his lips on hers, the warm press of his body, his fingers brushing her hair from her face. Just recalling it made her sigh from her head to her toes.

If you spend the whole afternoon in a boat making out with him, you won't get a lick of investigating done. And you've got a homicide to solve, girl.

What? Where did that _come from?_

The contradictory thoughts collided in her brain like a Ventura Freeway rush-hour pile-up.

Lance. Murder. Lance. Blue eyes. Muscles. Gotta catch the bad guy.

When "catching the killer" came out on top, she had to shake her head and wonder. *What's the matter with you, Savannah?*

But below in the courtyard, Merlin was untying the falcon and removing its hood. "Ladies, prepare!" he shouted. She and the others raised their gauntlet-protected arms and held them perpendicular to their bodies and out to their sides as they had been shown.

We'll discuss this later, she told herself.

Merlin lifted his arm. The bird flapped its wings, left the falconer's gauntlet, and headed straight for Savannah.

In spite of her former misgivings, Savannah felt the thrill of victory as the bird sailed toward her. It wasn't noisy and clumsy like the pigeon she remembered so well. This animal soared silently, effortlessly, like a disembodied spirit from an ethereal plane. On wings of silver and black that glistened in the sun, it flew and flew and—

Flew right past her.

A big wave of "agony of defeat" slopped over her, as she watched the falcon pass her by and land on Carisa's arm. For a moment the bird seemed to be biting at the other woman's hand, tugging at her glove with its beak.

Then Merlin whistled, reached into a pouch at his side and pulled out a piece of meat. When he held it up, the falcon wasted no time returning to his master's arm.

"I won!" Carisa shouted, jumping up and down on her balcony. "It came to *me!* It came to *me!* I won the afternoon with Lance."

"Now, now, boys and girls, we have to be gracious when we win," Savannah grumbled. "She must have been absent the day they taught that in kindergarten."

"Hey, Savannah," she shouted, "I'll bet you thought it was coming to *you,* didn't you! Ha, ha! But it came to *me!*"

Savannah tossed her head and lifted her chin a notch. "Yeah, well, don't bust your corset laces there, girlie. The game ain't over yet."

With Alex and the two-man crew busy at the lake with Carisa and Lance, Savannah and the other contestants had the afternoon to themselves to commiserate and bemoan the falcon's choice.

"She looks more like a rat than any of the rest of us," Leila said as they all sat on stools around the kitchen island, nibbling on the lunch leftovers. "That's why the hawk went to her."

"Aw, she was just lucky," Brandy replied. "It had to go to somebody and it chose her."

"Luck had nothing to do with it." Savannah was standing with her head inside the refrigerator, looking for anything that might have a bit of chocolate in it. Mary had delivered a decent lunch of salads and sandwiches, but she needed at least a token dessert—like a simple slice of triple-layer fudge cake, with a big dollop of French vanilla ice cream or whipped cream to go on top. "Carisa cheated," she told them, "plain and simple."

The other girls gasped.

"Cheated!" Brandy exclaimed.

"What do you mean, cheated?" Leila wanted to know.

Roxy jumped off her stool. "No way! I couldn't think of any way to . . . I mean . . . how did she cheat?"

Savannah reached into the refrigerator and pulled out one of the steaks she had seen earlier when preparing their late-night meal. It had been wrapped tightly in cellophane, which was now hanging loosely around it. A corner of the steak had been sawed off.

Tossing the meat onto the island in front of them, she said, "I thought I saw the falcon take something out of her hand when it landed on her arm. So I checked her gauntlet after the contest. It smelled like raw meat. And that steak there was whole earlier."

"Oh my!" Brandy exclaimed, shaking her head. "That just wasn't even fair!"

"That rotten bitch." Roxy shook her head in disgust. "I wish *I'd* thought of that. You wait until she gets back. I'll give her a piece of my mind!"

Brandy turned to Mary, who had been sitting at the end of the island, quietly studying a long to-do list. "Mary, can she do that? Are you guys going to let her get away with cheating?"

Mary shrugged. "All's fair in love and war, right?"

"You mean we can *cheat?*" Leila nearly dropped her sandwich. "Why didn't you tell us that?"

Mary gave them a mischievous grin. "Hey, it's every lady for herself here. If you want Lance, you have to be willing to fight for him."

Savannah couldn't help noticing a nasty little look that played across Leila's face. It was brief, but evil enough to send a little chill down her back. Yes, she'd definitely watch out for Miss Leila.

"So, what's on the agenda for tonight?" she asked Mary. "Another make-believe banquet with make-believe food?"

"Sorry about that," Mary said, looking genuinely embarrassed. "I tried to tell Alex and Tess before that you women would want real food at these dinners. But Tess said it would cause you to bloat and you wouldn't look as good in your costumes, and Alex said you'd be too nervous to actually eat anyway."

"Too nervous to eat?" Savannah shook her head. "That'll be the day you bury this ol' girl."

"And there's no way anybody could bloat in those corsets," Brandy said. "Your head might explode, but—"

"That's for sure," the rest agreed.

"Okay, okay." Mary jotted something on her list. "I'll tell Alex to put out at least a platter of fruit along with the fake stuff. And we'll set up a craft table off camera like we discussed earlier."

"Make sure you've got some pastries on that table," Savannah said. "And maybe a big platter of fried chicken."

Mary stood and picked up her notepad and pen. "I'll get on it right away. And you girls spend plenty of time primping before the banquet. I'll send Kit up to you for last minute touch-ups on your hair and make-up. You'll want to look good . . . what with Lance having to make his decision tonight."

"His decision?" Roxy choked on her apple.

"Yes. Tonight's the first cut. One of you has to go home."

A heavy silence lay on the room as they watched Mary leave. The women looked at one another with varying degrees of suspicion and dislike.

Finally, Brandy said, "Well, I don't know about you, but that's enough to kill my appetite for food tonight."

"Mine, too," Roxy replied.

"Yeah, for sure," added Leila.

Savannah nodded thoughtfully. "Yes, it definitely might take the edge off a body's appetite." She turned back to the refrigerator. All the more reason to find that big piece of chocolate cake now . . . just in case.

But before she could find it, or anything else that could be classified as calorie-dense and triglyceride-ridden, Dirk walked into the kitchen. She noted that his presence caused an instant hush of the female chatter in the room. All the ladies seated at the island gave him wary looks, which he ignored.

Dirk was accustomed to being greeted with little or no enthusiasm when he entered a room.

"You busy?" he asked Savannah. Before she had time to reply, he added, "The bimbo's here, and she says she's got something that. . . ."

He glanced over toward the threesome at the island and seemed to think better of finishing his statement.

Knowing that "the bimbo" meant Tammy, Savannah quickly forgot all about food. She slammed the refrigerator closed. "I'm all yours," she said.

He winced slightly at her words, and again she saw a flicker of hurt cross his eyes.

Somewhere deep inside she felt it . . . either a heartstring twang or maybe just a guilt chain getting yanked. She'd always had trouble distinguishing one from the other when it came to those she loved.

And she *did* love Dirk. She had decided long ago that it was possible to love someone and still entertain grisly, homicidal thoughts about them on a daily—sometimes hourly—basis.

"Let's go," she said, heading for the door. "See you gals later. Better get a beauty nap this afternoon. One of us is going to be sent packing tonight, and it ain't gonna be the Georgia peach!"

"What was that all about?" Dirk asked as they left the kitchen and headed down the hallway.

Savannah grinned. "That, darlin', was me psyching out the competition."

"Do you mean to tell me you actually intend to win this stupid contest?"

"I'm going to catch Tess's killer, get paid for doing it, *and* win that diamond tiara. You just wait and see."

Dirk stopped dead in his tracks and turned to her, a

scowl on his face. "You want a romance with that long-haired pansy?"

"Naw. I just want the crown and the paycheck," she said. "Lance isn't my type. Far too muscular. Those bulging biceps, the well-defined pecs—way over the top for my taste."

Dirk's scowl melted into a grin. "Oh, good."

They continued down the hall, and Dirk's step was considerably lighter.

"Yes," he said thoughtfully, "I can see where all those muscles would be a real turn-off for a woman."

Savannah turned away so that he couldn't see her smile, and she bit her lower lip. Finally, the urge to giggle passed and she was able to say with all seriousness, "Oh, yeah. A real turn-off for most normal women like myself."

Dirk grunted his approval.

She had to add just one more little jab. Just one. "Sorta like those porn stars with the outrageously big boobs," she said, "a *real* turn-off for most normal guys . . ."

She stole a quick sideways glance at Dirk.

He was staring straight ahead. And the look on his face could only be described as a definite return to "cranky."

Chapter

"Where is Tammy?" Savannah asked as she and Dirk exited the dining hall through the front door and made their way across the courtyard.

"She's with Ryan and John in their apartment in the gatehouse."

"What's she got?"

"She wouldn't spill it. Said she would only tell you or the whole Moonlight Magnolia gang—her words, not mine. That kid can be a brat sometimes."

Savannah chuckled. She was accustomed to hearing similar comments from "the brat" about "Dirko." To hear Tammy and Dirk talk about each other, she might have thought they hated one another. But having been raised in a family of nine children, she recognized the dynamics of sibling rivalry when she saw it.

When they entered the modest, two-room apartment that had been billed as the "gatekeeper's quarters," they found Tammy, John, and Ryan sitting in the humble accommodations on cushions that functioned as chairs and a sofa.

At first glance, Savannah thought the cushions were

covered with silk, but as she sat on one, she realized the fabric was only a cheap taffeta. The longer she stayed at Blackmoor Castle, the more she realized that no expense had been spent when decorating it. The place definitely suffered only the delusion of grandeur.

A low wooden table provided the "other" furniture in the main living area, but Ryan and John had spread a white linen cloth over the rough-hewn top and on that sat an elegant silver tea service. She recognized it instantly as their own, which they must have brought from home.

"Good afternoon, love," John greeted her. "We thought you might enjoy a spot of tea and a biscuit after your grueling morning."

Savannah knew better than to get her hopes up at the mention of biscuits. While tasty, what John was offering had little to do with the delicious, fluffy, white goodies that Granny Reid had turned out by the panful every morning of Savannah's childhood.

When John said biscuits, he meant cookies. He was British; he couldn't help himself. Savannah loved him anyway.

He passed her the delicate china plate covered with dainty, chocolate-coated wafers. So what if they weren't hot out of the oven, the kind you had with butter and sorghum molasses? Food was food to a starving woman, and with the way things were done around here at Blackmoor Castle, only the good Lord above knew when she would eat again.

"Good to see you, kiddo," she told Tammy. "What have you got for us?"

"I went to see Dr. Liu, like you said," she replied.

"You talked to the doc?" Dirk wanted to know. "I called her four times already today, and she wouldn't even pick up the phone."

"Gee, wonder why?" Savannah grinned. "Reckon you might have made a nuisance of yourself?"

Dirk gave her question half a second's serious thought, then shook his head. "Nope, couldn't be that. Between you and me, I'm beginning to think she just doesn't like men. And I'm starting to think maybe she plays on the other team." He gave an off-handed wave toward Ryan and John. "You know, the team you guys are on. Follow me?"

Ryan gave him the deadpan look. "Sure, right behind you. It's not exactly hard to keep up."

John poured himself a cup of tea and chuckled. "As a matter of fact, old chap, we're frequently several paces ahead of you."

"Laugh all you want, but there's something up with that broad. In all the years I've known her, she's never made a single move on me."

"Oh yeah, Dirk, that's got to be it," Tammy replied. "Dr. Liu's a lesbian. After all, what's not to like about you?"

"My point exactly." He grabbed a handful of cookies—five, to be exact—Savannah was counting.

"So, what did she say?" Savannah asked Tammy. "Was she finished with the autopsy yet?"

"She wasn't done, but by the time I left, she was well on her way. Tess died as a result of a blow to the back of the head."

"We already knew that," Dirk said, munching happily.

Tammy bristled. One of her least favorite things in the world was having Dirk burst one of her bubbles. Unfortunately it was one of his favorite pastimes. "Well, Mr. Smarty Pants," she said, "I'll bet you didn't know she was hit twice, not just the blow to the head but a second one across her back."

Dirk took a slurp of Savannah's tea. "Yeah, we knew that, too."

Savannah slapped his hand away. "Could you show a little maturity? We're all adults here. Give your fellow investigator the respect she's due and keep your icky, stinky boy germs to yourself." She turned back to Tammy. "What else?"

Tammy gave her a big, knowing smile. "The weapon left a distinctive mark on the body, one that might help us identify it."

Everyone at the table perked up instantly, and Dirk nearly choked on his cookie.

"That's great!" Savannah said. "What sort of mark?"

Tammy reached under the table and hauled out her briefcase. "Well, it just so happens. . . ." She pulled out her notebook computer and set it on the tabletop. "I took a couple of pictures of the wound with that new digital camera you guys gave me for Christmas and downloaded them onto here."

They waited in suspense as she loaded the program and the photos. "Of course," she said, "these are unofficial photos, and Dr. Liu will disavow having given me permission to take them if—"

"Yeah, yeah," Dirk interjected, "and the file will self-destruct in five seconds." He hummed a couple of bars of the *Mission Impossible* theme.

"What?" Tammy said.

"Nothing," Savannah replied, leaning over, trying to see the computer screen. "He's just showing his age. Ignore him and keep . . . doing whatever you're doing there. I've got to see this."

Ryan and John peered over Tammy's other shoulder, as curious as Savannah and Dirk. "I have a feeling," Ryan said, "that our killer regrets having struck that second blow."

John nodded. "It does cast doubt on the accidental

death scene they attempted to stage with the fallen ice cream."

"And," Tammy added, "if they hadn't lost their temper, or whatever, and hit her the second time, we wouldn't have this detail of the weapon. The blow to the head caused the skin to split apart, and Dr. Liu probably wouldn't have noticed the subtle pattern on that wound."

She made a couple of adjustments, then scooted back from the computer, allowing them all a closer view. "There you go. Take a look at that."

Savannah leaned forward and squinted at the screen, cursing her own vanity that she wouldn't admit she needed reading glasses.

The photo was of Tess's bare back and a dark bruise that ran from one side to the other at a slight angle.

Tammy reached for the computer, gave the keyboard a few clicks, and a second, closer shot appeared.

"What would you guess," Savannah said, "about an inch wide?"

"About that," Dirk replied. "And all the way across her back. A long weapon."

"Like a pipe or rod," Ryan said.

Tammy brought up the next shot which was closer still. For the first time they could see the fine detail that made the bruise so distinctive.

"There," she said, pointing to the screen, "look at that."

At even spaces along the long, dark bruise were thin, diagonal lines that were even blacker, crossing over the original wound.

"What would cause something like that?" Savannah asked, thinking out loud. "It looks like the weapon had some sort of decoration or . . ."

"Something wrapped around it," Ryan suggested, "candy cane-style."

"Something that protruded a bit," John added, "and cut deeper into the flesh than the rod itself."

Dirk shook his head. "So, that's what we're looking for? A bloody candy cane?"

"Hey, don't knock it," Savannah said. "It's more plausible than Killer Fudge ice cream run amuck."

She laid a hand on Tammy's shoulder. "Good work, darlin'. You're already earning your keep. Now, where are those maple bars?"

"As you ladies know, one of you will be going home tomorrow morning." Mary stood at the head of the table in the dining hall, dressed in a serving wench's costume. And on her thin body the outfit looked like an empty laundry bag on a coat hanger.

Some women were meant to wear medieval garb, Savannah decided as she sat in her assigned seat at the table and watched the proceedings. And some weren't. Poor Mary would have looked better in a suit of armor.

And Mary seemed terribly ill at ease before the camera. In Tess's absence, she had been pressed into service as the hostess who explained the game rules to the contestants. But in spite of Kit's makeup skills, the heavy wig of dirty blond curls, and the low-cut bodice, Mary Branigan looked more like a teenage boy in drag than a medieval beauty.

Savannah had to admit that she might have considered Mary a bit more attractive if she were only delivering better news. The idea of somebody getting eliminated from the game that night was a depressing prospect. Not that Savannah wouldn't be tickled pink to be rid of Roxy or Carisa, but the idea of going home with her tail tucked between her legs was enough to take the buzz off her maple-bar sugar high.

Looking around the table at the other contestants,

she could see they were as thrilled about the prospect as she was.

"Tonight, after the banquet, Lance will make his decision, and tomorrow morning, you'll be informed of his decision," Mary was saying, as Alex prompted her, from his position behind the cameraman. "But before that fateful moment tomorrow morning, you will dine on yet another traditional medieval feast, entertained by jesters and court musicians as lords and ladies were in days of yore."

Fateful moment? Days of yore? Savannah stifled a giggle. *Whoever wrote this fateful script ought to be drawn and quartered.*

From the self-satisfied smile on Alex's face, she had the feeling that he was responsible.

Personally, she didn't see any Broadway lights or Tony Awards in his future.

"In a moment, we'll bring out the 'Man of Your Dreams,' " Mary was saying. "Keeping in mind that this may be your last evening with him, I suggest that you make the most of every moment you have. And may the best ladies still be with us when the light dawns tomorrow morn."

Gag or giggle, Savannah thought, *tough choice.* And she was pretty sure that doing either would break Alex's rules. He had laid down the law before the camera started to roll that they should stay "in character." They had been told to refrain from talking about their cell phones, their favorite episode of *The Sopranos,* or their latest bikini waxing because, as Alex had so delicately put it, "Yapping about all that modern shit ruins the classy, dignified mood we're trying to create here."

"And now ladies," Mary continued, "I present to you, his lordship, the Man of Your Dreams, Lance Roman."

Savannah felt her pulse rate quicken and her cheeks

flush when the door to the outside gardens opened and Lance walked into the room.

Tarnation, but that man is hot, she thought as he came toward them, walking with the grace of a danseur or matador. Tonight his costume was black with silver studding, his doublet leather and his boots up to his well-defined thighs.

She felt herself sigh all the way to her toes.

As the girls around her chattered to each other and words like "hunk" and "gorgeous tonight" floated in the air around her, she ignored them and watched him closely. As he approached the table his eyes quickly scanned the group, then came to rest on her. He smiled at her. It was the briefest of smiles, so small that she didn't think anyone else even noticed. But she had noticed . . . and she knew.

He likes me. He does! He really does like me! The voice in her head sounded a lot like a thirteen-year-old who was amazed that the most popular boy in school had asked her to be his girl.

Her heart pounded as the reality of the situation hit her. This gorgeous, sexual mountain of manhood was genuinely interested in her as a woman! Whether the contest was cheesy, the script abominable, the production values in the toilet, it didn't really matter. She had a chance for a real romance here if she wanted it.

She could see it all, her future spread before her. Herself an old woman—old, but still stunning, of course—rocking in her chair before a fireplace. Beside her, Lance in his matching rocker—old, but still stunning, of course—their grandchildren playing at their feet. The little boys with dark hair and square chins like Gramp's. The little girls with blue eyes and dimples like Granny's and—

"Boy, we had a hot afternoon, didn't we, Lance?"

Carisa's voice cut through her cozy little fantasy like

one of the swords on the wall, and Savannah felt an overpowering urge to grab an enormous candy cane, if she could find one, and beat the dickens out of her with it.

What did she mean "hot" afternoon?

Hot, my hind end. She'd damned well better be talking about the weather, Savannah thought as she watched Carisa jump up from her chair and scurry over to Lance. She grabbed his arm and led him to his chair at the head of the table, where she settled next to him, holding tightly to his hand.

One look around the table told Savannah that she wasn't the only one who was harboring homicidal thoughts toward Carisa. Roxy looked like she could start spitting nails at any moment, Leila's nostrils were flaring as though she had just smelled a decomposing skunk, and even the gentle, ladylike Brandy was wearing an expression usually reserved for gunfighters who were about to blow a hole in an opponent's forehead in the middle of Main Street at high noon.

Lance was the only one who was hard to read. After that first, quick, friendly glance her way and their brief connection, he had donned a pleasant, but neutral, expression that said nothing about what was going on behind it.

"It was hot, wasn't it!" Carisa repeated, squeezing his hand. "We had such a go-o-od time all alone in that boat." She glanced around the table at the other girls to make sure they were listening.

They were.

So were Alex, Mary, Kit, the cameraman and the sound guy.

Yes, this conversation was far more interesting than any horror story about a bikini waxing gone bad.

And in the far corner of the dining hall, Savannah

saw two other people standing in the shadows who hadn't been there a few moments before. The light was dim in that end of the room, but Savannah knew their silhouettes all too well. Dirk and Tammy had come to watch the taping.

Having Tammy watch was fine with Savannah. But she wished Dirk would take a hike. Didn't he have something better to do . . . like investigate a murder?

Carisa grabbed Lance's hand and squeezed it, prompting a response. "Wasn't it? Didn't we have a great time?"

"Yes, our afternoon was lovely," he said without enthusiasm. "Thank you."

"Oh, the pleasure was mine," Carisa cooed. "At least, half of it," she added with as much suggestibility as she could pack into five words.

Lance made a small movement with his arm as though trying to extract himself from Carisa's death grip. But she held fast.

Savannah noticed, but when she glanced around the table to see if the others had, she decided they were too busy casting death looks at Carisa to even see Lance.

Alex waved an arm, catching Mary's attention. She nodded and announced in a loud but shaky voice, "Ladies and gentleman, let the banqueting begin."

An hour later, the so-called banquet had begun. A couple of jugglers were performing, tossing lit torches back and forth to each other, playing more for the camera than for those at the table. A pair of minstrel types played a lute and a flute, performing graceful tunes that sounded more authentically medieval than anything else at Blackmoor Castle.

But just as at the "meal" the night before, precious little eating had been done.

The plastic pig with the apple in its mouth had been recycled. Savannah could swear that he actually looked dusty and bored tonight. *How very appealing,* she thought. *Good thing I loaded up on maple bars and chocolate cookies this afternoon while I had the chance.*

And with Carisa continuing to brag about her romantic afternoon on the moat with Lance, Savannah didn't have much of an appetite anyway. She had already decided that if Carisa used the word "hot" once more to describe their time together, the woman would be taking the pig's place, stretched out on the table with the apple shoved in her mouth. If she was lucky, it would be in her mouth.

Brandy leaned closer to Savannah and said, "Do you really think they got it on the way she's saying?"

"I doubt it," Savannah replied. "My Granny Reid always said, 'Them that's got the least, brags the most.' She's probably just blowing wind up our sails . . . or trying to."

"I can't stand her," Brandy confided in the same tone one would use to confess a deadly sin. "I'm sorry, but I just don't like her one little bit. How about you?"

"I took her out of my will a long time ago, and if she keeps it up, she's getting scratched off my Christmas list, too."

From the other side of the table, it sounded like a battle was heating up between Leila and Carisa. "I think you should just shut up for a while, Carisa," Leila was saying. "We've all heard just about enough out of you." She turned to Lance and said in a whiny, tattle-tale voice, "Lance, can you make her be quiet for a while and let the rest of us have a chance to talk? She's hogging the show."

Alex raised his hand as though to halt the proceedings, but seemed to think better of it and allowed it to continue. On either side of him, Kit and Mary looked totally disgusted with the whole affair. The far corner of the room was empty; Dirk and Tammy had left long ago. And Savannah couldn't blame them. If she could have slunk away without being noticed she would have.

But only if she could have snuck off with Lance.

He seemed even more ill at ease than the girls as he held up one hand in referee fashion. "Ladies, ladies, please, I don't think we should—"

"But we're just sick of her and her bragging," Leila continued, her pretty face screwed into an ugly pout. "Ever since she won that stupid bird contest, we haven't heard the end of it. And she's got a lot of nerve boasting about anything when we all know she cheated to win!"

Carisa jumped up from her seat. "Cheated? I did not cheat! That bird came straight to me! How could I possibly control that?"

"Steak!" Leila shouted. "You sneaked a piece of raw steak into your glove. That's why the falcon came to you!"

Instead of denying it, Carisa smiled coyly. "So? That isn't cheating. That's just being smart. You would have done it, too . . . if you'd thought of it."

"She's got you there," Savannah added, chuckling.

"Oh, shut up, Savannah." Leila's face flushed as her anger built. "And that's not all. I overheard something the first hour we were here. Carisa, I heard you talking secretly to Tess. I heard you offer her money to fix the contest so that you could win."

"Cut! Cut!" Alex started waving his arms wildly. "You can't say that kind of thing on camera!"

"But it's true," Leila insisted. "Carisa did that. I heard every word of it."

"Where were you?" Carisa asked, not bothering to deny it.

"Under the main staircase, sitting in that little alcove. I heard it all."

Alex walked over to Carisa. "Is that true? Did you ask my wife to throw this contest in your favor?"

Carisa flipped her long hair behind her. "Yeah, okay, I did. But she wouldn't do it. In fact she was really nasty to me about it, said that if she fixed the contest at all, she'd fix it so that I wouldn't win. And I—"

She snapped her mouth closed, as though sensing she had said too much. A heavy silence fell on the room.

"That's true. I heard Tess say that," Leila said smoothly. "I also heard Tess use a particularly nasty racial slur when she referred to you. And you told her that nobody called you that without paying for it." Leila looked across the table at Savannah. "And a few hours later, Tess was dead. Kind of suspicious, wouldn't you say?"

Savannah studied Leila for several long moments before answering. "Did you happen to mention this to Detective Coulter when he questioned you?"

Leila shrugged and glanced away. "Well, I didn't think it was all that suspicious until now."

"Now that she's irritating you by bragging about her afternoon with Lance," Savannah added.

"All right, enough of this," Alex said. "If you two want to fight about the contest, that's one thing. But you're not going to drag my dead wife into it."

Lance stood, placed one hand on each woman's shoulder and gently pressed them back down into their seats. "Let's get on with the taping," he said. "Or we'll be here all night."

Turning to Alex and the crew, he said, "I feel like dancing with a lovely lady. How about some music?"

Reluctantly, Alex turned to the musicians and nodded. They began a particularly lovely version of "Greensleeves." Leonard lifted his camera into position, and Pete swung the microphone boom over Lance's head.

"Say that again, Lance," Alex told him.

"I said . . . I feel the need to dance with an especially beautiful lady right now."

Intuitively, Savannah knew what was coming next. So she wasn't surprised when he walked over to her chair and held out his hands to her. "Would you dance with me, Lady Savannah?" he said, smiling down at her, his blue eyes warm and inviting.

"Why, kind sir," she said in her most sultry Southern drawl as she slipped her hand into his. "It would be my pleasure."

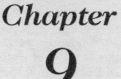

This is one of those moments that I'm going to remember for the rest of my life, Savannah thought as she glided across the floor of the dining hall, Lance's arms around her, moving to the beautiful, ageless song. "Greensleeves" would never be the same for her again. And that was just fine.

"What are you thinking?" he asked as he pulled her a bit closer to him, so close that she could feel the heat of his body. She was surprised to find that his warmth was not only delicious on a sensual level, but it was somehow comforting, too.

And considering that the camera was on them and everyone in the room was watching their every move, she wondered at the fact that she could feel anything intimate toward him.

She glanced over at Pete and saw that he had his microphone boom over the musicians, for once, not trying to record everything she said. Perhaps she could have some sort of "real" exchange with Lance after all.

"I was thinking," she said. "That this is a rocking-chair moment."

He looked confused and shook his head. "Sorry, I don't get it."

"A rocking-chair moment . . . one of those particularly lovely moments that I'll remember someday when I'm ninety years old, sitting in a rocking chair, recalling the amazing life I've led. I'll take my favorite memories out of my mental scrapbook and relive them one by one."

"And this is one of those?"

"Absolutely. How many women get to live a fairy tale, complete with a castle and Prince Charming?"

He had the modesty to blush, and she found that terribly appealing. "It's pretty nice for me, too," he said.

"What? Having all these women fighting over you?"

"No. That sucks. Having a private conversation with you." He smiled down at her in a way that made her weak. "Like this morning in the garden. Now *that* was a rocking-chair moment."

She returned the smile. "Oh, that one's going to make it into the top ten. No doubt."

Glancing over to the table where the other four women sat, she saw that they were all shooting visual darts at her. Poison-tipped darts. She felt a bit like a monkey in a jungle full of jealous Amazons.

And of the foursome, the most evil looks were coming from Carisa, whose jovial mood had gone south the instant Lance had asked Savannah to dance.

"Carisa says she had a lot of fun with you this afternoon," she said, testing the waters.

He sighed and frowned. "Well, I guess that's good. Somebody needed to."

She tried to hide a smirk. "Oh? You didn't have a perfectly lovely afternoon on the moat?"

"Please. What do you think? Would *you* enjoy an afternoon with Carisa? Any afternoon? Anywhere? She's a bimbo. And believe me, as a guy who's been accused of being a 'himbo' often enough, I know one whcn I see one."

"Hm-m-m." Savannah decided to test the waters at the deep end. "So . . . might she be the one going home this evening?"

A flicker of irritation crossed his face and something else that she couldn't quite read. Maybe frustration?

"Not necessarily."

"But if you obviously don't like her . . ."

"Unfortunately, not everything is so obvious."

Savannah lifted one eyebrow. "Are you saying this contest is fixed? That your choices aren't your own?"

She had waded in too deep. Instantly his expression became guarded. "Let's just say that this whole thing is about as 'real' as that pig over there on the table. Don't invest any of your heart into it, Savannah. It's a game. A TV show. That's all."

She looked up into his eyes and saw a deep sadness there, reflecting far more than just his disgust with a badly produced television program.

"It's all a big game, a big fake," he continued. "This show, the book covers, the image . . . just part of the big fantasy factory."

"What you do is real, Lance," she offered, her voice soft and low. "Creating fantasy is real work, important work. It's a hard, cold world we live in, and sometimes we need to escape. Sometimes we need that more than food or water or a roof over our heads. You help us do that."

He said nothing, but looked down at her with an intensity that told her he had heard what she'd said. Really heard her. And her words had affected him on a deep level.

The song ended, but he didn't release her. In fact, he pulled her tightly against him and laid his cheek alongside hers. "Thank you, Savannah," he said, his lips against her ear, his voice husky. "For a rocking-chair memory."

"You're welcome, milord," she replied, allowing herself the luxury of melting against him for a moment. "The pleasure was mine."

"Who do you think is going to get the axe tonight?" Brandy asked Savannah as they stood at the craft table at the opposite end of the dining hall and munched on bits of cheese, crackers, grapes and strawberries.

"Don't know, but we should find out pretty soon." She scooped a bit of brie onto a savory herb cracker and popped it into her mouth. She washed it down with a swig of passion fruit-flavored iced tea.

At that moment, Mary walked by, and Savannah motioned her over. "Thanks for the layout," Savannah said, motioning toward the table of goodies.

"Why are you thanking me?" Mary asked with a sly grin.

"It was either you or Alex." Savannah pointed to the brie and fruit. "And this isn't guy food; it's lady food."

Mary laughed. "He was going to order some pastrami heroes and barbecue-flavored chips. I thought an intervention was in order."

"Bless you. Bless you."

"Who do you think Lance will send home tonight?" Brandy asked, toying with a strand of her copper-red hair.

Mary shrugged, but a gleam in her eye told Savannah that she might have some insider information. "Don't ask me," she said. "I'm just the secretary/hostess/mistress of ceremonies/food gofer around here. They don't tell me anything."

"When is Lance going to announce the winner . . . I mean . . . loser?" Brandy wanted to know.

Mary looked over her shoulder at the center of the room where Lance was dancing with Leila.

He had been dancing with her for a while . . . nine minutes to be exact. Savannah had been keeping track.

"Pretty soon," Mary said. "Leonard should have about enough footage of him dancing with everyone by now. Then we'll meet outside for the 'fare thee well' scene."

"Fare thee well?" Savannah asked. "Really? That's what we're calling it?"

"That's it," Mary replied dryly. "Don't blame me. Mr. Jarvis runs the show. I just do as I'm told."

"I think it's cute," Brandy piped up. "I like everything around here. I wouldn't change a thing."

Eh, pucker up, Buttercup, Savannah thought.

As though on cue, Alex yelled, "Cut! We've got enough. Everybody get outside. We've got to wrap this up before the sun sets. Move it!"

"Mr. Scorsese wants us to 'move it.' I guess we'd better," she muttered under her breath.

But Brandy heard her. "I *like* Alex!" she gushed. "I like him a *lot.* I think he's neat. I think *everybody* here is neat."

"Well, ain't that nice," Savannah said, much too kindly. "How very sweet of you."

"Why, thank you." Brandy's big eyes were wide with sincerity—and pure naïveté, undiluted by common sense or a modicum of insight.

"Gr-r-r-r, God save us from Pollyannas," Savannah mumbled as she walked away, following the crew out the door. "Butt-kissin' fluff-heads who don't even know when they've been dissed. How much fun are they?"

* * *

When the ladies, Lance, and the crew walked outside the keep, they found Ryan and John standing in
the middle of the courtyard, next to the carriage with
its black horses. On the ground in front of them, sitting
end to end, were five old travel chests, complete with
leather straps and brass fittings.

Alex quickly had everyone arranged: Mary in front
of the chests, the ladies shoulder-to-shoulder behind
her, Lance standing to the side, and the cameraman and
soundman in their usual positions—under everyone's
noses, in their hair, and on their nerves.

At Alex's prompt, Mary began her spiel. "Ladies, the
time has come that you've all been dreading . . . when
one of you will have to say good-bye forever to
Blackmoor Castle, and more importantly, to the man of
her dreams.

"Lance is going to give each of you a key and tell
you which trunk is yours to open. Inside four of these
trunks, you may find a gift, specially chosen for you by
Sir Lance, himself. But, inside the fifth trunk there is
no gift. It contains one lady's clothing and belongings,
because as soon as the trunks are opened, that lady will
be helped into the carriage by our coachman, and taken
home. If you—"

"Wait a minute!" Leila said. "You packed somebody's clothes and put them in there without our permission? You touched our stuff?"

"Cut!" Alex threw up both hands in exasperation.
"Cut, cut, cut! What's the matter with you? We're trying to work here! You can't just shout something out
like that and interrupt what we're doing!"

"And you can't just pack up our personal belongings
without us even knowing about it! I don't want you
handling my lingerie, my jewelry!"

"It's not your junk!" Alex's face was an impressive

shade of purple. Savannah wondered if that vein pro-
truding from his forehead was actually going to pop.

Suddenly, Leila's face was all smiles. "Really? It's
not mine, so I get to stay, right?"

Alex ran his fingers through his thinning hair.
"What I mean is, it isn't anybody's real clothes. We just
threw some junk in there for the shoot, okay?"

"Then nobody's really going to have to leave?"
asked Brandy. "That's so nice!"

"No, no, no." Alex shook his head. "Somebody's
going to get the boot, but they can come back and get
their real crap out of their room, later tonight after
we're done."

"Oh." Brandy wilted.

"Let's try this again," Alex said, "and this time, everybody shut up. Don't say anything until you're supposed
to."

"What are we supposed to say . . . when it's our time
to say something?" Brandy wanted to know.

"Just use your common sense," he said. "If Lance
says something to you, say something back, but don't
stop the works to ask questions. Sheez. . . ."

Again, Mary delivered her speech, and this time she
finished without interruption. Then it was Lance's turn.

He walked over to the women, holding five golden
keys that dangled from chains draped over his hand.
Stopping at Carisa, he handed her one. "Will you accept this key from me, milady?" he asked.

"I will, milord," she said, gazing up at him with love-
sick eyes.

Savannah hoped to God she didn't look like that.
She'd seen more sophisticated expressions on cocker
spaniel puppies.

Next he handed a key to Leila. "Will you accept this
key, milady?" he repeated.

"Sure." She snatched it out of his hand.

He gave the third one to Brandy, the fourth to Roxy, and finally, he came to Savannah. "Will you accept a key from me, Lady Savannah?" he said, giving her that half-sweet and half-naughty smile that she was beginning to adore.

Okay, she told herself, *it's the same smile he uses for all the book covers.* But she didn't care. *He doesn't seem to be giving it to any of the other girls, so that makes me special, right? Well, maybe?*

"I accept your key with pleasure, sir," she replied, slipping the chain off his hand and allowing her fingers to brush over the inside of his wrist, briefly touching his pulse spot.

Mary stepped forward again. "And now, ladies, Lance will point you to your trunk. You will go to it, open it, and see what you find inside. Good fortune to you all."

Lance started with Savannah, leading her to the trunk on the left. She knelt in front of it, fit the key into the lock and turned. The lid sprang open and she saw a glint of metal inside. No clothes, just something that shone like finely polished brass. She reached inside and retrieved her gift. It was an antique magnifying glass, the type used by all of the old traditional sleuths. Tammy would have loved it.

The handle was decorated with an ornate filigree and set with a few cabochons that looked like lavender jade. It was very simply beautiful. She was so pleased that before she even thought about it, she stood on tiptoe and kissed his cheek. "Thank you, Lance," she said. "I love it!"

He looked genuinely pleased. "I hoped you would. I picked it out myself," he said, his voice too low for the others to hear. "I chose it because you're a detective, and I think that's really unique and special. You're the only one I've ever known."

Alex motioned for Savannah to return to her place.

She did, holding the magnifying glass against her chest. She got to stay! She got to stay, and she had a cool present, too! Not a bad turn of events.

But she watched with acute interest as the other girls opened their trunks one by one and found their own gifts, none of which she thought compared to hers.

Brandy received a decorative hair comb, which Lance told her had been chosen for her because of her long, beautiful red hair. Savannah noticed that he didn't tell her that *he* had chosen it. She preferred to think that Mary had picked it up at a discount store's jewelry counter.

Roxy was given a hot pink paisley scarf with an orange fringe. She seemed moderately pleased with it. Again, Savannah couldn't imagine Lance buying it.

Mary stepped into camera range and said, "Now, there are only two trunks and two ladies remaining. Lance will lead you to your trunks and together you will unlock them to see who will remain with these other three and who will be sent home."

She moved aside and Lance walked over to Carisa and Leila. He led them to the remaining two trunks, and they followed him with subdued enthusiasm.

Together, while the camera rolled and everyone watched with bated breath—or at least pretended to have bated breath—they walked over to the closed trunks and knelt before them.

"Open the remaining trunks," Mary said.

Savannah stood on tiptoe, trying to see inside the chests the moment they were open. But she didn't have to see the interiors to know who had found a gift and who had discovered that she had been sent packing.

"Oh, a mirror!" Carisa shouted, pulling a pretty, silver hand mirror from inside her chest. "I got a mirror! I don't have to go home! Yayyy! It's you, Leila! You're the one who's outta here!"

And she was absolutely right. Leila was kneeling in front of her trunk, which was piled high with medieval costumes. She simply stared at the contents for a long time, looking as if she might cry, scream, or faint. In the end she did neither, but stood and turned toward the rest of the contestants.

"I didn't want to win anyway," she said, slamming the lid closed. "This is a lame, stupid contest and it's keeping me away from my work. I can't believe I turned down a Victoria's Secret shoot for this!"

"Cut!" Alex yelled. "Is it too much to ask that you people remain in character for five minutes? I can't take this! I can't stand it!"

Ryan stepped up to Alex and put a calming hand on his shoulder. "It's all right, Alex," he told him. "You can edit out anything you don't want. Really. Let's finish this next part, us getting her and her trunk into the carriage and me driving away. Ten minutes tops. Okay?"

"I have a lovely cognac to offer you," John Gibson added. "As soon as we're finished here, I'll pour you a nice snifter and—"

"A snifter of cognac?" Alex didn't look impressed. "How about a fifth of Jack Daniels?"

John smiled and stroked his mustache. "That could be arranged as well."

Alex seemed to rally at the thought of booze. He took charge with renewed spirit. "Let's get you into that carriage and out of here," he said to the disgruntled Leila. "And then I don't want to look at any of you again until tomorrow."

Savannah stood and watched quietly as they finished loading the trunk and Leila into the coach, camera rolling, recording the "Fare Thee Well" for posterity. The other girls had left the scene already, gloating over their victories and their gifts.

She had to agree with Alex; she had her can full of these people. She just wanted to go to her room, take a leisurely bubble bath, hit the sheets, read a few pages of a romance novel, and get the night's sleep that she had been denied for what seemed like a couple of dog years.

One glance over at the garage told her that even Dirk had left for the time being—probably gone to the station house to file his reports.

Tammy had gone back to her house to feed the cats but would return to spend the night in her own room, adjoining Ryan and John's quarters in the gatehouse.

A little time to herself. That was all Savannah needed. And a jasmine-scented bubble bath. And about twelve hours of dead-to-the-world sleep. And while she was wishing . . . how about the answer to who killed Tess Jarvis? That would be nice, too.

"What are you thinking?" said a distinctly male voice. She turned to see that Lance was standing beside her, watching her. She hadn't noticed. She decided she must be even more tired than she thought.

"I was thinking that I'm exhausted and that I wished to hell I knew who committed that murder in the cellar."

"Is that all you were thinking?"

She smiled up at him. "And that I'm glad I'm not leaving in that carriage right now."

"Because you want to stay here and win my heart . . . or because you want to hang around until you solve the murder?"

Savannah knew what he wanted to hear. And she knew what to say if she wanted to win this contest. But it wasn't her way to speak only half her mind.

"Both," she said. "I want both."

"Fair enough." He nodded and smiled. "I suspect you'll accomplish one of them anyway."

She lifted one eyebrow and her dimples deepened. "Which one?"

He laughed and said, "We'll see. We'll see."

Then he walked away and left her standing there with her magnifying glass . . . and questions that would probably keep her awake tonight, no matter how relaxing that bubble bath might be.

Savannah stood at the window of her upstairs bedroom, holding her magnifying glass and fingering its delicate filigree as she looked out on the castle's courtyard. The sun had set, but strategically placed lanterns lit the towers, gate, and walls. Although the lights were electric, like the ones in the hallways, they flickered like torches, casting strange shadows on the walls. Perched on corners and along the walls, gargoyles grinned wickedly, their faces seeming to move as the light danced on their hideous features.

Again, Savannah was struck by the fact that the castle appeared more eerie than romantic, and she speculated about the wealthy Texan who had built this monstrosity. Was he a Dracula buff or a big fan of Frankenstein?

And she wondered if he was the fellow Brandy was speaking to on the phone. It had certainly sounded like it from this end of the conversation. But why would he have placed Brandy in the contest? Had Tess and Alex known about her connections when they had accepted her into the competition?

At the thought of Brandy on the cell phone, Savannah remembered that she, too, had a phone call to make. Tammy had told her earlier that Granny Reid had called Savannah's house and wanted to know how the taping was going. Tammy had promised Gran that she would have Savannah call her that evening.

Savannah glanced at the clock. With the time difference between California and Georgia, she couldn't wait any longer or Gran would be in bed. Besides, she could use a good dose of Granny Reid. She depended on her occasional fix to stay focused and balanced in life.

Carefully, she laid her magnifying glass on the dresser, then fished her cell phone out of her purse.

Her grandmother answered on the second ring. "Hello, Savannah girl," said the sweetest voice Savannah had ever heard.

"How did you know it was me?" she asked as she kicked off her shoes, lay down on the bed and untied her corset lacings.

"Your rings have a happy sound to them," her grandmother said, "I can always tell it's you."

"Aw-w-w, it's more likely that you finally got caller I.D."

Gran chuckled. "You're too smart for your britches. Always have been. I got call waiting, too. I got tired of your younger brothers and sisters telling me that I was living in the Stone Age."

"How do you like it?"

"The call waiting is a nuisance. I can't talk to more than one person at a time, so it's more trouble than it's worth. But the caller I.D. comes in handy when those old men from the home try to call me."

Savannah smiled. Gran had been running from the "old men in the home" since Grandpa had died, many years ago.

"They're still after you, huh, Gran?"

"Oh, lordy yes. They never give up, and I know what they want, too."

Savannah heard the suggestive humor in her octogenarian grandmother's voice and thanked her lucky stars that she had been raised by this lively, loving old woman.

"What is it they want?" she asked, knowing that the question was expected. It was part of a frequent game they played. One of many.

"They want my pension check, the one your grandpa left me; that's what they want. And they're not going to get it either. I'm going to spend it all on myself."

"That'll be the day," Savannah said, "when you splurge on yourself. You're more likely to give it to somebody who needs it at church or to one of those worthless, free-loading brothers or sisters of mine. And speaking of them, how's Vidalia doing?"

"About as good as can be expected for a woman who's too pregnant to see her feet. Had a big fight with Butch, though."

"Huh, oh. What did he do now?"

Granny sighed, sounding tired. "Well, it seems Vi worked up the nerve to go lay out in the backyard, get a little sun, and he told her there wasn't enough sun in the universe to tan that big white hiney of hers."

"That dad-gum yahoo. He gets her all riled up and then we have to deal with her. I'll give her a call and calm her down."

"I'd sure be obliged to you if you'd handle this one. I swear, Savannah, I must be getting old. I can't take those bawling fits of hers the way I used to."

"You? Old? Never. You're just getting smarter . . . and pickier about how you spend your time. You've got better things to do than referee Vidalia's marital spats."

"Amen to that. But enough about your sister; how's that contest of yours going? You got that boy down on his knee with a ring in his hand yet?"

"Now, Gran. You know I don't want a ring, just a crown with diamonds in it. Diamonds I can pry out and sell."

"Well, is he at least handsome enough to make the whole thing worth your time if you don't win the crown?"

Flashing back on her dance with the "man of her dreams," Savannah said, "Oh yes. Well worth it."

"Does he look like Sean Connery?"

Savannah laughed. Connery was Granny's standard for all time. Gran told everyone that in his youth Grandpa Reid had been the spitting image of Sean Connery with a bit of William Holden thrown in.

"Nobody's as good-looking as Sean Connery, Gran," she said, "except Grandpa, of course. But Lance is an excellent kisser."

She heard the little gasp of surprise on the other end. "Oh, is that right? You done givin' away the jewels already, Savannah girl?"

"Naw. Just a little nugget. Enough to keep him interested, but not nearly enough to gain myself a reputation as a 'maiden of ill repute.' Don't worry, Gran." She took a deep breath and decided to spill the rest. "And Dirk caught us kissing."

"Good."

Savannah was a bit surprised. "Good?"

"Yes. Good. That boy needs to see that if he's interested, he'd better stop sniffing around and get down to business. It would serve him right if somebody went and snatched you up, right out from under his nose."

"But Gran. You're forgetting something. I don't exactly want him to 'get down to business.' I like things the way they are between us."

"That doesn't matter. He ought to at least make an offer so's you can turn him down if you want to."

"Gran, I don't think that would—"

A huge crash sounded outside the window. She felt the bed shake beneath her. It sounded like part of the castle had collapsed.

"Oh, my God!" Savannah jumped up and ran to the window. "What was that?"

"What's wrong?" Gran asked. "You havin' one of them earthquakes?"

Savannah had felt the vibrations, but she knew this was no tremor. "No. It's not a quake, but something bad's happened. I'll let you know in a minute."

She looked out the window and at first saw nothing.

Then she spotted it, an enormous pile of broken statuary on the courtyard below and to her right. Although the figure had been smashed, enough pieces remained intact for her to see the evil grimace, some wings and claws. One of the gargoyles had tumbled off the roof of the keep.

"Part of the building fell off," she told her grandmother.

"A big hunk?"

"Big enough," she said. "Part of the decoration." Something told her not to tell her superstitious grandmother that she was hanging out in a castle where demons played a large part in the overall ambiance. What Gran didn't know . . . wouldn't cause Savannah any problems.

Savannah lifted the window and leaned out to get a better look.

Yes, the gargoyle was a goner; that much was sure. His days of guarding the castle were over.

But then she saw a movement. One of his legs was twitching. Twitching? No, it wasn't a trick of the light. There were at least one arm and one leg flailing away in that pile.

"What the hell?"

"Savannah!"

"Sorry, Gran, but I swear I saw something move

down there in that mess." She was already running back to retrieve her shoes from beside the bed. "I gotta go, Gran. Damnation if that ugly thing didn't go and fall on somebody!"

Chapter

10

Savannah ran out of her room and down the hall toward the staircase, hoping that, for once, she would be able to find her way through the dark maze of corridors and outside without too much backtracking. Whoever that was writhing on the courtyard beneath the broken statuary would be in desperate need of help.

Probably far more than she could give them, but . . .

At the second-floor landing, she nearly collided headlong with Alex and Roxy, who were also hurrying downstairs.

"What was that awful noise?" Roxy asked

"It sounded like it came from the courtyard!" Alex added, his usually high-pitched voice a few notes higher.

"It did," Savannah replied as they ran on down the staircase. "One of the gargoyles fell off the roof, and there's somebody under it!"

"No! Who is it?" Alex asked.

"Don't know. I only saw one leg."

"Do you think they're hurt?" Roxy said.

Again, Savannah was struck by the mental agility of

her competitors. "Considering that they're lying under a ton of stone or plaster or whatever, I don't suppose they're feeling too good," she replied dryly.

"But how can a gargoyle just fall off the building like that?" Roxy wanted to know. "I figured those things were stuck on there good!"

"We could have hoped," Alex said. "I'm going to have a talk with R.R. about the safety of this place! If one of my crew got hurt I'll sue his ass off!"

Roxy shot him a quick, warning look that Savannah noted . . . and decided to think about it later, post-emergency.

When they burst through the front door and into the courtyard, they found that Ryan, John, and Tammy were already there, having run over from the gatehouse. Ryan and John were lifting a particularly large piece of the statue from the pile.

"How bad is it?" Savannah shouted as she ran up to them. "Who is it?"

"Don't know yet to either question," Tammy answered as she, too, grabbed handfuls of the rubble and tossed them aside. "Whoever it is, they were moving just a second ago. But now . . ."

Ryan and John tossed the giant chunk aside, and more of the body was revealed. Savannah saw a corset and skirt. It was one of the ladies.

For an instant she considered that it might be Mary Branigan, and the thought made her sad. But the leg that was now completely uncovered was long . . . and dark-skinned.

"It's Carisa," she said, feeling no better. The sight of anyone lying there beneath the rubble was heart-wrenching.

She and the others began clearing the pile as quickly as they could, being careful not to jar Carisa or injure her further.

"Is she breathing?" Ryan asked as John gently brushed away the bits of debris from her head and chest.

Her face was covered with blood, her eyes closed. She was motionless.

"I can't be certain," John replied as he knelt next to the body. "This bloody awful light out here, you can't see a thing."

He bent over her and put his ear to her mouth. He held up one hand, motioning for silence. They all froze and waited.

"She's breathing," he said, "but barely."

"Has anyone called 9-1-1 yet?"

At that moment Mary and Brandy came running out of the keep and over to the pile. And seconds later Pete and Leonard ran around the side of the keep.

"What's happened?" Pete shouted.

Mary gasped when she saw the shattered statue and someone moving beneath it. "Is somebody hurt?" she asked.

"It's Carisa," Savannah said. "Go call 9-1-1 and tell them to send an ambulance, Code Three!"

Mary raced back into the building while Brandy stood by, wringing her hands. "Oh, dear! This is awful! Why is she under all that mess?"

"Why, indeed?" John said.

Ryan knelt next to him and felt for a pulse at her throat. "Thready," he said. "They've got to get here right away."

"I'll go get a blanket to cover her," Tammy said, already running back to the gatehouse.

Pete and Leonard did nothing except stand there with their mouths open, gaping at the mess and shaking their heads.

Savannah made her way across the rubble and joined Ryan and John, kneeling beside the body. She reached over and stroked Carisa's hair. "You're okay, honey," she told her, not knowing if she could even hear her, knowing she was far from okay. Loss of consciousness at the scene was never a good sign. And she could see from the unnatural angle of the woman's left leg that it was badly broken.

"We've got help coming," she told her as she took Carisa's limp, cold hand in hers. "Can you wake up for me? Can you open your eyes a little?"

Everyone watched anxiously, but there was no response.

"Carisa, can you hear me?" she asked. "Squeeze my hand if you can hear me. Try really hard, okay?"

Again, no reaction.

At that moment, another person appeared on the scene. It was Leila, holding a suitcase in one hand and a large make-up bag in the other. She walked over to them, a moderately concerned look on her face.

"What's going on?" she asked.

"Part of the building fell on Carisa," Roxy told her. "She's almost dead."

Savannah shot her a look. "Do you mind?" she said. "We've got an injured person here who doesn't need to hear that sort of talk."

"Oh, yeah. Sorry." Roxy didn't look all that sorry.

Leila strolled over to them, still holding her luggage. She took a quick look at Carisa, then at the mess. "Looks like one of those ugly devil statue things."

"Yes. That's what it was," Ryan told her.

Leila leaned back and looked up at the building's outer wall. "Probably from up there. Yep, one of them is missing. Too bad."

Savannah wasn't sure if she was referring to the demise of the gargoyle or Carisa's injuries. She suspected the former.

Leila turned to Ryan. "I guess this means I'm not going to get a ride any time soon out of here."

"No, I'm afraid we'll have to postpone your trip home for a little while," he said with a slightly contemptuous tone. "At least until the paramedics have arrived and taken your sister contestant to a hospital—one with a trauma unit."

"Damn," she said, "and me wanting to get out of this place as quickly as possible."

"Hey, life's rough," Savannah snapped. "You wanna hightail it out of here and stop making a nuisance of yourself?"

Leila lifted her chin a notch, turned on her heel, and marched back into the keep.

Tammy arrived, huffing and puffing from her sprint, a blanket under her arm. She handed it to Savannah, who gently draped it over Carisa's body and tucked the edges carefully around her.

Ryan felt for a pulse again. "Getting weaker," he said.

Savannah said to Tammy, "That ambulance is taking too long. Maybe you should go make a second call to 9-1-1. Make certain that"—she glanced down at Carisa, who showed no signs of consciousness, but one never knew for sure—"that they know how important it is that they arrive as *soon* as possible."

Tammy nodded and gave Savannah a knowing look. "I will," she said. "I'll make sure they get the message."

As Tammy ran away, Savannah looked at Ryan and John and saw her own deep concern registered on their faces. Standing several feet away, Alex and Roxy and Leonard and Pete seemed less worried

Brandy, however, was softly crying. "She's going to be all right, isn't she? She's not really hurt that bad, huh? It just looks bad, right? Her eyes are probably just closed because she's tired . . . from getting mashed and all."

"God, could you just strike her with a bolt of lightning, please?" Savannah mumbled, "And Lord, while you're in the neighborhood, answering prayers, could you also light a fire under that ambulance's tail?"

Everyone watched as the paramedics loaded Carisa into the ambulance and then sped away, lights flashing and sirens blaring.

Savannah had tried to read the paramedics' expressions, but in their business, blank faces were as necessary as surgical gloves and oxygen tanks. If the speed of their departure was any indication—and it often was—Carisa was in bad shape.

Once the ambulance had passed through the castle gate and disappeared in the distance, Savannah turned back to Ryan and John, who were standing behind her. "Do you think she'll make it?" she asked them.

"I don't know," Ryan replied. "I heard the paramedic say that her blood pressure is almost nonexistent. Sounds like internal injuries to me."

"And unfortunately," John added, "it's a bit of a distance to the nearest hospital. Her first 'golden hour,' when medical attention is the most crucial, is going to be long gone by the time they arrive."

Savannah looked around. Most of the castle's occupants were filing back into the keep, now that the major excitement had passed. Leonard and Pete had trailed away, and only Tammy remained. She was standing in the rubble, searching the ground with a flashlight.

"Nancy Drew's hard at work over there," Savannah said, nodding in her direction.

John chuckled. "Ah, she's a fine one, our Tammy. She would have done well in the Bureau with enthusiasm like that."

"Find anything?" Savannah asked as she walked over to her energetic partner.

"She was smoking."

"What?"

"Carisa was standing out here smoking when she got hit."

Tammy pointed her flashlight at the ground. Sure enough, there among the breakage were half a dozen cigarette butts, all the same filtered menthols. Tammy picked up a twig from the ground and poked at several of them, turning them over so she could get a better view. "These two are fresh," she said. "These three are older."

"Older?"

"Yeah, they're dusty and they look like they got a bit wet. Probably last night with the dew fall."

Savannah bent down and peered at the stubs. If she looked close, she could see the difference. The kid had a good eye for detail. "Okay," she said, "but how do you know she was smoking when she got hit?"

"Her lighter's right there, along with her pack."

Tammy shone her flashlight beam on a cigarette pack that had two cigarettes missing. Beside it was a silver lighter with the initials C. S. M. engraved on it.

"Smarty pants," Savannah said, grinning at her. "Got any other theories?"

"Yes. As a matter of fact, I do."

Ryan and John joined them, and Ryan bent to study the items on the ground.

"So, do tell us, love," John told her, "since you're on a roll, as they say."

Tammy leaned back and pointed her flashlight to the top of the building, where a line of gargoyles guarded the rooftop. The space created by the missing statue made the keep look like a mouth with a tooth missing.

"I heard Brandy say that Carisa was out here smoking last night after the shoot. If Brandy saw her, anyone could have. It would have been safe to assume she would do the same tonight."

Savannah nodded, following her line of logic. "And if they wanted to hurt her, they'd know where she would be."

"Exactly. And since those gargoyles are so close together, they could just estimate which one was directly over her and push it down on her."

Savannah thought for a long time. Finally she said, "Could be. Could be. We need to get up there on the roof to check things out. Did you call Dirk yet?"

Tammy made a face. "Yes, I called Dirko. I called him as soon as I'd called the paramedics. He said he'd be right over."

"We should wait until he gets here before we go much further," she said. "Certainly before we examine the roof."

"Yes, we really should," Ryan agreed.

"It's truly the right thing to do," John added.

"He'd get really mad if we went up there without him," Tammy said.

They stood there for a long minute, Savannah tapping her toe on the courtyard cobblestones. Then she said, "Let's go."

Ryan replied. "We're right behind you!"

It took a while for Savannah and her entourage to find their way to the roof, but several staircases and endless hallways later, they stepped out onto the flat expanse that was surrounded by a waist-high wall. Upon the wall at regular intervals sat the gargoyles, one uglier than the next. The gap in the chorus line was all too obvious.

As they had before walking up the steps, they

paused to check for any type of footprint. But the surface was fairly clean and free of dust or dirt that could register a print. Nothing was visibly disturbed . . . other than the tumbled statue.

"If you don't have gloves, don't touch anything," Savannah said, before recalling that no one in the troop needed that instruction. Normally, it wouldn't have occurred to her to warn them, except for the fact that they were blatantly violating and arguably contaminating a crime scene.

Together, they hurried over to the spot where the gargoyle had sat. All had retrieved flashlights from their cars, and their way was well lit. When they got to the wall, they all directed their beams onto the empty section.

"That's what I figured," Ryan said, pointing to a deep, even scrape mark about two inches wide across the stone. "They used some sort of pry bar. I didn't think one person, or even two could push that heavy thing off this wall by hand."

"Not without going over themselves," Savannah said, leaning over the wall and looking down to the courtyard directly below where the shattered statuary lay.

"I doubt they could budge it even if they had a running start," John said. "But thanks to the dynamics of leverage, it wouldn't have been that difficult to tip it just enough to send it over."

"Is there any chance at all that it fell off by itself?" Tammy asked. "I mean, it *could* have been an accident. And that mark might have been there from before, like when they set the statues onto the wall."

"Unless there was a five-plus quake," Savannah said, "that thing wouldn't have budged. And that scrape is as fresh as those cigarettes you found down there. It was pushed off."

"Speaking of quakes . . ." Ryan studied the line of remaining gargoyles. "It's not the brightest thing in the world to have these things just sitting up here, unsecured. This *is* prime earthquake country, after all."

"Maybe R.R. What's-His-Name is from Texas and doesn't know how much California loves to rock 'n' roll," Savannah suggested.

"R.R. Breakstone isn't known for taking a lot of security measures," Ryan replied, "other than having a gang of thugs around him all the time for personal protection. I doubt that he would worry a lot about having his guests injured at his castle—or them suing him if they did."

"Tough guy?" Savannah asked.

"One of the toughest," John replied. "May heaven help you if you cross swords with the likes of him. If he doesn't take you down, his so-called friends will."

"What are you saying?" Savannah was searching the area of the roof near the gargoyle's previous spot. "Are you suggesting that the owner of Blackmoor Castle, the eccentric Texan who built this spooky place, is in organized crime?"

"He's only been a Texan for two years," Ryan told her. "Before that he was a club owner in Las Vegas. And yes, the Bureau has been after him for years. That's a large reason why he left Nevada and moved to Texas, to escape some of the heat—legal heat, that is."

"But the FBI can follow and investigate him just as well in Texas as in Nevada," Savannah observed.

"But he's been keeping his nose very clean in Texas," Ryan said. "They think he's in with a ring that's smuggling dope through Juarez and El Paso, but they haven't been able to nail him with anything yet on his home turf in Dallas."

"I think Brandy is involved with him," Savannah told them. "I overheard her talking all lovey to him on her cell phone. Some of the things she said also made me think he placed her in this contest, like some sort of mole."

"I wouldn't be surprised." Ryan looked at John knowingly.

"I should tell you," John said, "that Alex, Tess, and R.R. have quite a history. He's bankrolled their last three projects, including this one."

"And he's fairly insistent that his investments pay off," Ryan added.

Tammy walked to the nearest gargoyle and shined her light along its lower edge. "Maybe that's why Alex was determined to keep the shoot going even after his wife died. He might be afraid to tell this R.R. guy that it was over."

"Very possible," Ryan said.

Savannah looked down at the spot where Carisa had been so badly injured and wondered how she was doing at the hospital. She wondered if the woman had even made it to the emergency room alive.

"So, what's Alex going to do now?" she said. "This show is cursed. His wife, a producer, is murdered, Leila gets ousted today, and Carisa is out of commission. Shoot, we're dropping like flies around here." She took a deep breath and sighed. "Makes you wonder who's next."

Savannah could hear the ruckus going on inside the dining hall long before she entered the room—excited, angry voices echoing down the corridors. Most sounded female. In fact, the only male voice she heard was Alex's nasal twang, shouting over the rest, or at least, trying to.

"I don't care what you think about it! I didn't ask you what you think I ought to do. I'm telling you what

I'm *going* to do!" he was shouting as Savannah stepped through the door and saw the unhappy group bunched near the fireplace. Roxy and Brandy stood in front of Alex, and behind him were Mary and Leila. It looked as though he was trying to keep the two factions separated and blood from spilling.

"But it isn't fair!" Roxy shouted, stomping her foot in a manner that reminded Savannah of her youngest nieces and nephews. But they were only three years old. Roxy had no such excuse.

"Lance told Leila to leave today," Brandy was saying in a voice that was several decibels lower but just as angry. "I think we should abide by his decision."

"She's out!" Roxy screamed. "She stays out! That's it; that's all! We aren't changing the rules halfway through the game."

"But we *have* to change the rules," Leila said, peeking over Alex's shoulder. "Carisa's dead, and—"

"She isn't dead," Savannah said, walking into the affray. "I just got off the phone with the hospital, and they say she's going into surgery to have her spleen removed, but she's alive. Let's don't measure her for a coffin just yet."

"Well, she's not coming back to the contest, that's for sure," Roxy said.

"I'm afraid she's right," Brandy added. "The way her leg was all twisted, I'm afraid that she's not going to be walking on it any time soon . . . even assuming she makes it through surgery."

So, even Miss Sunshine and Light isn't placing any bets on poor Carisa, Savannah thought. *Not a good sign.*

Roxy crossed her arms over her chest and stuck out her bottom lip. "And Alex here wants to put Leila back into the game, just because Carisa's out. I think it stinks! We were rid of her, and it should stay that way."

"You're just afraid of the competition, Roxy," Leila

shouted. "You know that Lance was starting to like me and—"

"Yeah, yeah, that's why he sent you home! Duh, Leila." Roxy replied. "Because he was so charmed by you. Hell, you're probably the one who pushed that monster statue thing down on Carisa, just so that you could get back into the game."

"Now, now. You shouldn't say an ugly thing like that." Brandy reached out and patted Roxy's arm. "When you find out it was just a simple accident, you'll feel so-o-o bad for accusing Leila like that."

Alex threw up both hands in his best director style. "Cut! Cut! Shut up and listen to me! I've got a lot of money invested in this show, and investors I have to answer to. We're going ahead. And in order to do that, we need more than three contestants, so Leila's back in. And I don't want to hear anymore about it!"

He left them and marched across the room and out the door.

Mary stepped into his place and quickly took control of the situation. "Ladies, ladies," she said, "we're all upset over the terrible things that have happened, and we're exhausted. What we all need is a good night's sleep, and everything will look brighter in the morning."

"She's right," Savannah said. "One hot bath and eight hours' sleep from now, I'll be a lot more cheerful and ready to do battle with you gals again. Let's hit the hay."

Brandy agreed, Roxy grumbled, and Leila looked far more satisfied than was decent, considering the circumstances of her reinstatement. One by one they filed away, leaving Savannah and Mary alone.

"You handled that a lot better than your boss," Savannah told her.

"Wouldn't take much." Mary smiled, but she looked

exhausted. "Are you going to your room now for that bath?"

"Not yet. Detective Coulter will be here soon, and I need to talk to him. After that, I'll be down for the count. But first, there's something I need to ask you."

"Sure. What's that?"

"Where's Lance?"

Chapter

11

"Lance?" Mary gave Savannah a blank look. But Savannah had seen that same look several thousand times before in her years on the police force. And she had seen it ten thousand times when helping her grandmother raise her eight siblings. She and Gran called it the "Who? Me?" look. And it had other variations, like the one Mary was exhibiting: the classic "Me? Know anything?"

"Yes, Lance," she repeated. "Where is he? Everyone was in the courtyard after the 'accident' except him. I just knocked on his bedroom door and he didn't answer. It was locked," she added, admitting that she had tried the knob.

Mary looked as uneasy as a cornered squirrel. She glanced right and left and swallowed hard.

"You can tell me," Savannah said. "I'm not trying to get anyone in trouble, but we have to account for everybody's whereabouts at a time like this."

"Okay," Mary said, "but you can't let it get back to Alex."

"I won't tell Alex a thing." *I might tell Dirk and all*

the rest of the Magnolia gang, she thought, *but Alex . . . no problem.*

"Lance went home."

"Went home?" Savannah's heart sank for a moment. Was the contest over after all? They could continue without a princess or two, but they only had one prince.

"To his apartment in Hollywood. Just for the night," Mary assured her. "He was worried that his neighbor might not be taking care of his dog, and, to be honest, he'd had about as much of Blackmoor Castle as he could stand and needed a break."

She thought of hearth and home and the comfort of unconditional kitty love. "I can understand that."

"He promised me that he'll be back before Alex is even out of bed tomorrow morning."

"But wasn't Alex asking about him tonight?"

Mary shrugged and looked sheepish. "He asked, but I told him Lance was sound asleep, resting up for tomorrow."

"When did he leave?"

"Right after the shoot. He sneaked away when Alex and I were going over tomorrow's schedule." Mary reached out and put her hand on Savannah's arm. "You won't say anything that will get him in trouble, will you? Alex gets all upset over even the smallest stuff. He'd have a fit over this if he knew."

"He won't find out from me, I promise," Savannah told her.

Mary relaxed. "Thanks." Then she added, "You know, Savannah, you're my favorite one of the contestants here. Always have been."

Savannah grinned. "Now, if only the 'Man of My Dreams' agrees with you."

"Oh, I'm sure he agrees with me," Mary said with a bit of sadness in her voice. "For all *that's* worth."

* * *

"This stupid contest is fixed," Savannah told Dirk as he examined the pile of rubble in front of the keep. "I don't have a popsicle's chance in Hades of winning it. Mary practically told me so herself, and Lance, too. I'll bet it's going to be that obnoxious Roxy—the advantages of sleeping with the producer—or maybe Brandy, who's in cahoots with the owner of the place, the guy who's paying the bills. A contest doesn't get any more fixed than that, now does it?"

"Whatever." He didn't look up, but tossed a few chunks of the broken statue aside as he rummaged through the mess.

"Don't you 'whatever' me, boy," she said. "This is important to me. Even if you do think it's stupid, you could at least pretend to be interested."

"No."

"No?"

"That's right. It *is* stupid. Grown men and women running around playing Knights of the Round Table and crap like that. It's dumber than dirt, and I'm not going to pretend to be interested when I'm not. Besides, it looked to me like you were doing all right, contest-wise, out there in the garden this morning."

Savannah wondered for a moment, *Just how big a chunk of plaster would it take to knock the tar plumb out of him?* And: *Is there any rule that two people can't get clobbered by the same fallen sculpture?* She figured it was safe to assume that one wasn't on the books.

Dirk glanced up at her and said, "What's that look supposed to mean?"

"What look?"

"You've got a puss on. What are you thinkin' about?"

"Don't aggravate me, boy, any more than you already have. I was wondering what the sentence would be for assault with a deadly gargoyle."

"On a cop? Forget about it. You'd get the needle. Now why don't you just forget about this friggin' contest for a few minutes, and tell me what the hell's going on around here?"

Savannah glanced around the dark courtyard with its flickering lamps that created more shadows than light. In the distant hills coyotes howled, adding a particularly unsettling note to the scene, which was eerie enough without any added sound effects.

"What's going on?" she replied. "Not much. We have one-and-a-half dead women in less than twenty-four hours, a slew of suspects, all of whom have secrets, and they make it no secret that they can't stand each other. I don't have the slightest idea who attacked these women; I'm pretty sure it wasn't me, but beyond that . . . And I'm wondering if I'm going to be next." She sighed. "Pretty much just your average day in the Middle Ages."

Never in all her living life had a jasmine-scented bubble bath felt so heavenly, Savannah decided as she slipped her aching body into the shimmering suds and felt the warmth melt away the tension stored in her joints and muscles.

Even away from home, she had to follow her nightly ritual, because it was one of the few hedonistic pleasures she allowed herself.

Other than Godiva chocolates.

Ben and Jerry's Chunky Monkey ice cream.

Irish coffees topped with extra thick cream.

Victoria's Secret's nightgowns.

And silk sheets with lavender sachets under her pillow.

Okay, she had to admit that she didn't really deny herself much when it came to fleshly delights, but a lady could have worse vices than a candlelit bubble bath.

Like stealing.

She had swiped a candle from the dining hall and brought it up to her room to complete her ritual. The small votive sat on a saucer on the edge of the tub, the only light in the room.

The suds glistened iridescent on her body and for a moment, there in the candlelight, the ugly realities of the world disappeared and she was nothing more than a woman enjoying her own beauty and sensuality.

Until her cell phone rang.

She had brought the phone and her gun into the bathroom with her and laid both on a stack of towels near the tub. With all that had happened, she had been reluctant to leave either behind.

Now she wished she had. She really, *really* wished she had.

If she'd only left the phone in the other room, she wouldn't have to kill whoever had called and interrupted her bubble bath.

"Dirk, this had better not be you," she said when the caller I.D. showed only "Private Number" on its display. "I told you I wanted to be left alone for a while."

"It ain't Dirk; it's me," said a female voice with a much thicker Southern accent than even her own. "You were supposed to call me. Gran said you would, and I've been waiting here by the phone for ages. Where have you been?"

"Digging a woman out from under a pile of rocks and trying to solve a murder," Savannah replied, settling back into the bath with the phone to her ear and resignation in her heart. If she knew her sister Vidalia, and she did—all too well—the bubbles would be long gone by the time this conversation was over.

Vidalia could gripe for ages.

"Yeah, right," Vidalia said. "You'd think you could come up with a better story than that one."

"Sorry, it was the best I could do in a pinch. What's shakin', sugar?"

"Me. I'm so big I jiggle all over when I walk."

"You're pregnant, sweetie. You've been pregnant twice before and you know this always happens. You'll lose the weight after the baby's born, what with nursing and all. You did before."

"Even my ankles are fat!"

"That isn't fat. You can't have fat ankles. That's water, darlin'."

"I can't stand this anymore. I'm tired of being pregnant. I want to back out of the whole deal."

"You've only got six weeks to go, and then all this will be a thing of the past. You'll have skinny ankles again. I promise. I'll buy you a pretty ankle bracelet for a baby gift. Lord knows, after two sets of twins, you've got baby clothes aplenty."

"I think Butch is in love with another woman."

Savannah pictured her brother-in-law, his head stuck under the hood of a car, grease up to his elbows, his only hobbies automobile repair, watching baseball from his recliner at home, and deer hunting. None were performed in particularly female-rich environs.

Besides, Butch—like most males who were involved with the Reid sisters—had a deep and abiding fear of his woman.

"I really doubt it, Vi. Butch is a good guy. And he wants to keep his genitals. It's probably just your imagination."

"He's been hanging out in a strip club."

"What?"

Savannah had expected anything but that. A strip club? Their tiny, rural hometown of McGill, Georgia, was only three blocks long. They considered themselves lucky to have a video store—three shelves of rentals on the back wall of Penny's Grocery & Drug Store.

There wasn't a proper, or improper, strip club within a two-hundred-mile radius of McGill.

"What are you talking about, girl?" she said. "Those hormones of yours have made you plumb crazy! What strip club?"

"Well . . . they've got these new uniforms out at the Chat-n-Chew Café. And they might as well be strippers. Their hind ends are hangin' out from under those short skirts of theirs and their T-shirts have always been too tight. Anyways, Butch has developed this sudden craving for their double-chili cheeseburgers. He's just gotta have one for lunch a couple times a week. He always has been an ass man. Don't tell me you didn't notice that about him."

Savannah rolled her eyes. "No, Vi, I can't say as I have noticed that, but if you say so. He's your husband. Maybe you oughta bend over a little more when you serve him his TV dinner of an evening. Give him a little thrill."

"No way! I'm never bending over in front of that man again for as long as I live. He . . . he . . ." Sniffle, sniffle. "He made a very rude remark about my backside. One that I'll never forgive him for."

"Oh, yeah. Gran told me about the 'not enough sunshine' crack he made. Not cool, but he was probably just teasing you. He loves your butt."

More sniffles. "How do you know?"

"Because you have four children already and another one on the way. Your ankles are swollen, you're crying all the time, you're accusing the man of going to a strip club just because he wants a cheeseburger for lunch, and he still comes home after work every day. He's a man in love with you. Butt and all. Believe me."

"Are you saying that Butch is some sort of saint for putting up with me?"

Savannah sank lower into her tub, feeling older than

Granny Reid. Much older. "No-o-o, Vi," she said in the least-exasperated voice that she could muster. "I would never suggest such a thing to you, and certainly not when you're pregnant. I'm just telling you that you've got a good husband and a good life. If I were you, I'd just wallow in that for a while and not worry about the waitresses at Chat-n-Chew or the size of your butt. Life's good, Vi. Really, really good! Enjoy it."

"Really?"

"Really, sweetie. You're beautiful and so, so loved. Put your feet up, have yourself a cold drink, relax and make your baby."

"Thanks, Van. I love you."

"I love you, too, darlin'. Take it easy."

"Okay. Bye."

Savannah punched the "Off" button and said, "Lordy, lordy, lordy . . . will those young'uns ever get raised?"

She laid the phone on the towels, silently daring it to ring again. Then she turned back to her bubbles—both of them. The rest were all gone.

The candle flame sizzled, flickered, and died, leaving her in total darkness.

"Well," she said with a sigh. "Now ain't that just ducky."

Savannah picked up her travel clock from the night-stand and pushed the button on the top. The light came on, the blue-green display showing 2:39 AM.

So much for dropping right off and getting a full night's sleep, she thought.

For the fourteenth time she fluffed her pillow, smoothed the sheets beside her and tugged her night-gown back down around her legs.

It had been a while since she had gone this long without sleep, and she was positively punchy.

The faces of her suspects floated before her, each with their own agenda . . . an agenda that might translate into a motive for murder.

And even more haunting were the victims. Tess's sightless eyes staring at nothing, her skull crushed. Carisa with eyes closed and her limbs twisted into terrible angles, and inside, deadly bleeding.

Okay, she told herself, going down the mental list again, *Alex and Roxy had a motive for getting rid of Tess, but why try to kill Carisa?*

Leila had the best reason to attack Carisa—in order to get back into the game—but she couldn't have been sure that would happen, and most people would have to be fairly certain they'd get what they wanted before they would actually kill somebody. And . . . why would she kill Tess?

She had to believe that one person had committed both crimes. What would be the odds that two murderers would both decide to strike in virtually the same time and place? The coincidence was far too great to really be considered.

Besides, it was disturbing enough to think that one killer was wandering around, walking and talking with decent folks, acting like a regular human being. It boggled the mind to think that two might be out there.

Without knowing the killer's identity and motives, no one at Blackmoor Castle could really consider themselves safe.

And not only was Savannah concerned for her own safety, but she took it personally when people got hurt, or worse, on her watch. She wasn't sure how she had failed Carisa, but she felt she had somehow. If she'd only seen something, heard something, put some pieces together that still eluded her, Carisa would be in her bedroom right now, scheming up ways to cheat in the next competition, as she should be. Instead Carisa was fighting for her life in a hospital, having her spleen removed.

Savannah hated whoever it was who had done this. How could anyone feel such a high degree of entitlement that they could rationalize killing another human being? Was there any more evil and selfish act than murder, taking absolutely everything from someone, even their very life?

That was why she loved catching them and putting them away where they couldn't hurt another innocent person. It was fun to nail a burglar, an embezzler, even a shoplifter. But catching someone who stole life itself—that was what she lived for.

And now she was trying to sleep in the very house where a murder had been done, most likely by someone she had seen and spoken to that very day. It was almost more than she could stand.

She sat up, threw back the covers, and got out of bed. Walking over to the window, she could feel the cool wooden floor under her bare feet, and the sensation was somehow soothing in the otherwise hot and stuffy room.

Sliding the window up, she felt a cool breeze sweep inside. She closed her eyes and let the night wind smooth her hair back from her face, caressing her skin. It made her feel clean, refreshed, her spirit less soiled by recent events.

Glancing down at the courtyard, she saw a shadow, a figure walking from the stable to the keep. The person passed beneath a lantern and she could see his face well enough to recognize him.

It was Dirk.

He was still on duty. With virtually no sleep the night before, he was still going, as obsessed as she was. This compulsion to grab the bad guys was one of the ties that had bound them together as friends.

That and a fanatical love of junk food.

She reached for her cell phone and punched in his number. Then she watched as he stopped in mid-stride in the center of the courtyard and pulled his phone from his pocket.

"What?" he barked—his usual gracious, chatty self.

"Look up and wave 'hi.' "

"To who?"

"To me, numbskull."

He looked up, scanned the front of the building, and stopped when he saw her waving to him from the third floor window.

Reluctantly, he waved back. Dirk wasn't comfortable with public displays of affection.

"What are you doing up?" he said with unconvincing gruffness. "You're supposed to be getting some rest."

"I can't sleep. You?"

"Me either."

"Whatcha doin'?"

"Thought I'd go down to that cellar again, check it out. See if I missed anything."

"Want company?"

"Sure," he said.

"I'm in my nightgown, and I'm not getting dressed again for anybody . . . not until sunup anyway."

Even in the semi-darkness, she could see him grin from ear to ear. "All the better," he said. "I'll meet you downstairs."

Chapter

12

"I don't like this stupid castle of yours," Dirk said as they descended the stairs into the cellar. "It's spooky and creepy, and this dungeon thing down here particularly sucks."

"Ah-h-h, ye have such a way with words, lad," she said. "Are ye sure yer not an Irish bard?"

"What?"

"Never mind. And it isn't *my* castle. I don't like it any more than you do. At least you don't have to sleep here."

"If I did, I'd be sleeping with a rosary on my chest and a string of garlic around my neck."

"But you aren't Catholic, and you don't like garlic."

"Well, I'm gonna start liking it and get real religious if I have to come down here in this torture chamber many more times."

Savannah looked around the so-called dungeon and decided he had a point. The large, rust-encrusted chains hanging from the wall, some of them with strange manacles, and other devices that looked a bit like bear traps, had obviously been placed there with the intention of giving the area a sinister atmosphere. And the decorator had been highly successful. All it needed was an iron maiden and a rack for stretching prisoners on to complete the ambiance.

"I know what you mean," she said. "This cellar reminds me of that S&M club we raided in West Hollywood."

Once again her eyes scanned the assorted devices on the walls for anything resembling Dr. Liu's description of the murder weapon. She knew it was pointless, having searched it at least ten times before, but she couldn't resist looking. Finding the murder weapon was paramount in any homicide investigation. You could learn so much about a killer by examining the tools of his trade.

"It's not there," Dirk told her, following her line of vision.

"I know," she said. "But I can't help looking."

"You'd think they'd just use something that's here, with all the choices," he said.

"Maybe they did. And then they didn't put it back where it belongs. And you know what that tells us about the murderer . . . ?"

He just gave her a blank look.

She smiled. "The killer's a man."

"Very funny. And this from a woman who lost her keys and had to call me at three in the morning to come jimmy her bathroom window open so she could get into her own house."

She stopped smiling and lifted her chin a notch. "Be that as it may. Shall we continue?"

"By all means. After you, Madame."

For several minutes they both walked around the room, saying nothing, studying the various markers and the scribbles on the floor left by the C.S.I. techs.

Savannah knew Dirk had memorized the layout as

well as she had, but it never hurt to go over it once more. Or twenty more times. Whatever it took until you found something that you had overlooked.

She knelt beside one of the four plastic markers that had been set on the floor to designate where blood drops had been found. The four markers were in a relatively straight line from the freezer on the far side of the room to the center. The two that were nearest the freezer door were the closest together, only a foot apart.

"These four drops were low velocity," she said, more to herself than to Dirk who had heard it all before from the C.S.I. team. "Probably dripped from the weapon."

"Or maybe the killer was bleeding, if he got injured during the attack," Dirk suggested.

"That's usually when the attacker is using a knife," she replied. "His hand gets slippery from the blood and slides down onto the blade. And besides, Tess had no defensive wounds. He came up behind her and whacked her before she even knew he was there. Otherwise, she would have turned to face him and been struck from the front."

"Unless she knew who was behind her, trusted him, maybe even talked to him and then turned her back on him."

"Maybe, but if the weapon was as large and heavy as the wound indicated, she would have probably gotten suspicious if they'd approached her with it."

Dirk nodded. "He probably snuck up on her when she was reaching for the ice cream. And, I want you to notice that I'm tolerating your calling the killer a 'him' like you always do until you find out it's a broad, even though it's blatantly sexist."

She gave him a sweet smile. "Oh yeah, we all know how often 'broads' kill men, compared to the other way around."

"It happens. And you'd better hope that this time it's a chick, because otherwise there's a one-in-four chance it was your boyfriend. More like fifty-fifty, because I don't think it was either that hippie cameraman or the pansy microphone dude."

"It's not fifty-fifty when one of the two male suspects is the husband. Odds are wa-a-ay in favor of her old man. They don't call it home-icide for nothing."

He opened the freezer door, turned on the light and looked around. "I gotta admit, I think it's Jarvis, too. What with you overhearing that conversation between him and the blond airhead, that's enough to convince me it was him. But that's not nearly enough to charge him. We really need the murder weapon."

"That's just the beginning of what we need. Especially now that we've got two victims. Have you heard anything new on Carisa's condition?"

"She's out of surgery. Still touch and go. Doctor said that even if she lives one of her legs is never going to be the same."

Savannah flashed back on the sight of the woman's horribly twisted leg and felt a little queasy, and more than a little angry at the person who was responsible.

"I don't think he was waiting for her here in the freezer," Dirk said, "for several reasons."

"The first being that he would have frozen his tushy off?"

"In no time. And besides, the inside of this thing isn't all that big. I don't think anybody could have hidden well enough that she wouldn't have seen them the instant she walked in and turned on the light."

"And if she'd seen them, she would have been attacked from the front, not the back."

"Right."

"So, either the killer followed her down here from upstairs, or was waiting for her." She walked over to a door halfway down the wall to her right. "My guess is that they were hiding in here."

Opening the door, she revealed a well-stocked wine cellar. "I already checked in here, and so did the C.S.I. team. We didn't find a thing except these dusty bottles."

"Neither did I," Dirk said. "The floor's clean and no footprints. No clear prints on the door handle or jamb. And it's pretty obvious that nobody's messed with the bottles because they're all evenly dusty."

Savannah bent over and looked once again at each shelf where bottles of merlot, chardonnay, cabernet, zinfandel, and other exotic wines she had never even seen lay, side by side. She would have to bring Ryan and John down here. As connoisseurs, they would truly appreciate the vast selection.

She, on the other hand, would have been far happier to see one tire iron, baseball bat, or maybe a pipe with some sort of band twisted around it—something that might have been used to crush poor Tess's skull.

"If there was anything in here, we would have found it," Dirk told her. "We're just wasting our time."

"Wasting *my* time, that's for sure. You're getting overtime. I could be sleeping and . . ."

Her complaint faded the moment she spotted something. It wasn't much, but she hadn't noticed it before.

"Hey, look at this," she said.

He hurried over to where she stood at the end of one of the long rows. "What is it?"

"It's what it's *not*. It's not dusty right there." She pointed to a spot about four or five inches across on one of the shelves that was about the same height as her knee. Although an even coat of dust lay on every other part of the shelf and its bottles, that one area was clean.

"One of the C.S.I. techs probably brushed against it with his lab coattail or something," Dirk said.

"Maybe, but it's also just about the right height for someone to step up onto." She pulled her nightgown sleeves down over her hands, put one foot on the clean spot and by holding onto one of the shelves, pulled herself up.

Looking around from her new vantage point, she suddenly became aware of a beam that stretched across the ceiling. When standing on the floor, it appeared to be flush against the ceiling. But from where she was standing, she saw a space of about three inches between the beam and the ceiling.

And she saw something else. A long, cylindrical shape.

"Hand me your flashlight, quick!" she said.

Sensing her excitement, he pulled the torch out of his back pocket, turned it on and handed it over.

She shone the beam into the dark space and saw a metallic flash.

"Gloves!" she said.

He got a pair from his pocket, handed them to her and then steadied her with his hands at her waist while she pulled them on. "Do you see it? Is it a weapon?"

"Sure looks lethal enough to me," she said, trying not to get her hopes too high, but whatever it was that was stuffed in that space was a dull, silver color, about a yard long and a couple of inches thick. And it didn't look like any sort of building pipe or conduit she had ever seen before.

Promising. Very promising.

While Dirk continued to hold her by the waist, she leaned over and reached for it. Carefully, she pulled it out by one end.

Holding it tightly, she jumped down from the shelf and stood there in the middle of the room, staring at her trophy.

"Look at that," she said.

"Yeah, if you hit somebody on the head with the end of that thing"—he pointed to one end of the rod that had a spiked iron ball attached—"you could brain somebody with it. No problem."

But Savannah wasn't looking at the end of the rod with the ball. Or the other end that had a heavy chain hanging from it.

She was looking at a metal rope that was twisted around the rod, diagonally, winding from one end to the other.

"That's the pattern, the candy-stripe pattern that Dr. Liu found on the body," she said. "How much do you want to bet that the bruises on Tess's back correspond directly to this pattern?"

"I wouldn't bet at all," Dirk replied. He pointed to the dark reddish-brown mess smeared near the ball end of the rod. There were even bits of hair and flesh caught in the rope twistings. "Just like I don't need a DNA test to tell me that's our victim's blood, tissue and hair."

Dirk put on a pair of gloves himself, took it from her and looked it over from one end to the other. "Good work, Van," he said. "You found the murder weapon! We've got it!"

"Yes, we've got it." She stared down at the ugly thing, trying to remember where she had seen it before. "But the question is," she said, "what the hell is it?"

"What a beautiful day it is outside!" Tammy said, chattering happily at Savannah's side as they walked down the stairs the next morning, heading for the dining hall and breakfast. "The sun is shining, the birds are singing, and—"

"Do you mind!?" Savannah snapped as they reached the landing. "You know I can't take your 'Zippidee-do-dah' routine first thing in the morning!"

Tammy continued, undaunted. "It's the perfect day for your . . . well . . . I can't say because it's going to be a surprise, and I promised Ryan and John I wouldn't spill the beans."

"I hate surprises. Especially the kind you get around here." Savannah tugged at the lacings on her leather vest. "I thought these new outfits that Mary gave us might be better, but this danged thing is nearly as uncomfortable as the corset."

"Yes, but it looks great on you," Tammy said. "The hose show off your great legs. Those knee-high boots look really hot, and that vest holds 'the sisters,' as you call them, right up there under your chin where they look their best."

She glanced down and saw that Tammy was absolutely right. This outfit would make any female look good, but it made her ample curves look altogether too good for common decency. Granny would undoubtedly have a conniption fit when she saw the show on TV.

Savannah could hear her already: "Savannah, girl, what in tarnation were you thinking, lettin' your bosom hang out there like that in front of God and everybody!? Why, I oughta take a paddle to you, young lady, runnin' around half-necked, lookin' like the Whore o' Babylon! I liked to've died when Elsie at church told me she seen you on the television set with your . . ."

Yes, Savannah would pay big-time when Granny saw *Man of My Dreams.* The most Savannah could hope for was that they would broadcast the show on Sunday or Wednesday night when Gran was at church. And if Savannah bribed and threatened her brothers and sisters enough, maybe she could convince them to "forget" to tape it for Gran. Fortunately, Granny Reid had never figured out how to work her own VCR beyond turning it on and off. Sometimes technical ineptitude in an octogenarian was a blessing.

"Yeah, the boots are pretty cool," she said, looking down at the soft-skin, knee-high boots that hugged and accented her shapely calves. "I feel a bit like Nancy Sinatra."

The blank look that Tammy gave her made her feel old.

"She sang a song about boots that was popular when I was a baby," she said. "I barely remember it."

Tammy shrugged and smiled. "Whatever."

"Yeah, whatever."

At the bottom of the stairs, they turned to head down a corridor leading to the dining hall, and Savannah nearly collided with the suit of armor that stood guard in the foyer.

A strange sense of déjà vu swept over her. "Wow," she said, stopping and shaking her head. "That reminds me of this weird dream I had before you woke me up just now."

"A nice medieval fantasy?" Tammy asked. "With Lance and romance and . . ."

"More like a nightmare. I dreamed this guy dressed in full armor was chasing me down the halls here, and it was like I was stuck in a maze. I couldn't find my way out of this place."

"That's not weird; it's perfectly natural that you would dream something like that. I got lost in here at least five times yesterday."

"But not with a knight chasing you."

"No, nothing that dramatic." Ever the kind heart, Tammy took Savannah's hand and patted it. They continued on down the hallway. "That must have been awful," she said. "Did he have a sword and a shield and everything?"

Savannah looked at her strangely before answering as she recalled the oddities of the dream that had been so vivid. "No. He didn't. In fact, that was what was strange about it. He was running after me, and when I looked over my shoulder to see if he was about to grab me, he raised his arm, like he was going to hit me with something. But there was nothing in his hand."

Tammy looked perplexed. "That *is* weird. But then, it was just a dream."

"*Just* a dream? Don't let Granny Reid hear you say that. She sets great store by dreams. She says, 'Your best common sense speaks to you in dreams and sometimes even the angels themselves, so you'd surefire better listen.' "

"But a knight chasing you through the halls, trying to hit you with . . . a handful of nothing?"

Savannah could almost see the little cartoon lightbulb switch on in her head. "I'll be damned!" she said. "It's that dad-gummed suit of armor."

She whirled around and ran back to the bottom of the stairs where the sentry armor stood, perpetually at attention.

His left arm hung straight down from his side, but his right was bent at the elbow. His right hand, a chain-mail gauntlet was slightly open, as though holding something. A weapon? A weapon that wasn't there?

"Didn't this thing have something in its hand when we first got here?" she asked Tammy. "I could've sworn it did. It wasn't just standing here, empty-handed, looking stupid like this. I'm pretty sure it was holding something."

"Like a sword?" Tammy was interested, but barely.

"No, I think I would have paid closer attention to a sword. It was more like a rod, something say—this long." She held her hands about three feet apart.

Suddenly, Tammy's eyes widened. "A yard long?" She stepped closer and looked at the glove, whose fingers were still curled as though holding an object that would have been a couple of inches across. "You mean, about the size of the murder weapon that you and Dirk found down in the cellar?"

"I'm sure he was holding something like that. And now he's not. We have to find out for sure."

Savannah left the armor and hurried on down the corridor with Tammy right beside her.

"The tape," Savannah said. "We need to get our hands on the tape that the crew shot there in the foyer when we all first arrived. That suit of armor is bound to be on there somewhere. Then we'll know for sure."

A wave of optimism that she hadn't felt in a while washed over her, energizing her body, which had been complaining about its lack of sleep and carbohydrate deprivation. Finally, a break!

"Yes, I'll talk to Leonard the camera guy and get him to show me the tape," she said, practically skipping down the hallway. "This is going to be great! I can't wait to tell Dirk! He's going to be so jealous that I figured it out, and I'll tell Granny about my dream and—"

"There's just one thing," Tammy said, uncharacteristically glum.

Savannah glanced sideways and saw the clouds of doubt gathering on her young friend's usually sunny face. "No," she said. "I'm not going to ask. Don't you dare rain on my parade, young lady. I want to feel this good at least until I get some coffee in me. Assuming those nitwits actually serve some real coffee this morning."

"Okay. I won't."

They walked on in silence, and Savannah's mood deflated moment by moment. They were nearly all the way to the dining hall when she couldn't take it any longer. She stopped in the middle of the hall and turned on Tammy with a vengeance. "All right. Go on. Spit it out. How can this not be good news, finding out where the killer got the murder weapon?"

"Oh, that's good news. It's just not great news."

Savannah propped her hands on her waist. "Well, Miss Prissy Pants, since it's the only news we've got, that makes it pretty darned great in *my* book!"

"Okay . . . but . . ."

"But what?"

"But if the killer was going to choose a weapon . . . well . . . that was pretty smart of them, huh? Picking a murder weapon that absolutely everybody saw and everyone had access to. Good move, don't you think, since even though you figured it out, we can't possibly narrow it down to anybody in particular?"

Savannah stared at her for a long time, a big scowl on her face. Finally, she said, "Thank you. Thank you very much for that bitter spoonful of reality. I think I liked you better when you were Mr. Bluebird on My Shoulder."

Tammy grinned the least sympathetic and remorseful smirk Savannah had ever seen. Then she sashayed on ahead and into the dining hall.

As Savannah watched her assistant's retreating figure, she couldn't help thinking how nice it would be to apply the sole of her left boot to the right buttock of that size-zero fanny. Just one or two swift kicks would suffice to reduce her internal conflicts, calm her jangled nerves, bring peace to her troubled soul.

Ah . . . 'twould be lovely.

"These boots are made for walkin'," she sang under her breath as she followed. "One of these days these boots are gonna. . . ."

Chapter

13

In the dining hall, Savannah and Tammy found Alex standing by the makeshift desk at the end of the room. He was speaking on the phone, and as they approached, Savannah was pretty sure she heard him say, "I can handle this, R.R. My wife just died; can you cut me a little slack here?"

One quick glance at Tammy told her that she had heard it, too. Tammy looked as alert as Granny Reid's bloodhound, Colonel Beauregard, when he got wind of a skunk.

As Alex watched them coming toward him, he quickly ended the conversation and hung up the phone. "Out in the garden," he said brusquely. "We're shooting the breakfast out there this morning. Get going. Everybody's waiting."

"Well, if they're waiting for me, they're probably waiting for you, too," she said a little too sweetly. "Why don't we mosey out there together and everybody can get started?"

He said nothing, but gave her a nasty look that made

her wonder what she might have done to knock his nose out of joint. She didn't have to wonder very long.

"I don't like that detective buddy of yours," he said before they had exited the dining hall. "He's grilled me four times already about Tess's death, and his bedside manner leaves something to be desired. He's all but accused me of killing her myself."

"He's not a doctor," Savannah said gently. "He's a detective who's investigating a murder. And, as unfair as it might seem, the spouse of a victim is always among the top suspects on a detective's list."

"Yeah, well, he's poking his nose into things that are none of his business. Stuff that has nothing to do with Tess being killed. You'd think he'd show a little respect for a grieving family member."

Savannah had to bite her tongue to keep herself from saying more. Dirk had his shortcomings, but she had worked with him for years and knew that he was always as kind and sensitive as possible to the bereaved . . . unless he was pretty darned sure they had something to do with the killing.

Tammy reached over and patted Alex on the shoulder. "You can't take it personally, Mr. Jarvis. Dirk comes across gruff, I know, but underneath all that, he's a sweetheart. He's just doing his job."

Savannah smiled to herself and tucked that little exchange away for safekeeping in her memory banks. It would be useful for blackmailing Tammy in the future. She would rather die than have Dirk know she had said something nice about him. Heaven forbid.

"So, he believes I killed my own wife?" Alex turned on Savannah. "Is that what you're telling me?"

"I don't know what Detective Coulter believes at this point," Savannah replied.

"Then what good are you? What do you think I'm

paying you for? I want you to report back to me exactly what's going on with every step of the police investigation."

Suddenly, he snapped his mouth shut.

Yes, she decided, Alex had said more than he had intended to.

Savannah's eyes narrowed. "I thought you were paying me to conduct *my own* investigation, and that's what I'm doing. Which reminds me: I want to have a look at some of the tape you've shot so far. Specifically anything that was taken in the foyer before we arrived or right afterward."

"I don't let anyone in the cast look at the dailies," he said. "They start complaining about the way they look and want this cut and that cut, or they start griping that I've got more of someone else and not enough of them, and—"

"I'm sure I look just dandy," she told him. "My interest is completely professional. When can I see them?"

"Uh . . . I guess this afternoon, after this morning's contest."

"Is the winner's prize an afternoon with Lance again?" Tammy wanted to know.

"Yeah, a horseback ride out into the hills."

Savannah raised one eyebrow. "And what makes you think I'm not going to be busy this afternoon with Lance? I might win this one."

Alex gave her an unpleasant little chuckle. "Call it a hunch," he said. Then he walked away, heading out the door to the gardens.

"Tell me this contest isn't rigged," Savannah said, watching him go. "I don't stand a chance."

"Aw-w, don't feel bad. You wouldn't want to win anyway," Tammy replied. "Not today's challenge."

"I wouldn't?"

"The prize is getting to ride horseback through the hills with Lance. Horse riding? *Horse?*"

"Oh, yeah. That's true. Even Lance isn't worth me climbing up onto one of those fly-bitten critters again. Especially for a whole afternoon. Forget about it. I'll let somebody else win."

"You'll *let* them?"

"That's right. If anybody other than me wins, it's because I *let* them. That's my story and I'm stickin' with it."

"Sounds good to me."

Ain't nobody *winning time with that guy but me,* Savannah thought when she saw Lance sitting at the breakfast table, a breathtaking smile on his face, the morning sun shining in his hair, muscles rippling against the thin fabric of his musketeer's shirt—not to mention the bulges in his tights that would have gotten even Granny Reid "hot and bothered" on a winter's night.

So what if I have to sit on a nag a mile above the ground, bouncing along until my butt aches and my bouncing boobs knock me unconscious? He's worth it.

She could have sworn that his eyes lit up when he saw her. To her surprise and delight, he stood and moved to another chair at the end of the table and pointed to the empty seat next to his. "Good morning, Savannah," he said, "I was starting to worry about you."

Ignoring the poison looks from the other women around the table, she not only sat next to him, but leaned over and gave him a friendly kiss on the cheek. "Good morning yourself, sugar," she told him. "Now, why would you be worrying about me?"

A look of concern crossed his face. He glanced around quickly, then said, "Well, you know . . . with what's happening around here. First Tess and now

Carisa. You never know who's going to wind up hurt or
. . . or worse."

"Carisa's going to be okay," Brandy said cheerfully.
"I called the hospital this morning, and they said she
turned the corner a couple of hours ago."

"What a relief," Roxy said dryly, adjusting her vest
and patting her hair. "I was awake all night worrying
about that one."

"Yeah," Leila piped up, "Carisa's going to be just
fine. So, we don't have to waste time talking about
her."

Suddenly, the crew appeared: Pete with his microphone boom; Leonard the cameraman; Mary holding
her clipboard, with a pen between her teeth; Kit lugging her make-up case; and Alex Jarvis with his atti-
tude.

"I agree," Alex said. "We've wasted enough time already. Let's get on with this. Maybe we can accomplish
some work today if we can keep the interruptions to a
minimum."

Savannah couldn't stand it. "Yeah, murder and
felony assault," she said, "those pesky interruptions."

"That'll be enough!" Alex shouted, his pasty face
turning a slightly pinker shade of white.

"Enough?" Savannah grumbled under her breath. "I
doubt it."

Under the table, she felt a large, warm hand close
around hers.

"Sh-h-h," Lance whispered, gently squeezing her
fingers. "We don't want you kicked out of here."

A rush of pure glee went through her, stronger than
anything she had felt since—she tried to remember—
ah, yes . . . since she had been fourteen and Tommy
Stafford had kissed her in a moonlit peach orchard.

*I'm going to win this stupid contest today, no matter
what it is,* she told herself.

The camera started rolling, and Mary stepped forward to tell them about their day. "Miladies, as you may have surmised from your costumes, today's activities are less genteel than our falconry competition of yore."

Savannah wondered if she could eat one of the apples on the table and actually swallow a bite without gagging. She decided to wait until Mary's monologue was finished.

"Today," Mary continued, "Cupid's arrows will fly. And the lady whose arrows most accurately pierce the target will be rewarded by spending the afternoon with the 'Man of Her Dreams.' She will ride with Lance into yonder hills, where the springtime daisies bloom, the perfume of wild lavender scents the air and . . ."

Archery? Oh, Lord, Savannah prayed, *just kill me now.*

"That was really nice of you," Tammy told Savannah, "to let Brandy win the archery contest like that."

"Oh, shut up. Don't you have some sleuthing or something to do?" Savannah lay on her back, sprawled across the floor of Ryan and John's quarters. Ryan had tucked one of the cheap pillows under her head and another under her knees. She could hear John in the kitchen and the sound of ice cubes rattling. He was preparing a cold compress for the inside of her left forearm.

Dirk and Tammy, on the other hand, were being less solicitous. Tammy was typing away on her laptop computer while Dirk stuffed his face with cookies and swigged a Coke.

"You just let the redheaded bimbo win?" he asked. "Why would you do that? I thought you wanted to win this contest and that dumb crown prize. I thought you liked this guy."

"She does," Tammy offered, "but she hates riding horses."

"The horse had nothing to do with it, and I didn't let her win." Savannah groaned as John gently laid a plastic bag full of ice on her bruised, swollen arm. "That Brandy chick is some sort of expert with a bow and arrow. Did you see her hit the middle of that big stupid red heart? Dead center every time! I wish I'd had my Beretta with me. I'd have shown her some target shooting."

Ryan unlaced Savannah's boots and slipped them off her feet. "Well," he said, "you should have suspected something. Your first clue was when she showed up with her own arm guard and quiver."

"Yeah." Savannah lifted the ice bag for a moment and looked at the dark purple swelling beneath it. "I wish I'd had one of those contraptions for my arm. Boy, howdy! When that string zings along your bare flesh, it about takes your hide off."

"I tried to get them to supply arm guards for all of you," Ryan said. "Anyone who knows anything about archery knows how important it is to protect your arm."

"Apparently, Miss Brandy Thomas knew a little about archery," Tammy said.

"Well, duh." Savannah replaced the ice and closed her eyes. "Like we just said, she—"

"She's the archery champion of Southwest Texas."

"What?" Savannah's eyes flew open. "What did you say?"

Tammy looked up from her computer. "I found a national archery championship here on the Internet. She's been number one the past three years in a row."

"Oh, man! Talk about a stacked deck." Savannah sat up and groaned as her shoulders complained about the unfamiliar exercise. "Who would have thought it would be so hard to pull one of those bows? Robin Hood and Little John made it look so easy in the movies."

"The bows you ladies were using had a draw weight of 36 pounds. They shouldn't have been more than 15 or 20 at most," Ryan said. "Again, I told them to chose their equipment a little more carefully, taking into account that you were novices. Well, except for Brandy, of course."

"Yes, except for Brandy." Savannah recalled how she and the other girls had fumbled with the bow and then mostly missed the target entirely, while the redhead had not even bothered to disguise her expert stance and smooth execution. "If Alex is tight with the owner of this place, this R.R. dude, and Brandy's his girlfriend, then setting up this archery competition had to be deliberate. They wanted Brandy to win, plain and simple."

"They probably just wanted to keep her happy," Tammy said.

"Or quiet." Savannah recalled Brandy's phone conversation with the castle's eccentric builder and Alex's call earlier that morning to the same guy. "Maybe this R.R. and Brandy know what Alex has been up to."

"And what's that?" Dirk wanted to know.

"Killing Tess, of course. You do still think he did it, right? He complained to me today that you keep grilling him."

"Grilling him?" Dirk gave a snort. "I haven't even come close to grilling that boy. I've been easy on him. Real easy. When I finally decide to light some charcoals under him, *then* he'll know he's been grilled."

"What makes you so sure it was Alex?" John asked as he settled down beside Savannah.

"We don't have that much," she told him, "other than the fact that he's been fooling around with that

Roxy hussy. And the stuff I overheard them say to each other there behind the falcon house could have been incriminating, though not conclusively."

"But," Dirk interjected, "it had to be somebody who knew Tess's ice cream routine. And that would have to be the husband."

"Or Mary, her personal assistant," John said. "She would be well aware of her mistress's habits."

"Or Lance," Tammy suggested. "He told Savannah he's known her for years."

"Or any of the crew members, who have all worked for her before," Savannah admitted with a sigh.

"The only people we can rule out are the contestants," Tammy said. "Because they had just met Tess here the first day of the shoot. Except for Roxy, who must have known all about her, since she knows so much about her husband."

"Actually," John said, toying with the end of his mustache. "You can't rule out the other ladies either. I distinctly recall hearing Mrs. Jarvis prompting her assistant, Mary, about the ice cream, reminding her to be certain it was available for her midnight indulgence."

"So?" Dirk said.

"She said it in front of the other ladies," John added. "The contestants were all standing there, except for you, Savan-nah."

Savannah's spirits sank a little lower. Brandy was out there somewhere, riding through the wild lavender-scented hills with the man of her dreams, while she lay there on some cheap pillows with ice on her wounded arm and a quiver full of suspects, not even one of which she could eliminate.

"This stinks," she said. "My arm hurts, and we've got nothing."

"Could be worse," Tammy chirped. "Your arm is

only bruised. I hear they had to put four steel pins in Carisa's leg and arm."

Savannah flopped back on the pillows and threw her good arm over her eyes. "I'm tired," she said. "If somebody would please smack Pollyanna over there with her own computer, I'd sure appreciate it."

"I don't know who's going to be voted out tonight," Brandy whispered to Savannah, "but I don't think it's going to be me."

Savannah glanced around at the other women who, like her, had been told to exchange their musketeer vests and boots for full-length, velvet gowns . . . again with laced bodices. They looked uncomfortable, nervous, and basically out of sorts as they waited for the inevitable thinning of their ranks.

Standing in the courtyard in front of the keep, waiting for Lance to place one of them in the waiting carriage and "banish" her from the "kingdom," Savannah was amazed how a dress that had practically no front to speak of could be so blasted hot.

She was pretty darned sure that the merry maids of old England hadn't sweated this profusely in their finery. If they had, they would have outlawed velvet gowns and taken up wearing more sensible garments. Like gauze loincloths. But then, they hadn't been living in Southern California in August either.

Next to the carriage stood Ryan and John, looking as uncomfortable in their livery as the ladies were in their gowns. And beside the carriages sat the trunks. As before, one of the girls would have her "belongings" loaded into the carriage along with her and her shredded dignity and driven away.

Under the circumstances, Savannah didn't really

G.A. McKevett

want to hear Brandy chattering away about how she was sure that she wasn't the one who would get the boot.

But her curiosity got the best of her.

It always did.

"Oh?" she said with as much kindly interest as she could feign. "Then your afternoon riding went well?"

Brandy rolled her big eyes. "I should say so. I'm a bit of a cowgirl myself, you know. I was raised on a Texas ranch, so I was right at home on the horse. Lance complimented me several times on my riding, in fact."

Savannah's nostrils flared ever so slightly, but she smiled. A little. "Well, isn't that just so nice of him."

"We decided we have a lot in common, Lance and I. Besides just riding horses, that is."

"Hm-m . . . do tell." She gave her a sideways look and added, "Is Lance an archery champion, too?"

Brandy looked down and decided it was time to pick some lint off her skirt. "Uh, no. He's not, I mean, *I* was a long time ago, but he . . . no."

"Lucky break for you, having the competition be archery. Coincidental, I'm sure."

"Oh, of course. No one would, you know, have arranged something like that if they'd realized one of us was sort of good at it."

"Good? Oh, sugar, don't be modest. You were magnificent! You looked like the goddess Diana herself, standing there with that bow."

Brandy's cheeks turned nearly as red as her hair, but she didn't reply.

"And when you brought out your own arm guard, I knew the rest of us were dead in the water. That's like when a guy in a pool hall cracks out his own cue. You know you're about to get hustl—I mean, beaten."

"Where is the crew?" Roxy interjected, shifting

from one foot to the other. "I'm tired and I just want to get this over with so that I can go back to my room and relax. If they make such a big deal about us being here on time, they should be, too."

"Yeah, I'm a little tired of the disrespect I'm getting around here," Leila added. "It's enough that you have to worry about getting attacked or even murdered, but to keep us waiting out here in the sun in these heavy, hot dresses . . ."

Her voice trailed away as the maligned crew appeared en masse. They all looked tired and as eager to be finished with the day as the rest.

Alex glanced around then scowled. "Where's Lance?" he snapped at Mary.

"I don't know," she said. "He was in his room half an hour ago with Kit. She was having to adjust his costume; it didn't quite fit. I'm sure he'll be along any— oh, here he is now!"

She looked enormously relieved as Lance hurried out of the keep, looking stunning in a dark hunter-green ensemble. Again, he was wearing the customary musketeer's shirt with a deep vee neck and billowing sleeves along with a tunic, leggings, and knee-high boots. But this time the outfit included a full cape of the same color that swept the ground behind him when he walked.

He, too, looked tired, and Savannah noticed that Kit had made him up more heavily than usual, perhaps to counteract the signs of fatigue.

"Good evening, ladies," he said as the camera rolled. He walked from Roxy to Leila, to Brandy, and then to Savannah, bowing and kissing each woman's hand in turn.

Once he had greeted them all, he took his place beside the carriage and Alex bellowed the traditional,

"Cut!" Then he turned on Lance. "You were late again! And I told you I wanted you to wear the blue outfit tonight!"

"I'm not late *again,*" Lance said calmly, but there was a fire in his eyes as he returned Alex's glare that suggested he might be a bit fed up with Alex's barking. "Because this is the first time I've been late. And it was unavoidable. A problem with the costume. The blue one didn't fit, and Kit and I couldn't make it fit. So, it's this one or my jeans and UCLA sweatshirt. You pick."

"I guess it'll have to do," Alex said. "Mary, do your spiel."

Mary laid her ubiquitous notebook on the ground and stepped into camera range. "Ladies, we have drawn near, once again, to say 'Fare thee well' to a sister who has grown so dear to our hearts. And as wrenching as this will be, it is a necessary evil because . . ."

Wrenching? Savannah thought. *Scraping the hide off your arm with a bowstring, that's a wrenching evil. Getting rid of one of these bimbos. That I can handle.*

Of course, there was the possibility she would be the one leaving, but she didn't even want to think about that.

She glanced around at the other women. None of them looked the least bit worried. They practically reeked of self-confidence.

As Lance handed each of them a trunk key, she tried to read his face. But all she could see in his eyes was a deep unhappiness that made her want to take his hand, lead him off to a private place and ask him what was going on.

But with the possibility that she might be the next to leave dangling over her, it wasn't exactly the time to pull his head onto her bosom and encourage him to "Tell Momma all about it."

As attractive as that prospect might be.

One by one, they were instructed, as the night before, to open their trunks and see if they had received a gift, or if their belongings had been packed for their departure.

This time their presents were less original—scented soaps—and Savannah had the distinct impression that Lance hadn't chosen them personally. Mary seemed far more interested in whether or not she liked her lavender, Roxy her gardenia, and Brandy her carnation.

And, once again, it was Leila who found her trunk filled with costumes and junk jewelry.

Leila was even less gracious than before, as Ryan and John performed their unhappy tasks of lifting her trunk onto the back of the carriage and ushering her inside.

"Okay, okay," she shouted out the window. "I can take a hint. You don't have to tell me three times. This is it. I wouldn't come back again if you begged me to."

As Ryan drove away in the carriage with Leila inside, Savannah looked around and didn't see anyone who looked as though they were "wrenched" to see this sister go.

Lance, who had supposedly elected to have her leave, was the only one who appeared the least bit disturbed by the curses that floated back to them from the departing carriage—suggestions about where they should spend eternity and what they might do for entertainment while there, preferably with their next of kin. He seemed downright embarrassed.

Savannah couldn't really blame him. This wasn't exactly an Emmy-winning documentary on the human condition that they were filming here. And at this point she was fairly certain she didn't want Granny's hound dog to see it on TV, let alone the rest of the nation.

"Well, that's that," Alex told them. "You're on your own for the rest of the evening, but I suggest you hit the hay early. I want you at breakfast at seven sharp. We've got a big day tomorrow."

A couple of the ladies groaned, Savannah included.

"Hey, Savannah," Alex said, as she and the others turned to walk away.

She stopped. "Yes?"

"If you just have to see the dailies, now's the time. Leonard can show you the ones of the foyer there, like you wanted."

"I want to see the tapes, too!" Roxy wailed.

"Yes, if Savannah gets to see them, we should all get to see them," Brandy said. "It's only fair, and I know you want to be fair, Mr. Jarvis."

Alex wasn't buying it. "He's not showing them to her so that she can see how she looks. It's part of her investigation into Tess's murder. She's checking out something having to do with the foyer when we all first got here."

"Really? What is it? What are you checking for? Who do you think did it? Why do you want to see the pictures of the foyer?"

Instantly, everyone was crowding around her, asking questions all at once. She felt a bit like a goldfish that had been dropped into a tank full of piranhas.

She didn't answer any of them. Instead, she walked over to Alex, took his arm, dug her fingertips into his flesh and said under her breath, "Thanks a lot, Al. And while you're spilling beans, why don't you just go ahead and tell them who really shot President Kennedy."

Chapter

14

"Why are you so interested in shots of the foyer?" Leonard asked as Savannah and Dirk leaned forward in their chairs and stared at the images on the tiny screen before them.

While Savannah hadn't expected to watch the dailies on a full movie screen with a bucket of popcorn on her lap, she had hoped for something better than this small, fuzzy, flickering screen that had given her a headache after the first three minutes of peering at it.

Leonard and Pete's apartment and makeshift "studio" was in a cottage that was little more than a shed at the far end of the garden. Its accommodations, or lack thereof, made Ryan and John's place look palatial. Small, dark, sparsely furnished, and reeking of something that smelled like gym socks and stale pot smoke, the room wasn't Savannah's idea of a fun place to spend the afternoon.

The sooner she got out of here, into the fresh air and away from Leonard's questions, the better. One glance at Dirk told her that he was thinking the same thing.

"Don't worry about it," Dirk said. "Are these all

you've got? Nothing taken in the entrance there, by the foot of the stairs?"

Dirk had been getting grumpier by the moment as the grainy images danced on the screen, showing them everything except the suit of armor in question.

"That's about it," Leonard said, "unless you want to see some of the stuff I shot when we were first scouting out the location."

"Does any of that include the foyer?" Savannah asked him.

"Probably. Hang on."

For several tiresome minutes they watched Leonard search his footage, until he finally found what they had been hoping for all along. A brief but clear shot of the entrance and Sir Knight of the Empty Hand.

Only his hand wasn't empty. He was holding something long with a spiked ball on one end and what might have been a chain hanging from the other.

"Wait! Right there!" Dirk said, leaning closer to the screen until his nose was practically touching it. "Can you make this picture any bigger? Zoom in or something?"

Leonard looked alert and interested for the first time since they had begun. "What part? What are you looking at in particular?"

Savannah cringed. If there was anything Dirk couldn't stand—well, actually, there were a whole lot of things that Dirk couldn't stand—it was someone questioning him about his own investigation. Especially when he had nothing solid yet.

"Just zoom in, wouldja?" Dirk snapped. "Don't worry what I'm looking at."

Leonard bristled. "Hey, I'm doing you a favor here. I'm spending time I don't have to—"

"Yeah, yeah," Dirk replied, "and I'm doing you a

solid favor by not searching this room for the dope that I could smell the minute I walked through the door, so let's get zoomin', huh?"

With only minor grumblings, Leonard adjusted the view on the screen, and Savannah and Dirk saw all they needed to see: the medieval weapon from the cellar in all of its nasty glory, down to the distinctive diagonal wrappings.

Dirk turned to Savannah and grinned. Then he scowled at Leonard. "I need a copy of that," he said.

"Well, I don't know if I can . . ."

"Or you can just give me the original tape right now."

Leonard peered at Dirk through the scraggly strands of hair hanging over his eyes. "Don't you need a court order or something legal to take stuff like that?"

"I can get one in an hour, if I need to," Dirk replied. "But if I have to go to all that trouble, I'm going to make it worth my while. Hell, I might even have to take every bit of tape you've got on this whole stinkin' show, and how's old Alex gonna like that? Especially when I tell him that all you would have had to do is make me one measly copy of one little section of—"

"Okay, okay. I'll do it this afternoon."

Dirk gave him a half-smile. "I'm so glad. You're a fine, upstanding citizen, helping law enforcement this way." He headed for the door and motioned for Savannah to come with him. But he paused with his hand on the knob and turned back to the less-than-thrilled cameraman. "By the way," he added, "you don't touch a joint, pipe, or bong until you've got that copy made for me, you hear?"

Leonard cast one quick, furtive glance at a backpack that was lying on the cot in the corner. "Yeah, sure, man. That's cool."

"And one more thing," Savannah said. "We'd appreciate it if you could just keep this whole business between the three of us. Okay?"

Leonard looked relieved to change the subject. He actually gave her a big, goofy grin. "Yeah, sure. No problem."

Once outside with the door closed, Savannah turned to Dirk. "How long do you think it'll be before he tells his tokin' buddy all about it?"

"At least until he sees him again. You know what they say about three people being able to keep a secret."

"Yes," she replied. "They can do it if two of them are dead."

As Savannah was walking through the front door of the keep on her way inside to find Tammy, she ran nearly headlong into Roxy.

The blonde had changed out of her velvet gown and, like Savannah, was wearing her comfortable clothes. But unlike Savannah's simple shirt and linen slacks, Roxy's shorts and halter top were skintight and didn't have an inch of fabric to spare. Savannah had seen more modest attire on some of the MTV entertainers.

She wondered for a moment if maybe she was missing something by not dressing in similar fashion. After all, it was eye-catching, and they all wanted to catch Lance's eye.

But then, her Granny's advice came to mind: "Don't show it all, Savannah girl. Let 'em wonder. 'Cause men are gonna wonder; it's their nature. Wonderin' is their favorite pastime. They'd rather speckle-ate on it than actually see it." When the young Savannah had asked her grandmother, "Why?" her granny had smiled a wicked little grin and said, "Because they know full well that their speckle-ation is bound to be rosier than the reality o' the sit-chi-ation."

That explanation hadn't made a lot of sense to Savannah at the time, but over the years she had grown to appreciate the truth and wisdom behind her grandmother's words.

So, she didn't spend long wondering if she should head upstairs and put on a tube top and short-shorts like Roxy's. There were all sorts of ways to compete.

"You're just the person I wanted to talk to," Savannah said, deciding to jump into the deep end and see what she could find underwater. Maybe a she-shark?

"Me?" Roxy didn't look thrilled. "I'm busy."

"Me, too. But there's always time for a little girl talk. A bit of old-fashioned chinwagging."

The blonde's eyes lit up ever so slightly at the mention of gossip. "Oh? Is it good?"

Savannah's eyes narrowed. "The juiciest. Girl, you're just not going to *believe* who's sleeping with Alex!"

Roxy's mouth dropped open wide enough for Ryan to drive the Blackmoor carriage through. When she didn't answer, Savannah replied for her, "Surprise! It's *you!*"

"That isn't funny," Roxy snapped, when she had pulled Savannah into the cubicle under the stairwell and checked to see that no one was within earshot.

"I don't think so either," Savannah replied coolly. "I mean, he's a married man. And even if screwing another woman's husband doesn't bother you, it just ain't smart."

Roxy propped her hands on her hips and tossed her head. "Oh, yeah? Well, a lot you know about it. It just so happens that Alex is going to marry me one of these days soon! So there!"

"Hmmm, and if that's true, and he actually marries you, what a prize you've got there! A man who fools around on his wife. Now, ain't you just the lucky one."

"You don't know what's between Alex and me. We love each other, and we're going to be very happy together now that—"

Her jaw snapped shut like a box turtle's.

"Now that Tess is dead?" Savannah said, finishing her sentence for her. When Roxy didn't reply, Savannah stepped closer to her, forcing her further into the tight little cubicle. "Did you kill Tess, Roxy?" she whispered. "Did you? Or did you help Alex do it? Did you guys bash that poor woman on the head and smash her skull in? Did you?"

Roxy's eyes were huge, her lower lip trembling when she shook her head and said, "No! No, of course not! I might have an affair with a man I love, even if he's married, but I'm not a killer. I'd never do something like that."

"Did Alex do it by himself?"

"No! Never!"

"Did he do it for you, Roxy? So that you two could be together?"

"We could have been together anyway. He was going to ask her for a divorce. He told me so."

"But if he had really been intending to leave her, he would have had to split everything he has with her. It would have been so much nicer for both of you to have it all to yourselves. Is that why he killed her, Roxy?"

"He didn't kill her!"

Savannah shoved her face so close to the other woman's that they could feel and smell each other's breath. "You can tell me, Roxy. Really, you can. I'm good friends with Detective Coulter. And if you tell him everything you know, he'll make sure that you don't get into any sort of trouble yourself. I promise. And you'll feel so much better."

"No! No! No!"

Roxy reached out with both hands and pushed Savannah as hard as she could. But Savannah had braced herself, and she didn't budge.

She was surprised when Roxy actually started to cry. "I don't know anything about anything," she blubbered, "And Alex didn't kill Tess. He wouldn't do something like that, no matter how mad he was at her. Do you think I'd be in love with the kind of man who could kill his own wife?"

"He was mad at her?"

"He was always mad at her. She was a real bitch, and nobody liked her. And he's not a bad guy for falling in love with another woman. He was lonely and hurt, and he needed someone, too. Alex wasn't the first to break their marriage vows. She was! He had it coming to him."

"She did? When? With whom?"

"Lance!"

Savannah hadn't braced herself for that one. She moved backward a step, feeling as though someone had just landed a roundhouse kick to her solar plexus.

"With Lance? Tess and Lance?"

She tried to picture it, Mrs. Orange Juice Commercial doing the nasty with Mr. Coverboy Hunk.

But she didn't try very hard.

Her mind flatly refused to go there.

"How long ago?" she asked. *Keep to the facts, Savannah,* she told herself. *Just the facts, ma'am.*

"For years."

"For years?" Her mind whirled like a carnival ride. One that made you throw up your cotton candy.

No. It just couldn't be.

"Off and on for years, ever since they got to know each other. So Alex had every right to take a lover. We weren't doing anything wrong, and we didn't kill her. So, you and that detective friend of yours can just go bother somebody else for a change. Maybe you'll even figure out who really killed her, and who hurt Carisa, too."

With that, Roxy, her tube top, and her short-shorts stomped off down the hall.

Savannah had seen a self-righteous huff. Having been raised in a family with seven girls, she certainly knew one when she saw it.

And Roxy's little hissy fit was as self-righteous as they came.

She hadn't killed Tess, she hadn't helped Alex do it, and if he had done it on his own, she didn't know anything about it.

Savannah only wished that *she* was as uninformed as Roxy. She would have paid a pretty penny not to know what she knew.

Way too much information.

Lance and Tess together. Yuck!

She had the terrible feeling that she might never look at one of his romance covers the same way again. The thought of Tess bent backward in his arms, her eyes locked with his in a lusty gaze, her bodice ripped, her orange hair aglow in the light of the setting sun.

Yes, Savannah decided, *I'm definitely going to have to bleach my brain to get rid of that mental picture.*

When you least expect it, things can take a turn for the worst.

Life is cruel.

Chapter

15

"All right," Alex shouted to the ragtag assemblage in the courtyard the next morning, "we've got to make up some lost time, so let's get this show on the road."

Savannah had wondered what form today's competition would take. They had been told to wear the same outfits that they had worn for the archery contest.

And now she knew.

"Swords?" Brandy looked like she was about to cry as Mary handed out the weapons of the day. "I don't like swords. I don't even like knives, and these are like really big, ugly knives! It's a phobia that I have."

"Get a load of Maid Marian there," Roxy said, as Mary presented the open case to her. "She's hot stuff with a bow and arrow, but the sight of a blade makes her sick. Go figure." Roxy chose her weapon, lifted it from the case and swung it through the air. She looked like a kid playing pirate.

Savannah also noted with delight that she looked like a rank amateur who had never picked up a bladed weapon before. *Okay,* she thought. *Brandy's afraid to touch a sword, and Roxy obviously has no idea how to handle one. Things are looking up for the gal from Georgia.*

Savannah had never fenced or wielded a sword herself either, but years ago in her karate dojo, she had fought many times with a wooden rod called a "jo." And even though a jo had no blade, it was amazing how much pain it could cause when your opponent landed it across your shins, your ribs, or even your arm.

Yes, this could be fun, she thought. *And more important than fun . . . profitable.*

"I don't want to do this," Brandy whined. "Really. These things look dangerous."

"Cut!" Alex threw up his hands. "Do you suppose we could get at least two full minutes done without one of you saying something stupid? Brandy, they have blunted blades. You couldn't cut hot butter with them."

He walked over to her and said, "Here, give me that!"

He snatched the sword out of her hand and struck his bare leg below his shorts with the edge. Then he held his hairy, unharmed calf up for her inspection. "See. Nothing. Okay, Brandy?"

She shrugged and looked partially placated. "Yeah, okay. I guess."

"Then with your permission, we'll continue." He marched back to his place behind Leonard. "Mary, go."

Mary walked over to Savannah and held the case in front of her. Looking inside, Savannah saw that one sword remained, nestled against dark green velvet.

It wasn't a particularly impressive bit of weaponry. This sword would never play the role of Excalibur in a movie, but she had to admit that when she took it by the handle and lifted it out of the box, she liked the feel of it. And while she wasn't ready to give up her Beretta and start packing a sword, she was surprised that she felt right at home with the thing in her hand.

A few swipes through the air and she was ready to go.

"Here are the rules of our warfare today," Mary told them. "And like the knights and noblewomen of yesteryear, we must abide by the code of honor."

Yeah, right, Savannah thought. *Honor, my foot. I'll knock Roxy's block off. Lemme at her.*

"You must make all good effort," Mary said, "to avoid striking your opponent in the head area. The only points awarded will be for body strikes. You will receive one point for every time your sword comes in contact with their torso area. The first person to gain three points wins the match. However, if your sword should fall from your hand for any reason, the match is over, and your opponent will win."

Savannah couldn't help grinning. This was going to be a piece of cake. A big, juicy piece of pecan-and-coconut-frosting German chocolate cake. *Off with her head,* she thought, looking at Roxy, who was twirling her sword like a baton. *Forget the knightly code of honor. That baby's gonna roll like a bowling ball.*

Mary continued, "The first contestant to win three matches will be our winner and will receive the most coveted prize thus far."

This time no one expected a luxury car or a fur coat. They knew, as usual, it was going to be time spent with Lance. Obviously, that wouldn't cost old Tight Wallet Alex any dough.

When no one inquired about the prize, Mary told them, "You will be given the opportunity to spend the entire night with Lance Roman, his guest in the Royal Chamber, a sumptuous suite in yon round tower." She pointed to a cylindrical structure that was part of the outer wall in one of the far corners of the compound. It didn't look especially sumptuous, but the idea of spending a night with Lance set her heart pounding.

It would have set her heart aflutter even more if she hadn't heard that nasty bit of gossip about him and Tess from Roxy earlier.

Yes, Roxy owed her. And Savannah figured that one clean, simple beheading would even the score just fine.

The other two women seemed impressed with the possibility of spending a night with Lord Gorgeous. Finally, something worth winning, even if you couldn't drive or wear it. Even reluctant Brandy seemed to warm to the prospect.

Mary closed the sword case and set it aside. "The first match will be between Lady Brandy and Lady Savannah. Noblewomen, stand here in front of me, facing each other, five paces apart."

Savannah and Brandy took their places. Savannah would have been happy to bloody her sword—figuratively speaking—on Roxy first, but Brandy would be good practice.

"Raise your swords," Mary shouted, "and begin!"

Savannah almost felt sorry for Brandy as she stood there, wide-eyed and scared to death, looking like a Georgia 'possum in the headlights.

But when she remembered how expertly Brandy had handled that archery bow, and how she, herself, had struggled with the blasted thing, Savannah decided there was such a thing as justice after all.

"Sorry, Brandy," she said as she advanced on her, sword held at ready, "but this one's mine. I won't hurt you."

And she didn't.

With one blow, she sent Brandy's sword flying out of her hand. It fell to the cobblestones, and the clatter echoed across the courtyard.

"Well done," Savannah heard a voice say from behind her. A beloved voice with a strong British accent.

She turned and saw John and Ryan, who were watching from behind the camera. They both applauded, as did Mary and Alex.

Brandy looked shaken as she walked over and picked up her sword from the stone pavement. As soon as she returned with it, Mary stepped before the camera and made another proclamation. "Our first match was won by Lady Savannah. Congratulations, milady." She curtseyed to Savannah, who supposed that the proper thing to do would be curtsey back, but with a sword in her hand, and her musketeer outfit on, she was feeling a little too macho for that curtsey crap right now. She was ready for her next opponent/victim.

"Our next match," Mary said, "will be between—"

Savannah and Roxy, Savannah thought, willing her to say it. *Lop, lop, roll, roll.*

"Lady Roxy and Lady Brandy. Noblewomen, take your places. And begin!"

This time Brandy seemed to come alive. Perhaps the competitive spirit that had won the archery trophies came to fore. Maybe she had realized that if she wanted to win, she couldn't just stand there like a scared Brandy Bunny. Either way, she charged at Roxy, sword high. And when she got within reach of her, she gave a mighty swipe with the blade.

Unfortunately, it missed Roxy and her sword, and Brandy lost her balance, almost falling on her face.

"That's it, Brandy!" Savannah shouted. "Go get her!"

Roxy looked as shocked as anyone at Brandy's sudden ferocity. Apparently the demure maiden from the Lone Star State had a streak of mean in her, too.

Roxy lifted her sword to defend herself from

Brandy's next attack, but received a sound thwack on the ribs from the side of her opponent's blade.

"Point one for Lady Brandy," Mary shouted.

"Ow! That hurt!" Roxy cried. "Alex! She's not supposed to just go at me like that, is she? If she doesn't watch it, she could—ow!"

"And point two for Lady Brandy," Mary announced.

When no one came to her rescue, Roxy flared. "Okay then!" she yelled. "You want to play rough?"

Undaunted, and invigorated by her mini-victories, Brandy charged her again, shrieking a war cry as she ran that would have done a ravaging, pillaging Viking proud.

At the last second, a rattled Roxy held her sword straight out in front of her and closed her eyes. Brandy ran straight into the point, which drove deeply into her left shoulder.

"Oh, my God!" Savannah said as Brandy staggered backward, then toward her, blood pouring from the wound. Savannah caught her in her arms, just as she started to fall.

A deep, terrible gash at least five inches long had been cut into the woman's flesh. Savannah could see bone and tendons exposed just before a gush of blood covered everything.

In a second, John and Ryan were on either side of her, and both of them helped Savannah lower Brandy to the cobblestones.

Roxy came running up, leaned over and looked down on her fallen opponent. When she saw the horrible cut she began screaming hysterically.

"What is it? What's wrong?" Savannah could hear Mary asking, as though from far away.

But she was concentrating on Brandy, who was staring up at her with eyes full of pain and confusion.

"What . . . what happened?" the wounded woman managed to whisper.

"You got cut, Brandy," Savannah told her as Ryan ripped off his shirt, wadded it into a compress and held it tightly against the wound.

In only seconds, the white fabric became dark red.

"What?" Brandy murmured.

"The sword was sharper than we thought," Savannah said, glancing up long enough to give Alex a withering look. "Your shoulder's been cut, but we're going to take care of you. Don't you worry, hon. Everything's going to be just fine."

Savannah's eyes met Ryan's for a moment, and the concern she saw there only confirmed her own fears. This was a very bad injury.

"Mary," she said, as calmly as she could manage. "You go fetch us some clean towels and a blanket or two. And Alex, call 9-1-1 and get an ambulance out here"—she shook her head as she watched them run away toward the keep—"again."

By the time Dirk arrived at Blackmoor Castle, the ambulance had already come and taken Brandy away. And he was in an especially foul mood.

"What the hell is going on around here!" he bellowed at the crowd still standing in the middle of the courtyard. "I leave for a few hours, and you've got another one down!"

Savannah resisted the urge to step out of the group and try to calm him. Dirk in a rage often produced results. And at the moment, she didn't really care if he shot the whole bunch of them on the spot.

That way they would be sure to get the guilty one.

"This was an accident," Alex told him. "A simple

accident, that's all. The girls were sword-fighting and—"

"You put swords in these people's hands knowing that they've been trying to kill each other? What's the matter with you, man? I oughta lock you up as an accessory."

"The blades were blunted," Alex protested. "My props supplier said they were perfectly safe, and . . ."

Savannah left Dirk to argue with Alex and walked away from the group, over to where the Brandy versus Roxy fight had been waged. There on the pavement both swords lay, exactly where the women had dropped them.

Roxy's sword wasn't difficult to differentiate. It was the one with Brandy's blood all over the blade.

Savannah still had one of the towels they had been using to staunch the blood flow in her hand. With the end that was still clean, she lifted the sword and looked at it more closely.

Yes, it was just as she had feared.

She walked back to where Dirk and Alex were still yelling at one another in front of their rapt audience.

Showing the weapon to Dirk, she said. "This sword is sharp, not blunted. Razor sharp. I've shaved my legs with duller blades than this. It's a wonder Brandy wasn't killed."

John stepped forward. "As it is, the young woman will undoubtedly lose the use of her arm," he said sadly. "She'll never draw a bow again."

"How could something like this have happened, Alex?" Ryan asked. "I checked those swords myself last night, and there were three blunted weapons in that chest. This sword wasn't one of them."

"How the hell do I know?" Alex shouted. "You're acting like this is my fault." He turned on Mary. "How about you? Why didn't you check those things before you handed them out?"

Mary's cheeks flushed, and behind her thick lenses, tears began to well. "They looked okay to me," she said. "I don't know the difference. You guys said they were exactly what we needed yesterday. How would I know to check them again?"

Dirk softened at the sight of her tears. It was one of his best personality traits, as far as Savannah was concerned, the ability to melt when a female started to cry.

"Okay, okay," he said gruffly. "We don't need to know who was in charge of what. Obviously, the exchange was made on the sly, sometime between last night when you checked them, Ryan, and today when Mary handed them to the women. Where were they stored overnight?"

Alex and Mary looked at each other. "They were in a case," Mary said, "and the case was left on a table in the dining hall last night."

"Was it locked?" Dirk asked.

"No. It just had a plain little latch on it," she replied.

"So, what you're telling me is that anybody could have gone in there at any time during the night and switched one of those weapons, and nobody would have been the wiser?"

Alex and Mary nodded in unison.

"And," Savannah added, "this place has swords of every kind hanging wall to wall. It's not as though a replacement would be hard to find."

"Great," Dirk said. "That narrows things down."

"But who would want to hurt Brandy?" John asked.

They looked over at Roxy, who was sitting on the front step of the keep, her hands over her face, wailing, as she had been since the moment she had inflicted the wound.

"I don't think she meant to do it," Savannah said quietly to Dirk, leading him aside, out of earshot of the crowd. "She's a basket case, and she looked as surprised and upset as any of us when it happened."

"But this was the little redhead who got hurt, right?" Dirk said.

Savannah nodded.

"She seemed like the nicest one of the batch. Who would want to hurt her?"

Savannah had been mulling that one over herself for the past hour. "Who says they wanted to hurt Brandy in particular?" she said. "Any one of us could have drawn that sharp sword. And any one of the three of us could have been killed with it."

"Comforting thought."

"Ain't it, though?"

Chapter

16

Savannah had never seen a vampire cowboy before. And after laying eyes on R.R. Breakstone, she decided it would be just fine with her if she never did again.

She and Dirk were walking from the gatehouse around sundown, having just conferred with Ryan, John, and Tammy, when they saw the hearse-style limousine pull up in front of the keep. A tall, gaunt man got out, looked around as though drinking in the scene, then headed for the front door.

IIis jet-black hair was straight and blunt cut just below his shoulders. He wore a black turtleneck, black trousers, black cowboy boots, a black Stetson, and an enormous silver inverted pentacle hanging from a thick chain around his neck.

He quickly disappeared into the keep, and his chauffeur drove the limo over to the stable.

"What the hell was that?" Dirk asked her.

"I suspect that was the owner of Blackmoor Castle," she replied. "How much you wanna bet his favorite color is black?"

"What do you suppose he's doing here?"

"I don't know. Let's go find out."

They hurried across the courtyard and into the keep.

The moment they opened the door they could hear a heated argument echoing down the halls.

". . . in the hospital and I want to know why! What's been going on around here, anyway?!"

"It was an accident, R.R. An accident. It wasn't my fault!"

Savannah recognized the nasal twang of the second voice as Alex's, and she surmised the first one with the slight Texas drawl must be R.R. Breakstone.

She and Dirk strolled down the corridor that led to the dining hall, trying to look nonchalant and not a bit like the eavesdroppers they were.

"Her doctor told me it was a sword injury! How the hell did she get stabbed with a sword?"

The sound of the quarrel was coming from a door about halfway down the hall. Savannah had seen it open once before, and it had appeared to be some sort of small parlor.

They stopped about twenty feet away and listened as the dispute continued.

"It was a mistake," Alex whined. "There was a problem with one of the swords not being properly blunted, and unfortunately—"

"Unfortunate? You call this unfortunate? It's tragic! Brandy will never have use of that arm again! The nerves were severed! She's ruined!"

"I'm really sorry that it was her who got hurt, R.R. She's the last person I would have wanted this to happen to."

"Oh, it would have been okay if it had been some other girl? Is it okay with you that there's another woman in the hospital with her arms and legs in casts?"

"No, of course it isn't okay. I hate that any of this happened. For God's sake, R.R., my own wife is dead!"

"Did you kill her?"

R.R. had lowered his voice, but Savannah and Dirk heard the question clearly enough. They looked at each other, then strained to hear the soft reply.

"No, of course not. Why would you even say that?'

"Because it wouldn't surprise me at all. The last time I saw you two together, you were fighting like pit bulls. I honestly came this close to pulling the whole project because I didn't think you guys could work together well enough to put a show together."

"I don't know what you're talking about. Tess and I had our differences, but no more than usual."

"Did she find out about Roxy?"

"She knew about Roxy all along. She couldn't talk. She got some on the side, too."

"Yeah, yeah, I know about her and Pretty Boy."

Savannah avoided glancing sideways at Dirk, because she could see in her peripheral vision that he was grinning. And if she slapped him—as she would have to do if she actually turned and looked at him—the men in the other room would undoubtedly hear it.

Half an hour ago, in Ryan and John's gatehouse apartment, Savannah had shared her new-found gossip about Tess and Lance with the Magnolia team.

All four had been surprised.

Only Dirk had been thrilled. And she wasn't likely to forgive him for that any time soon.

"This isn't about Lance," Alex was saying, "or Tess, or that Carisa gal, who's in the hospital. This is about a terrible accident that we all deeply regret, R.R. I know how much Brandy means to you."

"I doubt that," R.R. replied. "I doubt it because I don't think you've ever seriously cared about any woman in your entire life, including your wife. I'm crazy about Brandy. I'm going to marry her. And I promised her I'd get her into some serious films. This show of yours was supposed to launch her, get her face out there, get her recognized. Now she has nothing. Not even the use of her arm. And I'm holding you accountable."

Savannah and Dirk heard him walking toward the door, his cowboy boots resounding on the flagstone floor. They glanced around quickly and spotted a door about ten feet away on the opposite side of the hallway.

Ducking into the tiny room that served as a broom closet, they barely had the door closed behind them, when R.R. Breakstone marched out into the hall and past their door.

About a minute later, they heard Alex leave, too, exiting the other direction down the hallway.

"Well," Savannah whispered. "I think I like Mr. Breakstone a little more than I thought I would."

"Why? Because he said he was cra-a-azy about his woman?"

"That was a point in his favor, yes."

"You always were a sucker for that romantic crap."

"And because he jerked a knot in Alex Jarvis's tail. That right there is reason enough for me to love him, ugly long hair, vampire clothes and all."

"Do I have to remind you?" Dirk said. "He built this monstrosity of a place, those demon statue things on the roof, that dungeon downstairs with all the torture devices—this weirdo's idea of ambiance."

Savannah shrugged. "So he's a lousy decorator. Nobody's perfect."

Dirk had headed off to find R.R. to see if he could "squeeze something good out of the Satan-cowboy dude," and Savannah decided it was a good time to call her grandmother. The last time she had spoken with her, she had left her dangling, telling her only that a part of the building had fallen on somebody. Gran didn't like being left hanging. And even though Granny Reid was three thousand miles away, and Savannah had qualified as being a "grown woman" for more years than she cared to think about, she still feared raising Gran's ire.

So she decided to return to her room and make the call, steeling herself for opening words like: "Lord have mercy, girl! I was worried plumb to death, thinkin' all the awful things that might have happened to you there in that castle with all those Hollywood people. You know how Hollywood people can be! They're into more mess than the rest of us can even imagine, and you right there in the thick of 'em!"

But when Savannah reached her room, lain down across her bed and made the call, Gran sounded anything but indignant. She sounded exhausted and frustrated. Which meant only one thing: Vidalia and her young'uns were visiting.

"You got a houseful?" Savannah asked.

"Sure seems like it," Granny replied. "Lordy, but these twins sure have a heap of energy. Wish I had a tenth of it myself."

Savannah could just imagine. One set of Vidalia's twins could drive you crazy, but with both pairs at once, a person tended to just shut down mentally and tune out. It was a matter of sanity preservation.

And since Vidalia herself had shut down years ago, she wasn't exactly the most vigilant mother or the greatest disciplinarian in the world. As a result, her children were known the width and breadth of McGill, Georgia, as being unholy terrors.

"Today," Gran said, "I caught the two oldest ones in the garden, picking my tomatoes and eating them green. Heaven knows how many they ate because now their stomachs are all tore up. And the babies went from crawling to running around good now, getting into everything. They liked to've pulled my pole lamp right down on 'em a minute ago, and now they're foolin' with the knobs on the TV."

"What's Vi doing?" Savannah asked.

"She's resting, poor thing."

"I'll bet she is," Savannah muttered. Vi never missed an opportunity to rest, pregnant or otherwise, and between Gran's good nature in the daytime and her husband's willingness to care for his children in the evenings, Vi had "relaxation" down to an art.

"Put her on the phone, for me, would you, please?" Savannah said.

"I don't think you want to talk to her right now," Gran whispered. "She's not in the best of moods. She and Butch had another go-around this afternoon. That's why her and the young'uns are all over here instead of home. I think they might be spending the night. She's just steamed enough at him not to go home for days."

Savannah shook her head. That was just what her eighty-plus grandmother needed. Several days of Vi and the terrible twosomes.

"Let me talk to her, Gran. I'll take my chances," Savannah said.

A sleepy and grumpy-sounding Vidalia answered with a lackluster "Yeah?"

"Hi, honey," Savannah said, putting on her most cheerful, if somewhat disingenuous, big-sister voice. "How are you doing?"

She knew better than to ask, of course. But . . . what could you do?

"My ankles are lapping over my loafers, and my maternity clothes are all too tight. I thought this would be easier, just having one, but I swear I'm ever' bit as big as I was when I had the twins. And I'm getting worse stretch marks than ever before, even on my butt and boobs, because they're getting so big so fast that my skin can't keep up and. . . ."

Savannah closed her eyes as the litany continued and told herself, *Think happy thoughts. Go to a happy place. Happy thoughts. Happy place. Happy face.*

But all she could visualize was the firing range and herself blowing enormous holes in Happy Face targets with her Beretta.

Finally, Vidalia began to wind down. "And on top of it all, I've got pimples all over my chin. Like I don't have enough going on to make me ugly right now. I'm not worth shootin', I tell you, Van. Not worth the price of the bullet it would take to put me out of my misery."

To put us al-l-l out of your misery, Savannah thought.

"I just feel uglier than sin, and I don't think my body's ever gonna spring back from this one. This was the one that finally just ruint everything for good. I'm just going to be a saggy, baggy, scarred-up mess after this. I'm never puttin' on a swimsuit again!"

"Vi, Vi, Vi," Savannah said with a weary sigh. "What the heck are you talking about, girl? So what if you've got a few bags or sags here and there? You are a beautiful woman and—"

"Am not."

"Am, too."

"Am not."

"Hush up and listen to me. I don't like hearing you badmouth your body like you're always doing. It just ain't right. That body you're in is an amazing, wondrous thing, and you shouldn't go around telling it that it's not."

"But it's all sore and achy and swollen."

"And healthy and working and beautiful."

"It *ain't* beautiful! It ain't even passable pretty!"

"Vidalia, do you still have that thick black hair, the hair that's just like Gran's was when she was your age?"

"Well, yes, but . . ."

"And are your eyes that gorgeous shade of blue that we got from Grampa Reid?"

"I don't know what that's got to do with—"

"And don't you still have that soft, smooth skin that every one of us girls got from all those buttermilk soaks that Gran made us take?"

"I guess."

Savannah could hear her sister starting to melt just a little. In fact, she was pretty sure she had heard a sniff or two. And not the self-pitying kind. The self-appreciating type.

"Your ankles may be puffy, Vi," she continued, "but your legs and feet work. They get you where you want to go. Your hands work. So do your eyes and ears. And if you don't think those are all miraculous and wonderful gifts, go down to the old folks' home there in town and look around."

Yes, there was definitely some serious sniffing going on at the other end. Vidalia was listening to her older sister. It was a rare, red-letter day.

Savannah took advantage of the opportunity. Heaven only knew when it would happen again.

"Who cares," she added, "if your body doesn't look like one of those models on a magazine cover? So what if they're svelte and you aren't? *Your* body is making a baby, Vi. It's creating another life, a sweet little munchkin with ten fingers and ten toes and your nose and Butch's chin . . . right there inside it! If that isn't beautiful, girl, then I don't know what beauty is."

Before Vidalia had time to reply with anything other than more sniffles, a knock sounded on Savannah's bedroom door.

"Listen, sweetie," she said, "I've gotta go. Somebody's at my door. But you feel better, okay?"

"I will." Sniffle, snort. "I do already . . . a little."

"Good. Take the kids and go home to Butch. Ask him to rub your feet and ankles for you. I'll just bet he'll do it, if you ask nice."

"Okay."

Savannah said her good-byes, tucked the cell phone into her sweater pocket, and hurried to the door.

It's probably Dirk, she thought, *eager to tell me the latest dirt he's dug up on Lance.*

But when she opened the door, she was pleasantly shocked to see Lance himself standing there with a shy grin on his face.

"Oh, hi," she said.

"Hi yourself." He glanced right, then left, then down at his shoes. "I . . . uh . . . I was wondering if . . . well . . . I hear you won the contest this morning. Before Brandy got hurt, that is."

"I guess so. I had won the first match, but obviously, we didn't get to finish."

"But you were ahead, so that means you win the prize. If you want it, that is." Again, he studied the toes of his sneakers.

"You mean, the . . . round tower?"

"Yeah. The night in the round tower. With me. If you want to, that is. Only if you really want to."

Want to?

Suddenly, Savannah's head was spinning. She felt like a kid on the Tilt-a-Whirl at the county fair.

Spend the night with Lance Roman—Raff the Pirate of Wolf Cove, Tony the New York fireman in *Flickering Tongues of Flaming Passion*, Thunder Cloud of *Apache Lightning Strikes the Heart.*

Yes, she could practically see the carnival lights whirling past her, smell the cotton candy in the air, hear the screams from the roller coaster, feel her hot dog threatening to come back up in her throat.

"I don't spend the night with men I hardly know," she heard a voice saying, as though from far away, a woman's voice that sounded a heck of a lot like hers. "But I'd be happy to spend the evening with you . . . and see how quickly we can get to know each other."

Chapter

17

"I'm going to spend the evening alone with Lance," Savannah told Tammy as they walked from the keep toward the corner of the compound, "and for all I know, the guy could be a murderer."

"That's why you're playing it smart and telling somebody about it before you do," Tammy replied. For once, she was the one having to hurry to keep up with Savannah.

"For all the good that's going to do me," Savannah said. "I guess if he croaks me, at least you'll know who done it."

Tammy reached out and grabbed her arm, causing her to stop in the middle of the courtyard. "Are you really afraid of him? If you are, then don't go."

"I want to go." The words tumbled out before she even had time to think. "I'm not seriously scared of him or I wouldn't do it."

"If you're not afraid of him, you must not think he's our killer."

"Oh, he could be. Never say 'Never' about any of your suspects until a case is closed. I'm not afraid because I've got this." She patted the thick, velvet skirt of her gown.

"Your Beretta strapped to your thigh?"

"That's right."

Tammy grinned and started walking again. "What if you and he get frisky and he finds it on you?"

"Frisky? Tammy Sue, what do you think I am?"

"I know what you are, and I know that he's gorgeous; that's why I brought up the subject. And why do you always call me that? My middle name isn't Sue."

"I call you that because, where I come from, every girl's middle name is either Sue, Ann, Lynn, or Jo."

"What's yours?"

"None of your business."

They had reached the base of the tower and found a small, closed door with an arched top. Savannah paused, her hand on the iron handle.

"Are you going to be okay?" Tammy asked.

"Sure. No sweat."

"I'll hang around out here if you want me to. You know . . . listen for sounds of a struggle."

"Thanks, hon. But you go on back to Ryan and John. Tell them what's up, but don't let them interrupt us." She smoothed her hair and licked her lips. "How do I look?"

Tammy studied her by the flickering light of the courtyard lanterns, a sweet look on her face, but said nothing.

"Well?"

"You look beautiful, like one of those women on the front of those books."

"Really?"

"Yeah. Exactly like that."

"Gee, thanks."

"No problem. Just don't get ravished, pillaged, or plundered, and your bodice ripped."

"Or impaled on Sir Lance's sword?"
"Oh, m'gawd! Especially not that!"

When Savannah walked through the door and into the round tower, the first thing she saw—the only thing she saw—was a circular staircase in the center of the room. It reminded her of a lighthouse she had once explored years ago. Only it was darker inside the tower.

In fact, the few flickering torch lights that lit the way up the stairs might have provided atmosphere, but they gave no illumination to speak of. She had to be careful not to trip over her own feet or the hem of the full gown as she climbed the steep steps.

The stairs ended abruptly at what appeared to be a ceiling. But when she reached the top, she could see that the ceiling had a trap door in it, as well as a fancy bell pull hanging down from the crack in the door.

She gave it a hearty yank, and the sound of a bell echoed higher up in the tower.

"Open sesame," she said. And almost as soon as she had spoken the words, she heard a creak, and one end of the door above her head began to lift upward.

"Lady Savannah!" Lance said, extending his hand down to her and helping her climb the last few steps. "I was afraid you'd decided not to come after all."

"I wouldn't miss this for the world," she said as she stepped through the ceiling door and found that the ceiling was the floor of a small but charming room.

Unlike the rest of Blackmoor Castle, this room actually resembled what she thought a medieval castle might have looked like. At least, a deliciously luxurious one.

A large bed dominated the center of the room, and it was spread with a tapestry throw and animal skins: zebra, leopard, and tiger. And while she was sure they were faux fur, they were better than most, and looked inviting.

To her left a small fireplace blazed and on the floor in front of it were spread more fur throws and lush pillows of every jewel tone. She didn't need to even touch one to know they were covered in silk.

Near the fireplace a low table held a pair of ornate pewter goblets and a wooden bowl brimming with fresh fruit. On a plate beside it was an assortment of breads and cheeses.

The room had two large windows. One looked down on the courtyard below, and the other revealed a stunning view of the surrounding hills that were deep purple in the silver moonlight.

But as seductive as the room and its view were, it didn't compare to her host.

Lance had dressed the part, too, wearing a white cavalier's shirt, black leggings and knee-high boots. His hair was pulled back and tied with a thin strip of leather.

"I'm glad you're dressed up," he said. "I would have felt pretty stupid in this garb, if you'd been wearing jeans and a T-shirt."

"Same here," she said, turning from the window to face him. "I decided to take a chance and hope."

He smiled. "Take a chance and hope. That's the name of the game."

She looked around. "At least we don't have Leonard in our faces with his camera."

"And Pete up our noses with that fuzzy microphone."

"And, most importantly, no Alex screaming at us."

They both laughed. Then there was a long, awkward silence.

Savannah finally broke it. "So, without a director, how do we figure out what to do next?"

He thought for a moment, then said, "Why don't you come over here?" He led her toward the fireplace. "And sit down . . . about . . . there."

After seating her on a large, emerald-green cushion, he grabbed a couple of pillows, fluffed them and arranged them behind her back and at her sides. Finally, he covered her lap with a leopard-print throw and tucked the edges around her.

"And now," he said, "I'll make us some mulled wine. How does that sound?"

"Mulled wine sounds fantastic," she replied. "But only about half as good as a man who can actually *make* mulled wine."

"Well, don't be too impressed," he said as he took a hook from among some fireplace utensils, and used it to swing out a pot that had been hanging over the fire. "That's all I know how to make . . . other than roast hot dogs and cook hamburgers on a grill. The mulled wine is my sister-in-law's recipe."

"Your sister-in-law?"

"Yes, I was discussing the details of this gig . . . er, job . . . with my brother and his wife, and she suggested I learn how to make it, thought it might come in handy to know that sort of thing in a castle."

"Thoughtful lady."

"Very. My brother married above himself. But then, all guys do, huh?"

She laughed. "I think I've heard it said before."

He threw a small spice bag made of cheesecloth into the pot and swung it back over the fire. In only moments, the smells of cinnamon, cloves, and nutmeg filled the room.

"Have you ever been married, Lance?" she asked.

"No. I've never been lucky enough to find the right lady at the right time. How about you?"

"Nope."

"I'm surprised. You're pretty, a very nice woman. And you seem . . . oh . . . like the domestic type."

"Oh, I'm highly domesticated. I just do all that cooking, cleaning, and gardening stuff for myself and my friends."

"When you aren't chasing down the bad guys with your cop buddy, that detective."

"Definitely. I like catching bad boys even more than I like cooking and eating, and that's saying something."

As the wine heated over the fire, he sat down on a cushion beside her and looked into her eyes. "Thank you for coming, Savannah. I'm really glad you're here."

"Why?" Savannah said. She knew that blatant suspicion wasn't exactly the sort of sugar you caught flies with, but on the other hand, she had never been one to hold back. Questions, opinions, suggestions, and demands—they all came spilling out of her mouth at any time of the night or day.

He looked confused. "What do you mean?"

"I mean, why did you invite me here tonight?"

"You won the sword fight."

"The sword fight was cancelled due to Brandy's accident. There wasn't really a winner."

"Well, you were ahead at the time, and that's close enough for me."

He moved closer to her, reached out, and let a strand of her hair slip through his fingers. "I like you, Savannah. I like you a lot."

"I like you, too," she admitted as he wound yet another curl around his finger.

"And I enjoyed the time we spent there in the garden."

She could feel her cheeks getting hot, and it wasn't from the ambient heat of the fireplace. "I enjoyed being in the garden with you, too. It was truly a lovely experience."

His fingertips left her hair and trailed down the side of her neck, sending a delicious shiver through her whole body.

"You have very soft skin," he said, his voice husky. "And it's a nice, ivory and pink sort of color. What do they call that? Peaches and cream?"

"More like peaches and mashed potatoes."

"What?"

"If you are what you eat, I'm mostly peaches and mashed potatoes. That's pretty much what we ate there in Georgia when I was growing up. There was plenty of both around."

He laughed and shook his head. "I've never met anybody quite like you, Savannah."

"And you're not likely to again," she said. "So you'd better treat me right."

His fingertips moved on down her throat, then brushed lightly across the top of her breasts just above the edge of her bodice.

The simple gesture went through her, like a wave of hot liquid Fourth of July sunshine.

He leaned over and kissed a spot on her neck just below her ear. "I would treat you better than right," he breathed against her skin, "if you'd let me."

Be careful, Savannah girl, a voice said deep inside. *Be careful with this one. He's much too good to be true.*

She knew the voice was her own common sense, but it sounded a lot like Granny Reid.

She reached down and caught his hand in hers. Lacing her fingers through his, she said, "I like you a lot, Lance. As I said before, I enjoyed . . . no, way more than enjoyed . . . the time we spent together in the garden the other morning. And I'm not going to pretend that, after a few of those heart-stopping kisses of yours, I wasn't ready to drop my sails in total surrender."

He smiled. "Now, that's a nice thought."

"It certainly is. And if we hadn't gotten interrupted, we probably would have made a very pleasant rocking-chair memory. Pleasant, but possibly a mistake, nevertheless."

"How do you know it would have been a mistake?"

"I *don't* know," she said, "and that's the point. I don't know because I don't know you. And as I said earlier, I don't sleep with men I don't know. Not even one who has a body to die for, the bluest eyes I've ever seen in my life, and who knows how to mull his own wine."

He said nothing for a long time. But he unlaced his fingers from hers and brought her hand to his face. And after several moments, he placed a sweet, lingering kiss into the palm of her hand.

"I understand, Savannah," he said. "And I didn't ask you to spend time with me tonight just so that I could get lucky."

He glanced down at her bosom, grinned, and added, "Not that the thought didn't cross my mind, but. . . ."

"But?"

"The bottom line is: I've been feeling really awful about what's been happening around here, and I just really didn't want to spend the evening all by myself."

She quirked one eyebrow. "And Roxy, Kit, or Mary wouldn't do?"

"Uh, no. If they were my only choices, I'd be perfectly content to be alone right now."

He released her hand, stood, and reached for a jar of honey. Again, he pulled the heating pot toward him and away from the fire. Then he scooped out a spoonful of the thick, golden liquid and allowed it to drip down into the pot.

She had to admit that it smelled divine. And she also

had to admit that sitting there by the fire covered with soft throws, reclining on pillows, and having a hunk serve her wasn't too bad, either.

Maybe being a private detective wasn't so awful after all. If she'd still been on the force, this little adventure never would have happened.

But as she watched him pour the steaming hot wine into the pewter goblets, she reminded herself that she had work to do here tonight.

Someday, she might kick herself for passing up a night in that giant bed with its exotic throws with this man whom a million women desperately wanted. She might wonder why it was more important to nail a killer than to be plundered by Raff the pirate.

But she doubted it.

Passion came in all forms.

"How's the investigation going?" Lance asked, as though reading her mind. He handed her a goblet with a small white towel wrapped around it. "Careful, those metal cups look good, but they aren't very practical for serving hot stuff. Something my sister-in-law neglected to tell me."

"It could be going better," she admitted. "If we knew who killed Tess and hurt the other girls, it would definitely be going better."

"Anybody in particular that you're looking at?" he said as he poured his own mug full.

She could hear the pseudo-casual interest behind his words. She saw that his eyes were avoiding hers as he performed his task.

And for that moment, she would have preferred to be deaf and blind, or at least nearsighted and hard-of-hearing.

"I really can't say," she replied evenly, but with as much stress-producing insinuation as she could pack into four words.

"Whoever's doing it," he said as he sat down again beside her, "it's a horrible thing. Those two girls maimed." He stared down into his wine for a moment, then added softly, "Tess dead."

She watched as he took a long, deep draught of the hot liquid. She sipped her own and felt its heat steal through her, soothing and comforting, as the spices filled her head.

But this wasn't the time to be soothed or comfortable, she reminded herself. This was the time to do some digging. As unpleasant as the prospect might be.

"Lance," she said, "I know about you and Tess."

He didn't look surprised. And he didn't look her way, but continued to stare down into his mug. "I figured you'd find out sooner or later," he said. "I was hoping for later."

"Were you in love with her?"

He glanced up for just a second, then back down. But in that brief instant, Savannah saw a hatred so raw and intense that it startled her.

"No."

His one word answer said little, but his eyes had said it all.

"So, it was more of a physical attraction?" she prodded.

"Are you kidding?" She could hear the rage now in his voice, and she had to admit that she was glad she had her gun under her skirt. "You saw Tess," he said. "Do you think I was attracted to her? Do you think anyone would be attracted to her? She was a bitter, nasty woman and it showed . . . it showed all over her. That's not attractive."

"No, of course not. I was just thinking, she might have been different when you first met her, ten years ago. People change."

"Yeah, Tess changed all right. She mellowed. She used to be worse."

Savannah toyed with her goblet, took a few more sips of the sweet, hot wine, and chose her words carefully. "Then why, Lance? Why the ongoing affair?"

"Because I'm a whore."

Whoa, she thought. *I wasn't expecting that.*

Again, she considered her next question before asking it. "Do you mean, you performed sexual services for her? She paid you to . . ."

"Yes. She paid me. Not like an escort service. Not three hundred an hour. It wasn't that honest."

"Then how?"

"She paid me by passing my name around at parties and getting me gigs, by making sure I got enough book covers to pay my rent and car payments, by including me in some project of hers from time to time, seeing to it that nobody forgot who Lance Roman was in the industry. She paid me by not hurting my career with a dropped word here and there, a rumor started, a lie told, those careless little comments that can destroy you overnight."

Savannah reached over and laid her hand on his arm. "She was abusing her power. And abusing you. I'm sure that must have made you very angry."

Did it make you angry enough to kill her, Lance? she added in her mind. *Did it get to be too much for too long and you let her have it over the head with a medieval mace?*

Again, he seemed to read her mind. His eyes met hers for a moment, searching and evaluating. Then his demeanor changed to defensive.

"I was angry," he said, leaning slightly away from her, "and I might have thought she deserved it, but I didn't kill her."

It was her turn to study, to search, to evaluate. And she didn't see innocence in his eyes. As much as she hated to admit it, she saw guilt.

"Are you sure, Lance?"

"Of course I'm sure." He set his mug on the floor beside him and crossed his arms over his chest. "I wouldn't do something like that. You know I didn't do it. You were with me when we found her."

"Yes," Savannah said softly, "you were there when I first saw the body."

"And I can't tell you how awful I felt, seeing her— someone I'd known, someone I'd been intimate with lying there dead, blood all over the place, that horrible gash in her skull. I'll never get over seeing that. Never. It'll haunt me till the day I die."

That part, she believed. His eyes were full of regret and sadness, guilt and horror over what he'd seen.

His soul was open and exposed, and she could see all the way inside . . . whether she wanted to or not.

"I believe you, Lance," she said. "I know it was terrible for you, witnessing something like that. I hope you find some peace as time passes."

"That would be good," he said, passing a hand wearily over his eyes. "But I can't see it happening. I don't think this nightmare is ever going to be over for me."

She set her mug on the floor beside his. Standing, she leaned over and gave him a quick kiss on the top of his head. "I'm going to go now, Lance," she told him. "Thank you for making mulled wine for me. I'll never forget it. I'm never going to forget any of the time we've spent together. You're very special, to say the least."

"So are you, Savannah," he said, rising to his feet. "I'll walk you back to your room."

"That isn't necessary. Really. But thanks. Stay here

and . . . try to find some peace, Lance. No matter what goes down, a body's gotta find some inner peace if they're going to make it through this life."

He bent his head and gave her a kiss on the cheek. "Good night, Savannah," he said as he opened the trap door for her and helped her down the first few steps.

"Good night, Lance," she replied.

"Thanks for everything," he called after her.

"Don't thank me, Lance," she whispered. "Don't thank me."

When she exited the tower, she turned toward the keep, intending to go to her room. But she saw a movement in the shrubbery off to her left, then more off to her right. A moment later, four figures emerged from the shadows and came toward her.

It was Tammy, Ryan, John . . . and Dirk.

"We were just hanging around out here," Tammy whispered to her, wrapping her arm around Savannah's waist, "You know—just in case you needed help."

"All of you?"

Ryan chuckled. "In case you needed a *lot* of help."

"At the first sound of a scuffle," John said, "we were prepared to storm the tower."

"That's nice," she said without enthusiasm.

Dirk stepped in front of her, blocking her path. "What's the matter, Van?" he said. And for once, he looked more worried, more genuinely concerned about her welfare than angry and jealous.

For some reason that she couldn't explain, she rushed to him and threw her arms around his neck. She buried her face against his shirt and breathed in the old, familiar, comforting smell of him.

"What is it, honey?" he said, pulling her away from him and holding her by the shoulders so that he could look down into her eyes. "What did you find out up there?"

"Lance did it," she told him, her voice breaking. "He killed Tess. I know he did, and I know why."

"Let's go back to our apartment and talk about this," Ryan said.

"Yes, let's," John added. "I'll make a strong pot of tea."

Savannah turned around and took one long look up at the round tower, a stately black silhouette against the moonlit sky. She closed her eyes and for a few seconds allowed the sadness to flow through her, as the warm mulled wine had only minutes before.

Through her . . . and then out.

"Okay," she said as she turned her back on the tower and its lonely occupant. "Let's go."

Lifting her chin and squaring her shoulders, she headed for the gatehouse.

Chapter

18

"When did you really know for sure that it was Lance?" Tammy asked Savannah.

The two women stood at Savannah's bedroom window, looking down on the courtyard, where Dirk was having a serious, late-night conversation with R.R. Breakstone.

"I was pretty sure soon after I got there, just from the way he was acting," she told her. "He wouldn't look at me when he was asking me about the investigation. I got the feeling he was pumping me for information, not discussing it with me as a friend.

"But," she continued, "I knew for sure when he explained how he felt when he saw her wound. The big, ugly gash in her head."

"He seemed sorry about it?"

"Yes, but that's not how I knew. He described the wound very accurately. And it was on the back of her head. When he and I looked at her there in the freezer, she was lying on her back, face up. We didn't turn her over until later, when Dr. Liu okayed it. And he wasn't around then. He had gone upstairs with Carisa."

"Could he have seen it later, when they were taking her out?"

"No. Dr. Liu suspected right from the first that it was a homicide. And she had already zipped the body into one of the bags with a lock. No one saw that wound except the doctor, the C.S.I. techs, Dirk and me."

They watched in silence a few moments as Dirk and R.R. seemed to be ending their discussion in the courtyard below. From the body language of the two men, it was obvious that their exchange had been a tense one.

"Are you okay about this?" Tammy asked as Dirk and R.R. concluded and parted ways. R.R. got into the rear of his limousine and it pulled away, while Dirk entered the keep through the front door.

"I guess," Savannah replied. "I'm just sort of surprised at myself. I thought I'd seen it all. I didn't think somebody could pull the wool over my eyes like that. I must be losing it, kiddo."

"Ah, you're not losing anything. You're better than ever. You just let starry-eyed love get in your eyes."

"More like lust. It was just an infatuation . . . nothing even close to love. Heck, I didn't even know the guy. Obviously. He was killing and hurting people right under my nose, and I didn't even know it."

"Speaking of 'people,'" Tammy said. "How about the attacks on Brandy and Carisa? Do you think he did those, too?"

"Probably. He can't be accounted for during those times, so he had opportunity."

"How about motive? You think he killed Tess because he was sick of her sexual harassment. But what about the other two?"

"I don't know why he hurt them. Maybe they knew he had killed Tess. Dirk will find out, now that he knows who to look at."

A knock sounded on the door, and Dirk called out, "Hey, open up in there."

"Speaking of Dirko," Tammy said, going to the door and letting him in.

"Well, did you get R.R.'s permission to search the premises?" Savannah asked him.

"I sure did. He wasn't big on the idea at first, but I talked him into it. Told him that if I could pin it on somebody good and solid, he might not get his ass sued off for that statue falling on Carisa."

"Good thinking," Savannah told him. "You always have been able to bring out the best in people."

"I like to think so." He gave her a strange, probing look and said, "Do you want a part of this?"

"No," she said. "You go search his room on your own. Let me know what you find."

"You sure?"

She nodded. "I'm sure. I'll wait for you here."

"Okay." He didn't look happy with her reply, but he didn't argue. "Me and John and Ryan are going to go shake his room up good and see what crawls out. I'll see you in a while."

"I'll be here."

"Me, too." Tammy said.

"You don't have to baby-sit me. Go give him a hand."

Tammy's face lit up. She lived for these moments.

Usually Savannah did, too. So she understood completely. "Go," she said. "I'm fine."

"If you're sure . . ."

"I'm sure as shootin'. Now get going before I take a stick to you."

Tammy didn't ask a third time. She and Dirk were gone in a flash.

This was the fun part of any investigation. After hours, days, sometimes even weeks and months of boring hours doing stakeouts, interviews that go nowhere, chasing down worthless leads, this was the exciting payoff: closing in on the bad guy, a person who thought he could hurt an innocent person and get away with it.

A person with sapphire-blue eyes, eyes full of hurt and anger. A person who was used and abused and had simply reached the end of his rope.

Savannah shook her head, hoping to clear the thought from her mind. *Just because you like somebody doesn't mean they get a "Get out of jail free" card for murder,* she reminded herself.

No, nothing justified that.

And Lance had chosen to submit to Tess's demands for whatever degree of success she had offered him. He wasn't the victim here. The victim was the one lying in Dr. Liu's morgue. And Carisa and Brandy, lying in the hospital.

Savannah left the window, walked over to her bed, and plopped down across it. At least she had changed out of that miserably uncomfortable gown and into her street clothes. She would be glad to have her entire life back, as soon as possible.

She was thoroughly sick of the Middle Ages.

As she waited and Dirk searched, she thought of the man in the round tower, who didn't know that his freedom could now be measured in hours or minutes.

And she wondered if he would ever find peace.

She doubted it.

Less than an hour later, Savannah heard a soft knock at her door. When she asked who it was, Dirk's answer was as gentle as his knock. "It's me, Van."

Opening the door, she saw him standing there with a look on his face that she knew all too well. It was the glow of deep, soul-felt victory.

He had found something. Something substantial.

Holding up three brown paper bags and a clear plastic one, he said, "Wanna see?"

No, she didn't want to see.

"Sure. Come on in."

He hurried over to her bed and spread his bounty across it. She could tell he was trying to hold his excitement in check, but he was doing a lousy job of it.

His eyes were glittering with barely restrained glee.

But she was grateful for one thing: There wasn't a smidgen of "I told you so" or "Ha, ha, I busted that dude you were kissing" in his demeanor. This was strictly a case of: "I solved a homicide. I got the killer!"

She decided to be happy for him, and why not? Dirk was the good guy here.

"Whatcha got?" she asked, sitting down on the bed beside his evidence bags.

Just the sight of those paper bags with their official seals, Dirk's writing scrawled on them: dates, locations collected, case number, and his signature—they all caused her own blood to pump.

"He had this stuff hid good," Dirk said. "Took us ages to find it, stuffed under a loose board in the floor of an old dresser thing, like that"—he pointed to the armoire in her corner.

"That's called a . . . ah, never mind. What did you find?"

"Bloody jeans and sweatshirt."

Savannah's stomach clutched. Bloody clothes. Yes, that was about as incriminating as it got.

"How much you wanna bet the DNA will come back as Tess's?" Dirk said as he opened one of the bags and let her look inside.

Sure enough, there was a pair of jeans in there. And even without taking them out, she could see a blood-stained hem.

He held the second one open, and she could see the cuff of a white sweatshirt, also bloody.

"And, in here," he said, holding up the plastic bag, "we've got support for that theory of yours about his motive. Check it out."

He handed her the bag. Through the clear plastic, she could see that it was a handwritten note. On it was scrawled, in a rough but decidedly feminine hand, "I'll come as soon as he's asleep. Your room. Be there and be ready. I'm not kidding, Lance. We'd better not have a repeat of last time."

She shook her head and laid it back down on the bed. "Not the most romantic rendezvous appointment ever made."

Dirk picked up the last paper bag from the bed and held it close to his chest for a moment, as he gave Savannah a strange, almost sad, look.

"What's that?" she asked, dreading his answer.

"I don't know if you want to see this one. In fact, I'm pretty sure you don't want to."

"Do I need to?" she asked.

He shrugged. "I guess that depends on how much you want to know about why he killed her. I don't think it was just because of the sexual harassment, not after finding this anyway."

Savannah knew she was going to have to look inside the bag. She had never been one to run from the truth. One of the rules she lived by was: "Turn on the light and look the monster in the face. Then you'll know what you're up against and how to fight."

Only a fool fought in the dark against an unknown foe.

"Open it up," she said.

He took out a pair of surgical gloves, opened the bag, and reached inside. He pulled out a pink plastic bag that had a logo on the front that she recognized as belonging to an all-female spa in Hollywood. A spa that catered to the rich and famous ladies of Los Angeles.

Savannah had seen their commercials many times on Tess's romance channel. Apparently, this bag and its contents had once been hers.

As he lifted an item from inside the pink bag, she saw that it was a commercially produced video tape. And judging from the bad art on the cover, it had been cheaply produced.

The picture on the front was grainy, but clear enough for her to see more than she wanted to. "A porn flick," she said softly.

"Yeah. Afraid so. An old one. Probably made about ten years ago."

There were two young men on the cover, locked in a passionate embrace. And even though the dark-haired man was young, his haircut dated, his muscles not nearly so defined or his facial features so chiseled, it was undoubtedly Lance Roman.

The cover credits listed him as "Rod Romano."

"Lance Roman is gay?" she said, more to herself than to him. "This guy that all the women are panting over, is gay?"

"I don't know." Dirk quickly put the video back into its pink bag and returned it to the evidence sack. "I doubt it. Ryan and John were the ones who found this, and they don't seem to think so, you know, from what they've seen and heard from him. They said sometimes the guys in these films are straight or bi. They're just doing it for the dough."

She nodded thoughtfully. "Lance was a little evasive about what he was doing when Tess 'discovered' him. I can see why. Wonder how many of these are out there?"

"Probably not many, or somebody would have

blown the whistle on him a long time ago. I have a feeling this might be one of the only ones around."

"And Tess had it?"

"That's what I figure. I have a feeling we're going to be able to lift one of her prints off either the bag, the cover, or the video itself."

"You're right about one thing," Savannah said. "This makes his motive much stronger. It's one thing for her to offer him some publicity, a role every now and then for sexual favors. It's quite another if she was holding this thing over his head. Having this made public would have destroyed his career overnight."

"Sure it would have. It would've been splashed all over the tabloids for a week, 'Macho Muscleman Is Gay Porn Star,' and then he never would have gotten another 'romance' gig again."

"And his disapproving dairy father would have found out."

"What?"

"Nothing. It's not important. What's important is that you've got everything you need there to nail him for Tess. How about Carisa and Brandy?"

Dirk got a nasty grin on his face. "Oh, I figure a few hours of chatting with me in the sweat box tonight, and he'll tell me all about why they had to go, too. By dawn, we should have all the answers."

"Are you going to go get him now?"

"Yeah. I don't suppose you want to come along?"

"No, I don't suppose so. This is one time you don't have to share your candy with me."

He gathered the stuff off the bed and headed for the door. "You did good work on this case, Van. We couldn't have done it without you."

She nodded, then turned her back to him and stared out the window at the far corner of the complex. At the round tower.

"Thanks," she said.

He left, quietly shutting the door behind him.

She continued to watch at the window. She watched as Dirk walked across the courtyard to the tower.

She waited for four minutes . . . she counted each one . . . as he went inside.

And she saw him come out again with Lance in cuffs and lead him over to the stable.

Three minutes later, she saw Dirk drive away.

In the dark, she couldn't see into the backseat of the Buick, but she knew Lance would be there, cuffed to the door handle. That was Dirk's style.

And she knew it was going to be a very long night for both men. Dirk wasn't kidding when he had called the interrogation room a "sweat box." The two of them would be wringing wet by the time Dirk had all the answers he wanted out of his suspect—and probably a confession, too, considering how much evidence he had against Lance.

She thought of the women Lance had hurt and decided, *This is a good thing. Justice will be done, and justice is a good thing.*

Oh yeah? Then why does it feel so bad?

Chapter

19

Savannah had seriously considered going home that evening. Tammy had offered to drive her. But it was the middle of the night, and both of them were exhausted, so they decided to go ahead and stay, then leave the next morning as soon as they woke.

Although they hadn't seen hide or hair of Alex, Roxy, Mary, or the crew, they didn't need a formal announcement to know that *Man of My Dreams* was officially headed for the sewer treatment plant.

When Savannah had crawled into bed, she'd assumed it would be difficult to fall asleep, considering the events of the past few hours. But instead, she was dead to the world in a matter of minutes. And though her head was still working overtime with strange, disturbing dreams, she was deeply under when a frantic pounding on the door jarred her awake.

"Savannah!" she could hear someone yelling in the hallway. "Please, help! Sava-a-annah!"

She stumbled to the door, nearly tripping over her nightgown's hem and jerked the door open just as a new volley of pounding began.

"What?" she said, trying to shake herself awake. "Who? What?"

"Savannah! Help!" It was Mary, standing there in her pajamas, tears rolling down her face, shaking violently. "It's Roxy!" she said between sobs. "She's hurt, and I think she's dead!"

Savannah rushed out into the hallway with her. "Where?" she said, her pulse pounding in her ears. "What happened?"

"The cellar! She's at the bottom of the steps! I think Leonard pushed her!"

Savannah was already running toward the main staircase. Mary hurried to keep up with her.

"Leonard?" Savannah asked as they reached the landing between floors. "Leonard the cameraman?" *But what about Lance?* she thought. *Dirk just arrested Lance. What the hell's going on around here?*

"Yes, Leonard," Mary was saying. "I was in the kitchen getting a drink of water, and I heard a noise from down in the cellar, like a big thud. Then the door flew open, and he came running out. He went into the hallway, and I think he was headed for the back of the house."

They reached the first floor, and Savannah motioned for Mary to stay back as she looked down the hall.

That was when she instinctively reached for her gun beneath her arm and realized she had left the Beretta on her nightstand next to her bed. Ordinarily, grabbing it would have been second nature, but she had been sleeping so soundly that she hadn't been thinking straight.

"Wait," she told Mary. When she saw no one in the corridor, she said, "Okay, follow me and stay close. How do you know it was Roxy?"

"I wanted to know why he'd come running out of there like that. I opened the door and looked down. I saw her lying there at the foot of the stairs."

"How bad is she?"

"I don't know for sure. I didn't go down there. But she wasn't moving."

Not moving, Savannah thought. *Not moving is never a good sign.*

They had reached the kitchen, and as she had before, Savannah held Mary back until she checked the room.

All was clear.

They raced to the cellar door. Savannah reached it first and flung it open.

It was completely dark and she couldn't see a thing.

Feeling the wall to her right, she located the light switch and flipped it on. The dim overhead bulb came to life, but did little to illuminate the stairs.

But there was enough light, just enough for Savannah to be confused.

"Mary," she said, staring down into the shadows. "Mary, there's nobody"—

Suddenly, she was flying forward, downward. And the cellar stairs and floor were coming up to meet her.

She heard a woman scream and vaguely realized it was her. Then she hit. One step halfway down, then another, and another. As though in slow motion she tumbled, feeling her body twisting and turning as one after the other of the sharp edges drove into her.

She tried to grab. Anything. But there was no handrail. Nothing.

The floor hit her with sickening force that knocked the breath out of her lungs.

A horrible pain shot through her leg and foot—a pain that seemed like white fireworks exploding inside her skull.

She could hear a voice, but it seemed like miles

away, getting farther all the time. And she knew what that meant. She was about to faint.

And if she fainted—

Stay here! she told herself. *Stay awake or you'll die!*

Even in her dazed state, she knew that she hadn't fallen. Mary had pushed her.

Even in the dim light of the dank cellar, she could see Mary coming down the stairs. And she knew she wasn't coming down to help her.

"Why?" she asked. The word came out more like a bleat than speech. Her leg was hurting so badly she could hardly bear the pain. It had to be broken.

Mary stood over her, looking down on her. But said nothing.

Then she left her and walked over to the wall.

Savannah heard a jangling that sounded like the rattle of rusty chains.

"Why?" she asked again. "Mary, why do you want to hurt me? I thought we were friends."

"Don't you say that!" the woman screamed. Her voice was high and shrill. She sounded absolutely crazy. "You *were* my friend. You were my favorite. I didn't think you would do it. Not you! I thought you were safe!"

There was more rattling at the wall, and Savannah could hear her huffing and puffing as she pulled at something.

"Do what?" Savannah said, struggling to sit up. She reached down to her ankle and could feel that it was already starting to swell. It felt like someone was stabbing at it with a steak knife. "What did I do to you?"

"You went to the round tower tonight with *him!* I thought you were the one person who wouldn't betray me. I never thought he'd even give you a second look, you being fat and old."

Fat and old? Well!

Ordinarily, Savannah would have been incensed, but at the moment she had bigger concerns than being verbally assaulted. Something told her that Mary wasn't messing with the stuff on the wall for her own amusement.

This was deadly business.

Desperately, Savannah looked around her for a weapon. Anything at all. But like the handrail, there were no weapons—there was absolutely nothing within her reach.

Again, she cursed herself for forgetting her gun.

"But I didn't betray you, Mary," she said, trying to sound sweet and conciliatory, not scared to death and furious. "What do you think I did?"

"I *know* what you did. I saw you go into the round tower. I know you were up there with Lance. And I know what the two of you were doing, too."

"Doing? We were talking, Mary. We talked for a while. That was all."

"Don't lie to me!" Mary screamed, again, sounding as if she were very nearly unhinged. "Don't insult me with your lies! I know why you went up there. I saw the way you were dressed. You were up there a long time. I know. I watched you from my window."

There was a loud racket as something came loose from the wall and clattered to the floor.

Mary leaned over to pick it up. "I watched and I saw your friends hiding there in the bushes, waiting for you to come out. To come out and tell them all about what you and Lance were doing up there in the tower."

She walked back to Savannah, lugging something that was large, long, and heavy.

Savannah struggled to get to her feet, but her wounded leg wouldn't hold her. It buckled and caused her another rush of agony.

She scooted across the floor as best she could on her bottom, until her back was against a wall. Unfortunately, the wall was bare.

Where's a good ol' mace when you need one? she thought. *Or even a bow and arrow? Hell, right now I'd settle for a rock.*

"Mary, I swear to you on my life that I didn't have sex with Lance. We didn't even kiss up there in the tower. I promise! We just talked about the case. About who had killed Tess and—"

"Well, now you know, don't you?" Mary stepped out of the shadows, and Savannah could see what she was holding. It was a six-foot-long Viking battle axe.

The thing looked so big that one good blow with it could probably cut a body in half.

Her body, if she didn't think of a way out of this. And quickly!

"You killed Tess?" she said. "I can understand that, Mary. Tess was an awful person. I'm sure if you killed her you had a really good reason. I'd never hold that against you."

"You don't know what she was doing to Lance. How she was making his life miserable! She was making him . . . do things with her. Awful things. And he didn't want to. He hated her. He told me so himself. Lance and I are very close. He tells me everything."

"Did he help you kill her, Mary?"

"No, he didn't know about it until I told him. I brought him down here"—she motioned with one hand toward the freezer—"and showed him. I wanted him to see what I'd done for him. How much I loved him. I wanted him to know that, thanks to me, he wouldn't ever have to worry about her again. And I told him where she kept that terrible tape in her house in Brentwood. I gave him the combination to the safe, so that he could go and get it that night."

"Which night? The night you said he went to his apartment?"

Mary nodded.

Tears were still streaming down her face. For just a moment, Savannah felt a pang of sympathy for her. She was obviously deranged.

But that didn't make her any less dangerous.

It made her more so.

"But why the other girls, Mary? Why did you try to kill Carisa and Brandy?"

"Because they were saying awful lies. They said they'd had hot, sexy afternoons with Lance, that he kissed them and did things with them. And he didn't. I know because I watched them, too, from the tower. He loved *me! Me,* not them! He knew they were just trying to win a contest. I didn't care about any of that stuff. I just wanted Lance for himself. But now the cops have arrested him! I saw them take him away in handcuffs. That's probably your fault, too!"

She lifted the heavy axe and raised it over Savannah's head. The look on her face was nearly as terrifying as the giant blade.

Savannah held up her hands, knowing that if Mary struck with that deadly thing, her hands would be no protection at all.

"Mary, please, don't!" she said. "Wait a minute. You can still have Lance. You can tell the police that he's innocent, and he'll be so grateful to you. I know he already loves you, but just think how much more he'll love you when he hears what you did for him!"

"But I'd have to go to prison."

"Maybe for a little while. But he will owe you so much. He can write to you all the time, call you, and come visit you in prison. You'll get out early on good behavior, and he'll be waiting for you as soon as you're released. It could work out, Mary. Think about it. This could be great!"

She watched the woman's eyes, watched the inner struggle registering there. Mary wanted to believe the lies. Desper-ately.

But not as desperately as Savannah wanted her to.

The axe was still posed over Savannah's head, and she could see Mary's arm starting to tremble from the strain.

"Put it down for a minute, Mary," she said. "I can't walk. I'm not going anywhere. Put it down and rest for a minute while we talk about this."

"I think you're lying to me about Lance. You're just saying that stuff so that I won't kill you."

Out of the corner of her eye, Savannah saw a movement. Someone was standing at the base of the steps. Someone who was moving closer and closer to them, sneaking up behind Mary.

It was Tammy.

She had Savannah's Beretta in her hand. And she was pointing it straight at Mary's back.

"Wait," Savannah said. "Just wait a minute."

She didn't dare look at Tammy. But she hoped she would understand.

"Wait for what?" Mary said. "I've waited too long already. If I'd taken care of you earlier, you wouldn't have been in that tower, in bed with *my* man, turning him against me."

"We really weren't in bed together, Mary. I promise you. He told me he had feelings for another woman. Now I know he was talking about you."

Tammy moved a step closer.

Mary's arm was trembling so hard that Savannah was afraid she would drop the axe on her, even if she didn't strike with it.

"Don't," Savannah said, still not daring to look at Tammy. "Not yet." Then, locking eyes with Mary she said, "Mary, if you hurt me, that's only going to add to your prison sentence. It's that much longer you'll spend in jail, away from Lance. They're going to figure it out. It's just a matter of time until Detective Coulter comes to get you. He's probably on his way here right now. But if you turn yourself in, if you confess and explain why you did it, I know Lance will understand. Everyone will understand. Nobody liked Tess . . . or Carisa or Brandy either, for that matter. Everything will work out, if you just end it here. Put the axe down, Mary. Put it down and I'll help you figure out what to tell the police so that they'll understand."

The axe wavered in the air for a moment that seemed like a year.

Finally, Mary lowered it a few inches and said, "Do you really think they would understand why I did it?"

"Of course. We've all been in love. We've all had to deal with people like those women. We've all had to step in from time to time to protect someone we care about. You were doing it for Lance. Everyone will understand that. And most importantly, Lance will understand it. He'll be so grateful."

Mary lowered the ugly weapon, inch by inch, then laid it on the floor, close enough that Savannah got her first good look at the blade's edge. It was extremely sharp. If she had been struck with it, she would have been instantly dismembered.

A moment later, there was a flurry of activity, and before Savannah knew what was happening, Mary was on the floor, her hands pinned behind her, and Tammy sitting on her back.

"I got her!" Tammy shouted. "I got her, got her, got her! Are you okay, Savannah?"

"Not really," Savannah said, feeling the darkness closing around her again. "Now that you've got things under control, I think I'll just . . . ."

She passed out.

Chapter
20

"Is there anything else I can do for you, Van?" Dirk asked Savannah as he adjusted the rose-print chintz cushion under her leg. "Anything at all?"

She had her injured leg propped on the cushy footstool, her lower calf and ankle surrounded by an impressive brace with lots of Velcro straps and buckles.

Although she was sitting in her favorite chair in her own comfortable living room, Cleopatra and Diamante in her lap, and Dirk and Tammy waiting on her, hand and foot, Savannah was almost inconsolable.

"Oh," she moaned. "This is the most painful injury I've ever had. This hurts even more than when I got shot in the butt that time."

Tammy looked confused. "You got shot in the butt?"

"No, she didn't," Dirk said. "She's delirious from that pain medication she's taking."

"I *almost* got shot in the butt once," she murmured, her head lolling on the back of the chair. Another groan of pure misery. "Don't you remember me almost getting shot, Dirk?"

"Yeah, I think I do. Here, have another piece of candy."
He shoved a box of Godiva chocolates under her nose.

"No," she said. "I don't think I could. It just hurts so
bad. I still don't have any appetite at all."

Dirk turned to Tammy, a look of deep concern on his
face. "Do you think this is normal?" he asked her. "It's
been two weeks now. Shouldn't she be healing quicker
than this?"

Tammy shrugged. "You know what they said.
Sometimes those torn tendons take longer to heal even
than broken bones."

"I know, but wow . . . she usually snaps back faster
than this. She's not even digging into those chocolates
I brought her! That's not like her at all. I'm worried."

He leaned over Savannah and brushed her hair back
from her forehead. "Savannah, honey, do you need
anything else? Some more flowers maybe? Those that I
brought you the other day look sorta wilted."

"Sweet . . . of you," she managed between gasps of
pain. "You don't . . . have to . . . oh-h-h!"

Dirk shook his head and turned back to Tammy. "I
just feel so guilty about all this. If I'd just taken the
time to question Pretty Boy there at the castle instead
of waiting until I got him to the station house, this
never would have happened. But I was just so hot to
drag him in."

Tammy placed a comforting hand on his arm. "I
know. But you did what you could. As soon as he told
you about Mary, you called to warn Savannah."

"Too late."

"Well, yes. By then she had already left her room.
She was on her way downstairs with Mary, unaware of
the horrors that awaited her."

"Oh, God!" He clapped his hands over his eyes. "I
can't stand to think about it."

"But at least you had the presence of mind to call me and Ryan and John and let us know."

"And you found her in time. I owe you big for that one, kiddo."

"Hey, when I saw her bedroom door open and her gun lying there on the nightstand, I knew something was wrong. She never would have left it out like that."

"And you were the one who found her down in that cellar with that maniac. I can't tell you how grateful I am to you. If anything more had happened . . . I don't think I ever would have forgiven myself."

"Ah, it was nothing. Ryan and John were searching elsewhere. I just lucked out, going into the kitchen and seeing the cellar door open. The rest is history."

"Well, I've put you in for some sort of civilian service award. The brass doesn't like me that much, so I don't know if it'll do any good, but. . . ."

"Don't you worry about it. Everything worked out in the end, and that's all that matters."

They both cast sympathetic looks at Savannah, but she seemed unaware of them . . . of everything but her own personal world of pain and suffering.

"I have to go now," Dirk said. "I've got an appointment with the district attorney. They're deciding whether to charge Pretty Boy with 'accessory to murder' or just 'obstruction of justice.' Like it matters. If there's even one woman on the jury, he'll walk."

"Probably," Tammy said. "As long as Mary gets put away, that's what really matters."

"Oh, she's going away for life. No doubt about that one."

"Come on, or you'll be late. I'll walk you to the door," Tammy said.

He leaned over Savannah and placed a kiss on her forehead.

She answered with a moan.

"I'll be back to see you again tomorrow, sweetheart. And I'll bring you some fresh flowers and maybe some ice cream. Is Chunky Monkey all right?"

She gave a weak nod. "And . . ." she murmured. "And . . ."

"And what, honey? What else do you need?"

"Some . . . books . . . if you don't . . . mind."

"What kind of books?"

With a shaking hand, she pointed to a stack of romance novels on the end table next to her chair.

"*Those* kind?" He scowled. "You want me to go into a store and buy you some of those stupid, pansy romance things?"

She nodded weakly. "If it's not too much trou—"

"No, no, it's no trouble. It's fine."

"And . . ." She reached for his hand. "One more . . . little thing."

"What's that?" he said gruffly. His enthusiasm and willingness to serve and protect seemed to be waning a tad.

"Blondes . . . only . . . blondes. Cover . . ."

"What?"

"I think," Tammy interjected, "that she only wants books with blond guys on the covers. You know, nothing to remind her of—"

"Oh, yeah. Gotcha."

Tammy walked him to the door where they said goodbye.

She stood at the door and watched through the peephole until he had driven away. "Okay, he's gone," she called out.

By the time she reentered the living room, Savannah had ripped off the brace, had her face buried in the box of Godiva, and was happily munching away.

"How much longer do you think you can keep this up?" Tammy asked.

Savannah looked up at her with wickedly innocent eyes. "What?"

"When are you going to let the poor guy off the hook and tell him you're really fine."

She picked up a dark chocolate walnut cluster, looked it over with a judicious eye, and popped it into her mouth. "He's a friggin' detective, gold shield and everything. I ain't gonna tell him squat. Let him figure it out on his own."

"You're just using his guilt to get an endless supply of Godiva, Ben and Jerry's, flowers, and now, romance novels. You're going to go to hell for this."

"Nope," she said, closing her eyes and savoring the treat. "I've bought that man snacks and fast food on stakeouts and fed him homemade dinners for years and years and years. The good Lord above knows that I so-o-o-o deserve anything that I can milk out of this situation."

Tammy laughed. "Well, then, I guess I can go home for the evening."

"Sure. You skedaddle and have a nice night. I'll be fine."

Tammy looked around at the bounty of junk food. "Yes, you will. And I'll see you in the morning."

"Thanks for everything, sweet pea."

"You're welcome."

A few minutes later, when Savannah was certain that she was alone and would remain so for a while, she reached beneath her chair cushion and pulled out her copy of *Love's Tempestuous Tempest*.

Opening the book, she shook out a one-page letter, opened it on her lap and read it . . . for the twentieth time.

Dear Savannah,

I don't even know how to begin this letter. But I want you to know that I'm actually relieved that you figured out the truth about me. Even though I'm in terrible trouble right now, the nightmare is over, if you know what I mean. I'll do what I have to do, and get through this. I don't know what the future will bring. Maybe, when I've paid whatever debt society deems fit, I'll wind up back at my father's dairy. There are worse lives to be lived. That's for sure.

But I wanted to thank you for some of the things you said. They meant more to me than you know. And, of course, for the rocking-chair moments. I'll always remember you.

Affectionately,
Lance

Savannah's cats shifted in her lap, one of them sniffing the letter, the other one trying to chew on the corner.

"What do you think, girls?" she said.

She listened for a moment to their synchronized purring. "Yes, I agree," she said, wadding the letter into a tight ball. She tossed it into the wastepaper basket next to her chair.

"How about another piece of chocolate, Diamante? No? Okay. I'll eat yours for you. How about you, Cleopatra? No? You girls are no help at all. I'll have to eat this whole box by myself. The only thing is . . . I need an Irish coffee to wash it down with."

She dumped the cats on the floor and started toward the kitchen.

But halfway across the floor, she stopped, turned, and walked back to the wastebasket. Reaching inside it, she retrieved the crinkled ball of paper and carefully smoothed it out on her lap.

Then she gently placed it back inside the book cover.

"You're right," she told the cats as she tucked the novel back under her chair cushion. "We *could* sell it on eBay. Now, how about that coffee?"

Despite New Year's resolutions to avoid irritating house-guests and nerve-wracking cases, California P.I. Savannah Reid finds herself playing host to her assistant's cranky cousin—in town for an unwanted makeover at a local spa—before the Christmas fudge is even gone. But when the spa's renowned plastic surgeon goes missing, murder's on the menu. And for Savannah, it's in for a penny, in for a pound . . .

Voluptuous and proud of it, Savannah can't understand why any woman would diet in pursuit of beauty, never mind go under the knife. She likes herself just fine the way she is . . . and so does her detective buddy, Dirk. Too bad her house-guest isn't as content. Abigail is livid that her cousin, Tammy, won an extreme makeover, complete with plastic surgery, at Emerge, San Carmelita's new luxury spa. Abigail's daunting enough when she's ranting about social pressures and medical butchery, but when she suddenly puts on a co-operative smile Savannah gets really nervous . . .

There's barely time to worry about it when Dirk brings her in on his latest case. One of Emerge's owners, renowned plastic surgeon Suzette Du Bois, is missing. And quicker than you can say Botox, Sergio D'Allessandro, Suzette's business partner and ex-husband, hires Savannah to find Suzette before the cops do.

As she broadens her search, Savannah begins to realize that some of the employees at this temple of perfection harbor serious inner flaws. There's Myrna Cooper, Emerge's receptionist, whose permanently surprised expression proves she fears aging almost as much as she despises her bosses. And publicist Devon Wright, Sergio's not-so-secret lover, was overheard threatening Suzette just before the doc disappeared. Add to the mix Jeremy Lawrence, Emerge's disgruntled and aggressively ambitious style consultant, and the picture is far from pretty.

When one of the suspects turns up dead, Savannah's had enough. She'd love nothing more than to wrap up this case, kick out her guest, and make friends with a nice strawberry margarita—or three. But first, she'll have to stitch up a killer who cuts to the bone . . .

Please turn the page for an exciting sneak peek at CORPSE SUZETTE coming next month in hardcover!

Chapter

1

"Wanna go watch Loco Roco?"
"Sure."
"Same place?"
"I'll be there in ten."

"There" was the Patty Cake Donut Shop, which frequently served as a meeting spot for Savannah Reid and her old buddy, Dirk. Police work could be lonely when nobody in the department was willing to be your partner. And Detective Sergeant Dirk Coulter was frequently a lonely man.

But generally not for long.

Now a private detective, Savannah had once been his partner in another lifetime . . . before she and the San Carmelita PD had parted ways under less than amiable circumstances. And once in a while, when she "got a yen," as her Southern granny would say, for an old-fashioned stakeout, she accepted one of his invitations.

He invited her constantly. He enjoyed her company and the homemade snacks she frequently brought along to fuel the long, tedious hours. She accepted once in a while . . . when there were no good forensic shows on TV and no unread romance novels on her nightstand.

But she always accepted when the subject was Loco Roco.

She was every bit as determined as Dirk to catch that lowlife doing something illegal, immoral, or fattening and put him back in the joint where he belonged. Roco had made a lifelong career of robbing convenience stores and on his last job had pistol-whipped a clerk into a coma. With Savannah's help, Dirk had arrested him, only to have the most serious charge thrown out on a technicality: prosecutorial error.

They'd never gotten over the disappointment that Roco was back on the street after only eighteen months. They knew it was just a matter of time until he lapsed into his old pattern, and they intended to be there when he fell off the wagon and violated his parole.

They had been watching Loco Roco for weeks. So far, he hadn't even jaywalked or spit on the sidewalk. To their consternation, he was Mr. Law-Abiding Citizen, while his latest victim was still in physical therapy, relearning how to walk. But Savannah and Dirk weren't the sort to give up easily.

And that was why Savannah arrived at their rendezvous spot in eight minutes rather than the estimated ten.

When she pulled into Patty Cake's parking lot, she found Dirk sitting in his old battered Buick Skylark in the rear near the alley. She knew the drill. He was waiting to see if she had brought any cookies, pie, brownies, or cake before he went into Patty's. Cheapskate that he was, he was hoping he'd only have to buy coffee. His mood—which usually wavered between morose and sullen—would plummet when she emerged from her classic Mustang, bagless.

Tough.

Her company didn't come cheap. The scintillating conversation, the benefit of her vast law-enforcement experience, the occasional slap upside his head to keep him awake . . . it all had a price. And the cost was two maple bars . . . or a giant chocolate-frosted Boston cream if she was in the throes of PMS.

He rolled down his window as she approached the Buick, a scowl on his face.

"No fried apricot pies?"

"You ate them all when you were over Saturday night," she said as she opened the passenger's door and brushed some Taco Bell wrappers off the seat and onto the floor.

"That was two nights ago. You've had plenty of time to make some more."

She slid in next to him and fixed him with a baleful eye. In her thickest Georgia drawl, she said, "Ye-eah, buddy . . . and I've had time to go clean that filthy house trailer of yours, wash your pile of dirty laundry, and perform an unnatural sex act on you that I'm sure you'd just love. But we both know none of that's *ever* gonna happen, so go get me some donuts, boy. Two maple bars *and* a Boston cream. And make it snappy!"

Dirk's jaw dropped. "*And*?"

"And."

"Now you're just bein' spiteful."

She grinned and winked at him. "You think?"

Half an hour later they were parked across the street from Burger Bonanza, watching the rear door of the fast food joint, waiting for a skinny, grungy thirty-year-old named Roco Tessitori to exit.

"How sure was his parole officer that he's going to get fired tonight?" Savannah asked as she licked the chocolate frosting off her fingertips.

"Sure, sure. The manager here called the P.O. this morning and said he was gonna let Loco go as soon as his shift's over. Said he's been late every day, doing next to nothing on the job, and he threatened one of the girls who works here. The manager figures his public service obligation's been fulfilled. He's done hiring ex-cons."

"And you figure our buddy's going to take his firing hard and go off the deep end?"

Dirk smiled, a nasty little grin that Savannah knew all too well. "Oh yeah. Loco's pretty predictable. When things don't go his way, he reverts to his old way of life. And besides, I'm feeling particularly lucky. I got two out of five on a Lotto scratch-off card this afternoon."

Savannah shot him a sideways glance to see if he was serious.

He was.

She decided not to mention that getting two out of five on a scratch-off was an everyday occurrence for most Lotto enthusiasts. No point in dampening Dirk's cheerful mood which for him was as rare as getting all five on a scratch-off card . . . while sitting naked on the back of a bull elephant . . . under a blue moon.

She took the last bite of her Boston cream and washed it down with her last sip of coffee. Okay. The food was gone; it was time for this stakeout to end.

"So," she said, "you figure he'll knock off another convenience store before the night's out?"

He took the empty donut bag, crunched it into a ball,

and tossed it onto the back floorboard. "Tonight. Tomorrow night. Next Tuesday. It'll happen, and it'll be worth the wait. After all, I'm a very patient man."

Savannah sniffed. "Yeah, right. This from a guy who has a conniption if he has to wait three seconds for a light to turn green, who pitches a fit if a waitress takes longer than five seconds to refill his coffee cup, who—"

"All right, all right. I . . . hey . . . heads up."

He pointed to the back door of the burger joint, where their quarry had just emerged, wearing a bright red uniform with the white "BB" Burger Bonanza logo on the back. Roco stomped across the parking lot to an old, decrepit Chevy. Opening the trunk, he peeled off the shirt and pitched it onto the ground.

"The boy looks downright disgruntled to me," Savannah said with a snicker.

"Oh, he's had better days," Dirk agreed.

They watched as the guy dropped the red pants, kicked off his shoes, and yanked the trousers off his ankles.

"Well, would you get a load of that," Savannah said. "Right down to his bloomers, here in front of God and everybody."

"I oughta bust him for exposin' himself right now," Dirk replied.

Savannah took a pair of binoculars from the glove box and focused them on Roco's rear end. "Or for wearing those briefs. They say 'kiss me under the mistletoe' and Christmas was two weeks ago. That's gotta be some sort of fashion felony."

Roco had thrown the pants onto the ground beside the shirt, then retrieved a pair of jeans from the trunk. In less than a minute, he was wearing the jeans and a black sweatshirt, and his sneakers were back on his feet.

As Roco got into his car, Dirk restarted the Buick and Savannah fastened her safety belt, happy for a bit of action. If there was anything she hated it was a boring stakeout once the goodies were gone.

A few seconds later, Roco peeled out of the parking lot, going out of his way to drive over the discarded uniform. They followed him onto the freeway, where he chose the northbound entrance ramp.

"He lives south of here," Savannah said.

Dirk smiled. "I know. Like I said, I'm feeling lucky tonight."

"I don't know what to make of this," Dirk said as Roco disappeared inside Kidz Emporium. Having followed him to a strip mall on the outskirts of town and the large toy store, they had parked a discreet distance away and watched as he entered the establishment.

Savannah shrugged. "Do you figure he'd go shopping for a nephew's or niece's birthday or whatever, right after getting fired from a job he badly needed?"

"Can't imagine it. Maybe he needs a video game to while away the idle hours now that he's unemployed."

Savannah got out her cell phone and called information, then dialed the store's number. "Security, please. Yes, hello. I'm with the San Carmelita Police Department"—she gave Dirk a sideways smirk—"and I was wondering if you could discreetly surveil a gentleman who's just entered your store and let us know what he purchases, if anything. Yes, Caucasian, thirty, black hair, dark eyes, six feet, one hundred and forty pounds, jeans and black sweatshirt. Sure. I'll hold. Thanks a bunch, darlin'."

A few minutes later, Savannah thanked the security

guard again, tossed the phone back onto the dash and chuckled. Elbowing Dirk in the ribs, she said, "You're right, big boy. Today's your lucky day. You're not gonna believe what that moron just bought."

Fifteen minutes later, they were still sitting in the car, but this time they were parked at the outer edge of a convenience store's lot. Roco was standing beside his car, fumbling with the small orange bag he had carried out of the Emporium.

"He's going to do it," Savannah said. "He's crazier than I thought. He's actually going to try to knock over a Quick Stop with a toy gun."

"I guess he's got some urgent bills to pay and can't take time to score a real piece on the street." Dirk shook his head and laughed. "Fine with me. Now I can let him go through with it and hang himself good before I have to intervene. Hell, he can't even give a clerk a decent pistol-whipping with a toy gun."

Roco tucked the plastic pistol into the front of his jeans, pulled his shirttail over it, and strode toward the store's entrance. Savannah and Dirk checked their own weapons in their shoulder holsters and got out of the car the moment he disappeared inside.

In seconds they were at the front door. They looked through the glass, ready to duck if he was facing their way. Having arrested him before, they were sure he'd recognize them on sight, and this was one crime they didn't want to interrupt . . . at least, not at first.

Timing was everything.

They slipped inside unnoticed and made their way along the wall that was lined with soda-filled refrigeration units. Savannah glanced down each aisle they passed, but other than Roco and the elderly lady behind the counter the store appeared empty.

Roco was hanging out by the candy display, making a show of choosing some gum. With a couple of packs in hand, he made his way to the front.

Weapons drawn, but pointed at the ceiling, Savannah and Dirk followed him.

He approached the clerk and slapped the gum onto the countertop. "Gimme these," he barked.

The clerk was a petite, silver-haired woman with bright blue eyes that narrowed at hearing his rough tone. "And will that be all?" she asked with forced courtesy as she rang up the sale.

"No, that ain't all." He reached into his waistband and pulled out the toy weapon. Pointing it at the woman's head, he said, "Gimme the money in that register, too, while you're at it. And hurry up about it, too, or I'll blow your fuckin' face off."

For a moment, Savannah had a horrible thought: What if the old lady died of sheer fright? What if she had a heart attack and dropped dead then and there?

Maybe they should have intercepted him before he'd gotten this far!

But over Roco's shoulder she could see the woman's face and the hot fire of anger that leapt into the elderly lady's eyes. Savannah decided not to worry about this one. She had seen that look in her own Granny Reid's eyes, and she knew this woman wasn't one to be scared to death . . . literally or even figuratively.

She felt Dirk tense beside her. He was ready to make his move.

She lowered her gun and trained it on Roco's back.

She wouldn't take the shot. Not with the clerk also in her line of fire. But Roco wouldn't know that.

In her peripheral vision she saw Dirk do the same.

In another second, he would announce and then they would—

Boom!

The explosion shook the store, and Savannah felt its reverberations throughout her entire body. Her ears rang as her brain tried to process. Instinctively, she dropped to one knee and ducked her head, her Beretta still pointed at Roco.

A gunshot.

She knew the sound all too well.

She did a split-second mental check to see if she had fired. No. She hadn't put her finger on the trigger yet.

A quick, sideways glance at Dirk told her that he hadn't fired either. He looked as confused as she was.

Roco had fired a shot?

With a plastic gun?

Roco. She looked back at him and saw an ugly, dark red stain appearing on the back of his thigh. He was starting to shake, violently. Then he dropped to the floor like a sack of flour.

Now Savannah had a clear view of the old lady behind the counter . . . all of her . . . including the Colt .45 in her hand that still had smoke curling from its barrel.

"That'll teach you!" the clerk said as she slowly lowered the weapon and laid it on the counter. "Try to rob *me* will you! And with a toy gun?! You oughta be ashamed of yourself. I'll bet you thought I was just some poor, helpless old woman. Well, I served in the Women's Army Corps, buster! You just held up the wrong woman!"

Dirk wasted no time rushing the counter and securing the .45 before Annie Oakley, Sr. could do any further damage with it.

Savannah holstered her own weapon and turned her

attention to Roco, who was lying on the floor, bleeding profusely from his leg wound.

So far, he hadn't said anything. He wasn't even moaning or groaning in pain. He looked like he was in complete shock as he stared up at Savannah with blank eyes.

"How bad is he?" Dirk asked her.

She looked down at the wound and saw that blood wasn't just flowing from it; it was spurting. Annie O. had hit an artery. "Pretty bad." Savannah turned to the clerk. "Do you have any sanitary napkins in here?"

"What?" The old lady looked confused. "I . . . uh . . . there are some tampons on that shelf there. I—"

"No, I need sanitary napkins . . . pads . . . if you've got them. To stop the bleeding."

"I don't carry anything like that."

"Paper towels?"

"I got regular old napkins over there by the coffee machine," the clerk said, "but I'm not getting them for you if it's to help him."

Dirk ran to the coffee station, grabbed a handful of napkins, and thrust them into Savannah's hands. She used them to apply pressure to the wound but the blood quickly saturated them, welling between her fingers. She silently cursed herself for not having a pair of gloves. "Roco, my man, you better not have AIDS," she muttered. "Call 9-1-1," she told the clerk. "Tell them to get an ambulance here, code three."

The lady shook her silver head. "I'm not calling anybody. I hope he bleeds to death right there on that floor. Then he won't be holding up some other poor soul who *hasn't* served time in the military."

Dirk made the emergency call himself.

He also brought an entire box of the napkins over to Savannah, knelt next to her, and tried to help her staunch the flow.

She glanced down at Roco's ashen face, his dark eyes wide with pain and fear. She had to admit; she felt just a little bit sorry for the guy . . . until she thought of his previous victims . . . the guy he had pistol-whipped, who still couldn't walk.

Then she decided that maybe Lady Justice wasn't such a bad old broad after all.

"Guess this *was* my lucky day," Dirk said as he tossed away a handful of soaked napkins and grabbed some fresh ones. He looked down at Roco. "*You*, on the other hand . . . you're going to the hospital and then right back to prison."

Savannah could hear sirens approaching. She could also hear the clerk talking on her cell phone. She was saying to somebody, "Yeah, I got him good. Right in the leg. He's the third one I've shot in only five years! Sure, let's get together tonight at O'Henry's and celebrate."

Savannah nudged Roco to keep him conscious. "Stay awake for me, there, buddy. Help's about here." She shook her head. "Boy, you're just havin' a bad night, aren't you? You get fired from a job, you pick the only convenience store in three states with a gun-totin' granny WAC behind the counter, you violate your parole, and get a hole blown in your leg . . . all in one hour. How piss-poor unlucky are *you*?!"

"I sure appreciate you letting my cousin stay with you," Tammy said as she brought Savannah a second hot-from-the-oven cinnamon bun on a china dessert plate. "I just don't have room for her there in that tiny little apartment of mine, and you have a nice extra bedroom upstairs. It's just so much handier, and you're so nice to do this for us and . . ."

She babbled on as she placed the roll on the end table next to Savannah's easy chair, then fluffed up a pillow and shoved it under Savannah's feet, which were resting on an ottoman. Still in her bathrobe, pajamas, and fluffy slippers, Savannah looked the picture of Saturday morning leisure. Except that it was Tuesday.

Tammy tried to grab the mug out of Savannah's hand. "Here, let me refresh that cup of coffee for you and—"

"Hey, hey . . . hold on." Savannah clutched the mug to her chest. "Not that I don't enjoy having my hiney kissed like this first thing in the morning, but the homemade rolls are enough. You don't have to wait on me hand and foot, too."

"I don't mind. Really, I don't. Here, is that enough cream in your coffee? Enough frosting on that bun?"

Savannah paused mid-slurp to watch her assistant over the rim of her Mickey Mouse mug.

Something was up.

Tammy Hart had been Savannah's so-called sidekick for years, a delightful addition to her Moonlight Magnolia Detective Agency, not to mention a close personal friend. Tammy was always energetic, eager to please, and beaming with exuberance—often more exuberance than the less feisty Savannah could stand.

But the tall, slender, athletic, and health-conscious blonde despised junk food of any kind. She considered the "three deadly whites," Sugar, Flour, and Salt, to be the greatest evils upon the face of the earth—far ahead of Lust, Gluttony, Sloth, Greed, or Envy.

So why would she appear on Savannah's doorstep first thing in the morning with a piping hot pan of cinnamon rolls? And why was she scurrying around like a chamber maid in a queen's court? A grumpy queen, who was likely to scream, "Off with her head!"

"Tell me more about this cousin of yours," Savannah said, keeping her voice even, her face expressionless.

Tammy shot her a quick look as she poured a dollop more cream into her cup. "Uh . . . Abigail? Mmmm . . . yes. Abby's well, she's . . . . What did you want to know about her?"

"What she's like. If you two were close growing up. And why you feel so guilty about dumping her off on me."

Bingo. Tammy's golden tan turned two shades paler. She spilled some of the cream onto the floor beside Savannah's chair.

Instantly Savannah's two black cats, a couple of mini-panthers named Cleopatra and Diamante, scrambled off the windowsill and began to lap it up.

"Guilty?" Tammy choked on her own spit—always a bad sign. "I just hope the two of you will get along. That's all."

"Why wouldn't we? You said she's a big girl, like me. She probably likes to eat and cook. We'll swap recipes."

"Well, actually, Abigail's bigger than you. Quite a bit bigger, in fact."

Savannah shrugged. "Good. Then she'll probably have better recipes."

Tammy set the creamer on the end table and sat down on the sofa. "Abby's really big. Really heavy. The family is all worried about her health. That's why I entered her in the contest."

"The makeover thing that new spa is offering?"

"Yeah. The place is called 'Emerge,' and the woman who runs it is this famous Beverly Hills surgeon, Dr. Suzette Du Bois." The guilt briefly left Tammy's face and her eyes sparkled with enthusiasm. "She's been running a spa for movie stars in the Hollywood Hills—"

"The Mystic Twilight Club . . . yeah, I've heard of

the place. But you have to have a bazillion bucks to even get through the gates."

"That's there, but this new place, Emerge, is for the average person."

"The average person with money to burn, you mean."

"Well, yes, I'm sure it's expensive, too. I mean, plastic surgery and personal trainers and fashion consultants, they don't come cheap, but what they can do there is amazing! The idea is, you go in as a disgusting old caterpillar and *emerge* as a beautiful butterfly!"

"And you're going to send your cousin, Abigail, through this . . . process?"

"Yes! I won it for her! Dr. Du Bois had a contest; people wrote in to enter the people they love and to recommend them for a metamorphosis. I had to write this long letter all about Abigail and how she deserved to enter the program and find the true, beautiful self she has hidden under all that . . . you know . . . inside."

Savannah took a sip of coffee, then said quietly, "Don't you consider Abigail beautiful, as she is?"

"Well, yes, but . . . she could be so much more . . . or less . . . or . . . You know."

Savannah stifled the urge to take offense. As a woman who carried some extra pounds above what the weight charts considered "ideal," she was a bit sensitive to disparaging remarks aimed at less-than-svelte folks. But she knew that Tammy, for all of her own weight-consciousness, wasn't really prejudiced against any group of people.

Tammy meant well. She had a good heart. And that was the only reason Savannah hadn't shoved the carrot and celery sticks that she was always offering up her left nostril.

You don't do serious damage to nitwits who mean well. It was a motto Savannah lived by, most of the time.

"How does Abigail feel about you entering her into this contest?" Savannah asked.

Tammy shrugged. "I haven't told her yet. I thought I'd wait until she gets here this afternoon. Then I'll surprise her with it. Don't you think she'll be thrilled? I mean, this is the chance of a lifetime! Who wouldn't be?"

Who wouldn't be thrilled to know that their cousin entered them into a contest for a total physical makeover— an ordeal involving torturous exercise, a starvation diet, and having your body carved, vacuumed, and stitched— the chance for a big, fat "caterpillar" to emerge as a socially acceptable "butterfly"? Yeah, who wouldn't be just jazzed about that? Savannah mulled that one over.

"When is Abigail getting here?" she asked with lackluster enthusiasm.

"I'm picking her up at LAX this afternoon. She's flying in from New York. I figured I'd bring her straight here from the airport. She thinks she's just here for a California vacation: some sun, some beach, Disneyland. Wait until she finds out! She's going to be so happy!" Tammy bounced off to the kitchen and quickly returned with yet another roll.

Savannah took it and held it close to her nose, breathing in the warm, cinnamon-scented sweetness. Yes, she intended to savor this frosting-coated bit of bribery. Because, in spite of Miss Tammy-Pollyanna's optimism, Savannah had a feeling that before Cousin Abigail's California visit was over, she was going to earn every stinking, guilt-laden calorie.

ABOUT THE AUTHOR

G.A. McKevett is the author of ten Savannah Reid mysteries and is currently working on the eleventh, CORPSE SUZETTE, which will be published in May 2006. She loves to hear from readers and you may write to her c/o Kensington Publishing. You can also visit her website at www.gamckevett.com.

Get More Mysteries by Leslie Meier